The Earl Caught Chelaine's Shoulder and Turned Her from the Railing . . .

"Get below to your cabin," he ordered. *"Now."*

"No!" She faced the railing again and looked out toward the sea.

"Have it your way, then." He circled her shoulders, swept an arm down beneath her legs, and lifted. He moved so swiftly, without warning, that for a few moments she was still, shocked into silence.

"Put me down," Chelaine growled through tightly clenched teeth. The Earl ignored her, carrying her effortlessly.

Rage supplanted caution. She swung without thinking, smacking his right cheek with an open palm . . .

The imprint of her fingers showed clearly, a reddened outline on the smooth bronze of his cheek. Not even sure why, Chelaine reached up, gently laying her cool fingers over the spot she had struck . . .

There was no resistance when he drew her close, cradled the back of her head and lowered his mouth to hers . . .

Dear Reader,

We, the editors of Tapestry Romances, are committed to bringing you two outstanding original romantic historical novels each and every month.

From Kentucky in the 1850s to the court of Louis XIII, from the deck of a pirate ship within sight of Gibraltar to a mining camp high in the Sierra Nevadas, our heroines experience life and love, romance and adventure.

Our aim is to give you the kind of historical romances that you want to read. We would enjoy hearing your thoughts about this book and all future Tapestry Romances. Please write to us at the address below.

The Editors
Tapestry Romances
POCKET BOOKS
1230 Avenue of the Americas
Box TAP
New York, N.Y. 10020

Chelaine

Donna Comeaux Zide

A TAPESTRY BOOK
PUBLISHED BY POCKET BOOKS NEW YORK

This novel is a work of historical fiction. Names, characters, places and incidents relating to non-historical figures are either the product of the author's imagination or are used fictitiously. Any resemblance of such non-historical incidents, places or figures to actual events or locales or persons, living or dead, is entirely coincidental.

An *Original* publication of TAPESTRY BOOKS

A Tapestry Book, published by
POCKET BOOKS, a division of Simon & Schuster, Inc.
1230 Avenue of the Americas, New York, N.Y. 10020

ISBN: 0-671-61721-4

First Tapestry Books printing March, 1986

10 9 8 7 6 5 4 3 2 1

POCKET and colophon are registered trademarks
of Simon & Schuster, Inc.

TAPESTRY is a registered trademark of Simon & Schuster, Inc.

Printed in the U.S.A.

For Thomas A. Williams
in appreciation of his friendship
and compassionate nature.

greens, accompanying the melodic rush of water rippling over the rocky stream bed.

Close by, two squirrels chattered in a battle over possession of the same nut, while a sea of fallen acorns surrounded the oak. A chorus of honking announced a flight of wild geese, and Chelaine arched back, anxious for a glimpse of the familiar brown and black fowl. Like an arrow pointing south, the graceful birds passed overhead in a V formation.

Eyes closed, Chelaine brooded over these signs of winter's onset. For the land and the wild creatures inhabiting the forest, it would be just another dormant season, a rest before spring brought renewal. Not so for her people. This autumn marked the beginning of an uncertain exile to shores both foreign and inhospitable. The Acadia of her childhood was gone. Against the dark of her shuttered eyelids, unbidden images came to haunt her. Like so many others, her sister's home lay in a scorched pile of fallen timbers, the recently harvested crops destroyed in ashes, the cattle that had fattened on the rich prairie grasses driven away to feed the British settlers.

There was no use dwelling on what could not be changed. Chelaine sat up, running a hand back through the unruly tangle of her brown waves, stretching her tired arms high overhead before she reached for the haversack. Washing at the stream and combing the snarls from her hair would banish her brooding mood. She drew forth a linen shirt and her comb, then rose to cross to the bank. Pulling off the buckskin shirt and setting it aside, she bent over the water and splashed her face. The icy water shocked her but it was invigorating. She cupped a handful and sluiced it over her throat and shoulders, briskly scrubbing to alleviate a shiver. Leaning back on her heels, she mopped at the beaded droplets and then donned the shirt, bothering to fasten only the middle buttons and gathering the tails to knot them at her waist.

Back at the blanket she settled down cross-legged and combed the damp tendrils back from her temples, then began the chore of pulling the comb through the snarls of the waist-length mane of hair. Suddenly she froze. Across the stream, a doe and fawn emerged from a thicket, cautiously approaching the bank to drink. The wind gusted, stirring her curls . . . or perhaps the animal caught her scent. The doe's head raised, her great, liquid brown eyes staring at Chelaine, white tail flicking. At last she lowered her nose, nibbling at the grass. Even as Chelaine exhaled a long-held breath, the deer tensed, glancing upstream, ears cocked and keenly attuned to some sound. As suddenly as she'd appeared, she wheeled and bounded off, her fawn scrambling to keep up.

Setting the comb aside, Chelaine came to her feet, listening. Now she heard the sound that had sent the doe sprinting for cover. A horse whinnied, then snorted and quieted. Moving a few steps forward, she strained to hear a footfall. Nothing, only another wickering snort. One horse . . . surely not a redcoat, not this deep in the interior. A *coureur,* perhaps.

Lt. Jeffrey Bead moved from the cover of a spruce, silently padding forward. Following the stream south to his camp, he'd sighted a deer gazing fixedly across the bank. Out of curiosity, he'd tethered his mount and circled behind a hill. The deer had vanished but the object that had drawn its attention, a slender girl clad in breeches and a clinging, linen shirt, stirred an intrigued smile.

4

She stared intently upstream and only when he was behind her startled at the crackle of a breaking twig. She glanced back and he had the briefest glimpse of wide, shocked eyes before she tensed to bolt. His right arm shot out, circling her narrow waist to catch her against him. A shriek of frustration broke from her as, arms flailing, legs kicking, she struggled to break away. Surprised by the vigor with which she fought, Bead started to laugh. "Hold still, you little wildcat!" he ordered, tightening his grip. A rapid flurry of French poured forth, one word close enough to its English equivalent to understand that she'd named him a bastard. Still chuckling, he clamped a hand over her mouth and swung her off her feet and about.

Though he wasn't a redcoat, the man who held her spoke English, reason enough to curse him even if he hadn't pounced on her. His amusement at her helpless struggles only added to her rage. She sank her teeth into the edge of his palm, biting hard. A resounding oath followed and her mouth was free but his arm lowered, banding her throat, almost choking her. She ceased fighting but writhed, incensed by the ease with which he held her.

The lieutenant's smile evaporated, his hand throbbing from the bite, but he loosened his hold on her throat to allow her to answer his questions. "Now, who are you and what—"

Chelaine tugged vainly at his arm, digging her nails into his wrist. "Let me go!" she insisted through tightly gritted teeth.

Surprised again, this time by the demand in English, Bead relaxed his grip slightly. "If I do . . . you'll behave? I've no mind to chase after you." In answer, she nodded curtly. He released her waist but held on to

5

her left shoulder, whirling her about to face him. The girl glared at his hand, then glanced up, and he was taken aback by how lovely she was. A cloud of fine, honey brown curls framed her flushed, oval face. A pair of long, thick lashes nearly hid the malice glittering in eyes the color of topaz. And, above a stubborn set chin, her delicate mouth stretched thin in an air of haughty contempt, all the more remarkable for the fact that she was his captive. "What in heaven's name are you doing out here on your own?"

"Fleeing beasts such as you," she retorted, then suddenly raised her knee, aiming a kick at his groin. The "beast" avoided the blow with an agile sidestep and thrust out a leg, hooking it behind her knees to send her sprawling backwards. Chelaine landed with a thud that knocked the air from her lungs.

Before she could recover, Bead was down and had her arms angled overhead, held there by laying his own atop hers. He shifted sideways, pinning her with his body. She cursed him again and wriggled, striving to wrest free, though his palms pressed her hands flat to the ground.

Chelaine gave one last indignant push and scowled. The man was not British, yet he spoke their tongue. Except for an irritatingly smug smile, he was not unpleasant looking. His hair was black as night, above a slightly crooked nose, his dark eyes crinkled in amusement. Bitterly aware that her own lack of caution made her his prisoner, she demanded to know who he was. "What do you do here?"

Her command of English exceeded what little French he knew, though her grammar lacked polish. Still, the queries sounded more charming for the soft accent. He grinned down at her. "I am, *chérie,* a colonial scout."

The revelation was as disturbing as if he'd said he was a regular soldier. She arched her wrists once more, straining, and grimacing at his strength. "Let me be," she pleaded, aware that he studied her with unnerving fascination, as if she were a captive butterfly. "I have no weapons."

"I wouldn't say that. My palm still smarts from your teeth marks." Shoving her wrists together, easily securing them with one hand, he lowered the other to brush back a silky tendril at her temples. "My orders are to bring in French refugees fleeing His Majesty's justice," he explained, his lips twisting wryly as he gazed down at her. "Since you're obviously one of—"

"Justice?" The term was a mocking distortion of the truth. "Your king is a filthy cur, a foreign devil . . ." She left off the useless cursing and arched a feathered brow in curiosity. "You are alone, yes?"

Bead tipped his head backward. "My men are camped downstream."

Though she was well aware of how she looked, the scout seemed entranced by her. Her lashes fluttered, then lifted high in an artful appeal. "Then you can let me go," she reasoned. "No one will know." He quirked a brow at the plea, and though it nearly choked her, she added, "Please?" His eyes warmed but he shook his head, continuing to toy with strands of her hair.

Drawing back a little, Bead glanced down at her shirt. The thin material clung damply to the swell of her breasts, accentuating their rounded firmness.

"I have nothing of value," she protested, disconcerted by the open appraisal, by the helplessness of her position.

"I disagree," he asserted, reluctantly dragging his

7

eyes from her enchanting curves. "You're a lovely little wench, a bit wild, but that makes you all the more desirable." His head lowered slowly, intent on pressing a kiss to the soft, sweet curve of her mouth. Just as his lips touched hers, she jerked away. Frowning, he caught at her jaw and forced her to face him. She wiggled, arms twisting with renewed energy, legs shifting in an effort to roll him away. "Stop struggling so," he snapped irritably.

"Then let me—"

He swooped, muffling her words as his tongue drove past her parted lips. His mouth ground against hers and she whimpered, helpless before the stirring exploration. Only when he had battled her attempts to evade his probing tongue and won did he finally raise back. The color on her cheeks had deepened, in modesty or anger, and her reddened lips had the look of a crushed blossom.

"You want your freedom," he said and before she could even nod, went on. "Well, I want something in return. Since your wriggling has already stirred my desire, all you need do is surrender. When I've had my pleasure, you can go, disappear into the woods, wherever you were bound for."

"I should let *you*—"

Her lovely eyes were rounded in shock. "It isn't a matter of letting me. You're mine whether or not you like the idea." Contempt flared her nostrils and he scowled. "I didn't have to offer you anything. How badly do you want to escape deportation?"

"What you want, it is rape—"

"It needn't be. I noticed a wedding band on your finger. All I want is what you gave your husband."

"But . . . but I am not . . ." Chelaine stuttered helplessly. "The ring, it was my mother's. You may have it if—"

The offer stirred his laughter once more. "At the moment you're more valuable than gold. I can't spend my passions on a worthless piece of metal when—"

Frustrated, Chelaine turned her face away, furious with him and herself—for the weak, betraying tears that trickled down her cheeks. She had no recourse. In a tiny voice trembling with apprehension, she whispered, "You will hurt me."

"Only if you fight. I don't believe your little lie about the ring, though it was quick witted. Your husband was probably deported . . . somehow you escaped. Satisfy me and you can still evade that fate."

How arrogant, how utterly galling of him! She would rather die than play the whore for an English bastard. Chelaine forced herself to relax, if only to lull him into believing she had given in to defeat. Though she longed to scrape her nails down his cheek, she suppressed the urge. Apparently he was taken in by her ruse. He released her wrists, lowering his mouth to hers again.

A sense of triumph came with her surrender. For a while he teased at her lips, and though she lowered a hand to push at his cheek, it was a feeble attempt at restraint. He rolled aside and watched the tantalizing rise and fall of her breasts. Each breath strained the shirt taut. Grasping the edge of the linen, he pushed it back, exposing the firm ivory mound peaked by a pale pink bud of flesh. Beneath his fingers the nipple firmed, and he gloated over the response.

Chelaine had never imagined that any man could humiliate her so. His hands were everywhere, cupping her breasts, sliding lower to drag at the waistband of her buckskins. Finally he seemed to tire of the crude

9

fondling and rose, sitting back on his haunches to tug at the leather thongs lacing her breeches. Again she sought to stop him; his eyes met hers, no longer amused but heavy lidded and sullen with determination.

"You do it then, if you're so skittish," Bead snapped impatiently. When she hesitated still, he tugged at the bow. She obeyed then, freeing him to attend his own breeches. They'd grown uncomfortably tight, the cloth constraining the swelling bulge at his crotch. He unfastened the buttons and dropped the flap, then hooked his thumbs beneath the short, woollen undergarment and shucked them along with his pants. His relieved sigh was cut short as he glanced at her. She had the laces half loosened but her fingers shook, working too slow. Shoving her backwards, he finished the task. At each contact, she cringed, giving him pause to wonder if she *was* the innocent she'd claimed to be.

Chelaine shut her eyes tight, detaching herself from the rough urgency of his hands. In seconds he'd pulled the last lace free and dragged the breeches down, jerking them past her hips, not satisfied until the material bunched around her knees. She almost gave in to an instinctive mindless panic then. Turning onto her side, she swiped at her tears and stifled a sob, reaching down to cover the curls at the base of her belly. He stretched beside her again, resuming his relentless exploration, pawing at her breasts before his hand slithered down her stomach, his fingers brushing past her hand to prod her thighs apart.

She could bear it no longer. Her nails scratched at his neck, scraping furrows and then digging into his chest. The stinging scratches drew a curse and he raised up, slamming his open palm across her face. The blow rocked her, leaving her stunned and too dazed to resist

10

further. A finger suddenly probed the vulnerable fold of flesh between her thighs, and she arched in pain, retreating from him. Hoarse from heavy, excited breathing, he chuckled as he lay beside her, pulling her close and draping his arm over her waist.

"Damned if you aren't a virgin," Bead mused aloud, pondering the fortune of finding so defenseless a beauty—and innocent yet. "Heaven seems to have had an ear for my prayers," he added.

Not so for Chelaine. She could not believe that God had anything to do with this awful torture. He found her mouth once more, his kisses brutally punishing, bruising her lips. She sobbed bitterly, hysterically struggling for breath. His hand swept over her hips, grasping her curves to press her closer, and the feel of his manhood elicited a moaning wail that seemed to give him some perverse thrill. He jerked his hips, rubbing against her, relishing her frantic efforts to retreat.

Fighting a nausea that churned her stomach, Chelaine went limp, depriving him of the delight he found in taunting her with the lewd stroking. Somewhere deep within her, a cold hatred burned like frostbite. She let him do as he pleased, yielding her mouth with a softness that surprised him. She had a fleeting glimpse of a conceited grin as the pressure against her derrière eased. His fingers returned to probe between her thighs.

Intent on one purpose alone, she endured the trespass. Arching her knee, she rested her calf on his leg, then lightly traced her fingers over his shoulder muscles, trailing down until her hand was close to her knee. She fumbled for and seized the hilt of the knife hidden within her boot, slowly easing it from the sheath. If, at

11

that moment, her assailant had raised his head and seen the blazing fury that narrowed her eyes to mere slits, he might have been warned. But he continued his probing, complacent in the belief that she was defenseless.

Chelaine scooted back, away from the intruding fingers but he caught at her waist. Raising her arm high, she struck blindly at his back. The blade glanced off something hard, a rib, and then sank deep, buried to the hilt in muscle and sinew.

Bead jerked convulsively, and as he arched back with a hoarse, strangled scream, his fingers thrust forward. Like an echo, Chelaine screamed, a jolt of pain tearing between her thighs. Small birds nesting in the surrounding trees took to the air, fluttering high in confusion and alarm.

Nearly faint, but desperate, she wrested the knife free and struck again, deep into the muscles of his shoulder. A twist of the blade brought another howl, then he shuddered and went limp. Racked by sobs, Chelaine pushed at his heavy body with all her strength, finally rolling free. On her side, with her knees curled to her chest, she rocked slightly, moaning at the ache radiating from the base of her belly. Suddenly fingers scraped at her thigh. She screamed again and whirled, ready to stab again.

Bead saw her through a haze, his eyes glazing over with pain. The girl had led him on, lured him into thinking she was helpless. What he could see of her features looked savage, as menacing as the knife she gripped. A dark mist rolled over him and he coughed, tasting his own blood.

Chelaine stared as a froth of pink saliva foamed at his

lips. Blood soaked his shirt, a stream of it pulsed from his shoulder. He shook once more and lay still. She collapsed then. Blood streaked her belly, the blade dripped with it, the whole world had taken on a crimson hue. With a quivering hand she wiped at her tears; her fingers came away with drops tinged pink. It seemed as if she were even crying tears of blood.

Wiping the knife on the blanket, she struggled to rise and wavered, then straightened. She pulled her breeches up and stumbled toward the bank, coming down on her knees with a force that renewed the aching throb. She laid the blade aside and thrust her hands into the water, the icy shock of it pushing away the hysteria. She hadn't been raped, she was alive . . . and *he* was dead.

She sat back, raising her face. The clouds had drifted away and the sky was tinted violet as dusk settled over the woods. Though he was dead, she hated the nameless man with such passion she wished he were alive, to kill him again. Suddenly she leaned forward, racked by spasms of heaving. Nothing came up, but the wretching continued for a minute, leaving her stomach muscles sore and cramped.

Weak and shaken, she struggled to her feet, standing still while the world tilted crazily. Finally she was able to take a tentative step and, if she proceeded slowly, walk. She fastened her breeches, and the pain came again. He had scraped her, cut her somehow with his nails. A strange calm replaced the hysteria now, stilling her racing pulses. She gazed back at the scene with an aloof detachment, seeing it as if she were a stranger who had happened along. The violence, the blood soaking her blanket, the awkward sprawl of his

13

body . . . none of it seemed real. Moving more steadily now, she circled him and reached down to pluck at her sack and vest. Leaving the blanket as his shroud, she turned and walked away, moving up the bank.

His mount was tethered beneath an elm, grazing on the meadow grass. The animal raised its head and then resumed grazing, shying only when she approached and he caught the scent of blood. Even then she might have lost the gelding if the reins weren't tied so tightly to a branch of the elm. She'd ridden since childhood—but on the sturdy ponies bred in Acadia. This horse towered over her. He was skittish at first, but once she was astride, he calmed. If he noticed she was lighter than his owner, it made no difference. The scout was easily forgotten. More so than for Chelaine, who, with each jostle of the saddle, was reminded of the brutal attack.

Riding on, pushing through the dark of night, she paused only to water the horse. There would be time to sleep later, when she was far from the man who had taught her a violent lesson: there were worse fates than deportation.

The sun was past its zenith and shone down from a cloudless sky, glittering silver on the azure waters of Baie Cristal. An unmarked, aged-looking schooner lay anchored off the land side of the bay. No flag flew from her mast, the sails were furled and bound; all in all, the ship had the faded look of a drab past her prime. Adding to its bare-bones, skeletal appearance, a body dangled from the mainmast spar. The man's head lay at an angle to his body, his face was swollen and mottled purple by the rope that had choked and snapped his neck.

The schooner had arrived at first light. Soon after, the crew assembled on deck to witness the hanging. Not a one of the thirty seamen objected to the captain's justice. Now the crew were climbing the bow ladders, finished with the task of ferrying the contraband cargo to shore. Henri Sully's men were still working, lugging the crates and powder kegs up a hill and over the slope to the camp they had set up a week before.

The ship's appearance was a deception, designed to hide her purpose. Four years out of a Connecticut shipyard, the schooner was fast and seaworthy, with a draft shallow enough to permit easy access to the many coves and inlets lining the rocky Acadian coast. In the British colonies she flew the Union Jack, and the log book showed a registry of Grand Exuma, Bahamas. In these waters, she always sported the white and gold fleur-de-lis of France and a pennant with the insignia of a large, black bird, the symbol of the elusive smuggler known only as Corbeau, the Raven.

Below deck, in the sparely furnished main cabin, Sully lounged in a chair drawn up to a plain-hewn, rectangular table. Corbeau sat opposite, between them a half-full bottle of Jamaican rum and two silver goblets. The remains of a meal had been pushed aside.

Corbeau glanced at his friend and frowned. Despite a healthy bronze cast to his round, full face, the young man looked haggard. He'd barely touched his food. Seeming preoccupied, he shifted restlessly and often. Above them the deck vibrated with the tread of boots; Corbeau heard his mate issue an order and the mast creaked, followed by a heavy thump.

"You're more troubled than usual, Henri," he commented, and reached to fill both goblets. As he set the bottle down, a stack of silver coins jingled to his left. He straightened them with an upward stroke of his long fingers, staring fixedly at the pile as a heavy dragging sounded on deck. "Perhaps Bontaine's death unsettled you?"

Henri looked up, surprised. "Such a sentence is not dealt out without good cause. I assumed, when you chose to, that you would tell me why."

"The man died for the only crime I will not overlook," the smuggler replied, his expression sour. "From the first, I mistrusted him. Jacques Bontaine was no more than a Marseille water rat." Raising his cup, he took a swig and held it, as if to dispel a bad taste from his mouth before he swallowed. "We had put in to one of the New England ports. For repairs. My mate saw Bontaine meet a stranger at one of the dockside taverns and after, followed the man." Corbeau's lips twisted cynically, his eyes cold as they met Henri's. "An unfortunate accident befell the stranger as he passed an alley near the customs house. The waterfront can be a most dangerous place."

"When did you confront the traitor?"

"After we sailed. He denied it, though the mate's word was enough to condemn him. After a search, we found these," a finger crooked at the shillings, "sewn into his collar." At a loud splash portside, Henri startled, then grimaced at his skittish nerves. Corbeau's forefinger flicked, sending the coins sprawling. One continued to revolve like a whirling top until he set his palm over it. "So much for the Judas."

"I'd have done the same," Henri affirmed. "Any Frenchman who would turn on his own deserves no less. I suppose he protested to the end?"

"No. Bontaine knew the penalty for informing. He chose to take the risk—for these coins. Small recompense for the cost he paid. I imagine he turned on me more out of spite. I warned him more than a few times that his drinking interfered with his duties." Corbeau swept the money aside, dismissing it. "If not the hanging, what troubles you then?" He and Sully had met often over the past several years. The younger man was his only contact with the Otter, the resistance leader, Le Loutre. After the fall of Ft. Beauséjour in June, Henri had seemed despondent, but then the strategic loss had marked the beginning of the British campaign. He hailed from Grand Pré—perhaps that was it. "Bad news from home?"

Henri sighed and tipped his cup, swallowing heavily before he lowered it, to gaze over the rim. Though they were friends, not even he knew the Raven's identity. Only the Otter did, and that was just as well. The secret was safe . . . except for the crew. With the punishment meted out that morning, their loyalty was assured. "Rumors . . . bits of news brought by the refugees. The Otter would not let me leave." He closed his eyes, resting his head against the chair back. "My sister and her sons are likely deported now, bound for God knows where. I try not to think what lies in store for them."

Servitude, indenture . . . at the least, a harsh life. Corbeau considered Governor Lawrence's "solution" to the French presence. Among the Acadians, there were two disparate factions—those, like Henri, who believed a mass uprising would have rid them of the British presence—and a greater number of colonists who chose to ignore English rule and now blamed Le Loutre's fanaticism for the miseries of expulsion.

"The Abbé was right, Henri. You could do nothing but risk capture yourself. Why lose one more good man? Still, I know how helpless this makes you feel. You look as if you haven't slept in days."

"I haven't." Henri stared into the cup, brooding, and

raised it again. Corbeau had done so much for the cause, he hesitated to ask a favor . . . yet with each passing day, his worry increased. With a great sigh, he leaned forward, resting his arms on the table. "It is my sister, Corbeau. She is missing."

"Yes, you said she was—"

Henri raised a hand, excusing himself for interrupting. "My thoughts are all ajumble." He ran his fingers back through his thick, wavy blond hair. "My older sister lived in Grand Pré. No, it is Chelaine, the younger, who concerns me more."

The name jogged a memory, but Corbeau couldn't put a face to it. "She wasn't at the village?"

Henri shook his head. "With me—at Louisbourg. Safe. We argued over Elise's safety. You must understand, Mama died in childbirth. Elise was the only mother Chelaine ever knew."

"Surely you told her a rescue attempt was impossible. The place is crawling with troops."

"I know . . . *she* knew. I had her promise she would not leave the fortress."

"But she went anyway." At a nod, he frowned. There was no gain from so foolish a venture. "How long ago?"

"Over a fortnight. On foot. She could have made it in four days and—"

"—allowing for skirting the patrols, another two days and four to return." His dark scowl happened to coincide with a glance at Henri.

Though there was no judgment in Corbeau's eyes, Henri flushed guiltily. "She no longer listens to me," he said defensively. "Michelaine is headstrong . . . no, *heart*strong. Emotional. Wherever her heart leads, she follows."

18

"This time, it has led her into a danger from which she may not escape." He refilled his cup. Like Bontaine, the girl had chosen her course. Unlike him, though, loyalty had spurred her. "Was she armed at all?"

"With a knife. Her skill is as sharp as the blade. And she can survive off the land." His mouth quirked wryly. "All she knows, I taught her." He rubbed a hand over his forehead and eyes. "She's a captive. I know it," a finger jabbed close to his heart, "here."

"She knows the terrain. Your impetuous little sister may be in hiding." The suggestion was more for Henri's benefit. The girl was impulsive. If she'd only listened. . . . Suddenly the name registered. His brows came together in concentration. "Chelaine—wasn't she the child—"

Henri's face flushed a dull red, his lips curled down. "She was. I'd hoped you had forgotten the incident."

"No girl has ever thrown her arms about me at first sight." Corbeau smiled, recalling the time more clearly. Then, alert to his friend's discomfort, he suppressed his amusement.

"Nor brazenly kissed you. Even then she was impossible to control. I laid a switch to her for embarrassing you—"

"I wasn't embarrassed," the smuggler insisted. He thought back, cocking a brow. "Surprised, but not embarrassed."

"*I* was," Henri complained irritably. "She had no right following me to our meeting. And was she satisfied with an introduction? Not Michelaine. You bowed most graciously over her hand, but it was not enough. Why do you think, at almost seventeen, she is still unwed?"

"Come, Henri . . ." Corbeau's stare was incredulous. "A brief kiss would not—"

"She's in love with you." Henri set his goblet down with a thump. "She was then and still is. Oh, she's had suitors, but each one had some unacceptable flaw. This one was too fat," he gestured with a flip of his hand, "that one too old, another vain. In her eyes, no other could match you. My Chelaine is all too stubborn."

The revelation of the girl's lingering infatuation stunned Corbeau. Admittedly, he was flattered, but more so, chagrined. Now it was he who leaned forward, disturbed. "You could have told her I was married."

Henri shook his head. "Still, you do not see . . . but how can you? One has to know Chelaine." He stared morosely at his cup and pushed it forward in an unspoken request. "My baby sister is spoiled. And beautiful."

Corbeau obliged with a tip of the bottle and, again, smiled. "With all modesty, Henri, I have known many beauties. As her brother—"

"You think I overstate her charms? Chelaine is . . . different. From so high," he held his palm level with the table edge, "she has always had her way. Whatever she wants, she goes after with a vengeance."

"And this is the girl you wish me to find? If I am able to save her . . . who will save me?"

Henri grinned. "You are safe, my friend. I did think to tell her you had married. Though she believed you lost to another, she measured every man's worth by you. Who could compete with such lofty standards?" His fingers nervously fidgeted with the stem of the goblet. "Corbeau, you have done so much. I would not ask your help, but she is so innocent. The thought of her in British hands . . ." He shuddered, unable to finish.

"She may yet turn up. Did she know of our rendez-vous?"

"Yes, but she would have been here by now."

"If she is a prisoner, she could be anywhere . . . Ft. Edward, even Halifax." It was senseless to search the countryside. "All I can do is sail for the colonies. Boston for a start . . . I have some connections there. If she is interned and up for indenture, I will buy her papers."

"But if she has already been indentured—by the time you find her?"

Corbeau shrugged. "I will offer for her."

"The man may not wish to sell."

This last objection was met with a wink. "There is always a way. I will kidnap her if need be. If your Chelaine is in the colonies, I will find her somehow. It may be spring, though, before I return with her."

"No."

The adamant denial puzzled the smuggler. "You want her safe with you, no?"

"Safe, but not with me. She obeyed only me and now . . . now I cannot trust her. I should have found her a husband, no matter what her objections. None of them was strong enough to curb her wild streak, though." He looked up, a brief smile flickering at his lips. "She needs a man, Corbeau. I would not strain our friendship by suggesting that you be the one." Drawing a heavy gold band from his finger, he set it on the table. "This was my father's. It will help with your expenses."

"Henri—you insult me! Would a friend do less?"

"Take it then and see her wed to one of our kind.

You've already taken some Acadians to our island colonies. This ring—and the one Chelaine has—will provide some dowry for her. Though I would not see her bound to a husband who uses force to dominate her, she must learn to obey. I tell you, I do not envy the man, whoever he may be."

"I cannot force her to marry."

"Tell her she has no home with me." He retrieved the ring and set it in Corbeau's palm, closing his fingers over it. "With this, I give her to your care. You will make her obey. I know you can." For the first time since he'd boarded, Henri looked relieved, the lines furrowing his brow easing. "One thing more—do not let her know you are a bachelor. Then, my friend, she will be yours forever."

Corbeau chose to take the warning lightheartedly, as it was surely meant. "I will remember, Henri. Now . . . you'd best describe this beautiful sister of yours in detail. We met but once and then on a dark clouded night, almost two years past."

Chapter Two

SEATED BEHIND THE CLUTTERED DESK IN HIS QUARTERS, Colonel Marion Pritchard fumed, his broad, jowled face florid with an almost apoplectic righteousness. "I assure you, this . . . this scandalous attack on your ship shan't go unpunished, m'Lord!"

Stephen Harte, earl of Braden, ceased swirling the brandy in his glass and glanced up, his dark, straight brows raised at the officer's embarrassed blustering. A pair of blue eyes, so light and translucent they looked like chips of ice, flickered with a hint of annoyance. "I've had your assurances before, sir," he replied, and with a bored sigh, set the glass on a table beside his chair. "You wrote that the whole of Nova Scotia was under our control. Otherwise, I shouldn't have bothered to sail for Halifax."

There was something arresting about the aristocrat, a presence that had nothing to do with his finely tailored clothing or the lean, sculpted features men envied, women found fascinating. Strength, confidence, an ease that came of his birthright—whatever the source, an aura of subdued power emanated from him. A corner of his mouth twitched impatiently now. "And though I would term it more scurrilous than a scandal, my ship was *not* attacked."

"But the scoundrel fired on you! Your bowsprit—"

"—has been repaired. The man knew what he was about—I'll grant him that. If he'd chosen to fire broadside, I shouldn't be here. The shot was more . . . a toss of the gauntlet. I'm less concerned by the damage than the fellow's bloody insolence. Exactly how much trouble has he been?"

"Corbeau?" Pritchard hesitated, cautiously phrasing his answer. "He's more a nuisance than the Otter. The Acadians were never fond of *that* madman, thank God! This rascal rather inspired them. They admired his daring, took an odd delight in his escapades. Just a day before you encountered—" He paused, chary of admitting more of the smuggler's successes.

"You were saying?"

"Sighting his schooner near Sable Island, two of our corvettes gave chase. They, uh, lost him."

"Lost him?" Braden turned his head slightly, his intent gaze challenging. "You mean he outran them?"

"In a manner of speaking, yes. The patrol followed him around the island and . . . and he slipped over the banks while they . . ." the color mottling his complexion deepened, "ran aground." The colonel sighed heavily. At any other time, the incident would have been just another plaguing affront, but the challenge to the earl's brigantine directly affected Pritchard's finances. Lord Braden had contacted him with a request that he act as his agent in presenting a prospective land grant before the Provincial Council. It meant a fat commission, but now the proposal was in danger of falling through. "I shall insist that the navy double its patrols."

Clearing his throat, he brought the conversation around to the land purchase. "There should be no trouble passing your request through channels, m'Lord. Governor Lawrence is anxious to resettle the peninsula as quickly as possible. It's an honor to have a man of your eminence invest."

"I'm interested in more than the Port Royal parcel, Colonel." Pritchard's face brightened, greed showing, and Braden continued, "I understand there are some very fertile fields near a place called Grand Pré. Is it cleared of the French?"

"At last report, the settlement and outlying farmsteads had been burned. The inhabitants went aboard the transports docile as sheep. Amazing lack of pluck in these people. Still, the better for us."

"Indeed. If they'd risen to the priest's call to arms, you'd still be fighting for their lands instead of arranging British settlement." The earl interlaced his fingers across his embroidered satin vest. "Well, what's to be done about this smuggler? I—"

There was a sharp rap at the door. Pritchard scowled, begging his guest's pardon for the interruption before he called out. His aide opened the door a crack, peering hesitantly around its edge. "What is it, man?" the colonel snapped. "I gave strict orders not to be disturbed."

"Yes, sir. It's Pichon, sir. He's here, insisting he must see you. Something about the prisoner, the rebel."

"Have him wait five minutes and usher him in, then.

Do him good to cool his heels." Corporal Miles saluted, relieved that he'd escaped a reprimand, then quietly retreated.

"Who's this Pichon fellow?" Braden inquired. "And why is he in such a pother over a prisoner?"

"A French turncoat. He came over to us while he was the commandant's aide at Beauséjour, reporting on the Otter's activities. Unfortunately the man couldn't deliver the devil into our hands. As for the rebel," he smiled, showing a row of uneven, yellowed teeth, "'tis a girl. He recognized her somehow among the interned women. She has a brother with the resistance—both he and the girl were at Beauséjour. P'rhaps I should bring him in now, eh? You might be interested in what he's learned."

"I would."

Pritchard called out again, a bellow that brought his aide to the door. Thomas Pichon pushed past the corporal, striding forward with an awkward attempt at a bow. "I am sorry to disturb you, Colonel, but—"

"Yes, yes, go on. I've a very important guest and . . . tell me what you've found out."

Pichon flushed. He had served the British well, and though he'd chosen to aid them and be branded a traitor, they seemed to have little regard for the sacrifice. He was still smarting from his questioning of the Sully girl, who had answered his inquiries with a curse and a stinging slap. "The girl, she will tell me nothing. I was, perhaps, the wrong man to interrogate her."

Pritchard glowered, his fair brows drawn together in disgust. "So, you learned nothing and this was important enough to disturb me? Did you consider threatening the chit with a lash?"

"Such punishment would make her more stubborn. I know she has only recently been with Le Loutre. Though she may not betray him, you may be able to learn something of Corbeau."

The officer visibly perked at the name. "And how would I gain that information?"

"Offer her the chance to stay in Acadia. From me, this promise means nothing. If you were to grant her the right, on paper, and pay her a portion of the bounty for his capture—"

"Assuming he can be captured." Braden's interest was as piqued as the colonel's, and he smiled as he settled back in his chair, stretching his legs to cross them at the ankles. "If he's as elusive and popular as Colonel Pritchard claims, the offer would be met with scorn."

Pichon glanced in the direction of the fireplace, noticing the guest for the first time. Irritated by the comment, valid as it was, he studied the darkly handsome man and suppressed his annoyance. Whoever he was, his clothing indicated wealth. The man lounged with casual grace in a chair that faced the desk, seeming to diminish its size by the breadth of his shoulders and his long legs that indicated a height well above average. His cool blue eyes gazed back with an aloof confidence that came of rank and privilege.

"Lord Braden's observation is most astute," the colonel agreed. "She won't cooperate, and so the matter is finished. Let her suffer deportation for her obstinate loyalty. We'll ship her out with the others. Once she finds herself indentured to one of our colonial farmers, she'll have time aplenty to repent."

"D'you really think she knows anything of Corbeau?" The earl's question addressed Pichon. The man's face had fallen at the decision, but now his eyes glinted with renewed eagerness.

"I believe she knows . . . m'Lord. If I had only some inducement—"

"There are other means of persuasion."

Pritchard listened to the exchange with mounting interest, more intent on watching the earl. "Surely *you* aren't thinking of going after the smuggler? The bounty is high, but for a man of your means—"

"If she reveals what she knows of him, the money can go to the girl," Braden said, and with a quirk of his brow, admitted, "Life has been a bit of a bore of late. One can derive only so much from Boston's social amenities. You forget that the smuggler tossed the first challenge. He thinks himself invincible." A chilling smile curved his mouth as the earl set his fingertips together, flexing them. "I have reason enough to prove him wrong."

"Whoever the bastard is," Pritchard interjected, "he knows the coast so well—"

"I can study a map as well as any ship's captain. You *do* have an accurate survey of the coastline?" At the answering nod, his smile broadened, baring a row of even teeth that appeared more white for the contrast with his bronzed complexion. "I suggest you have the girl brought here. She may even agree to Pichon's proposal . . . if it's properly broached."

Braden certainly did have cause to hunt down the smuggler, and though he led the life of an indolent nobleman, his enviable, well-conditioned physique intimated a man who was active and in his prime. As unexpected as the offer was, Pritchard found himself excited by the prospect. A feather in his own cap if the plaguing devil was brought to justice. "You heard His

Lordship, Pichon. Have the girl brought here. Immediately."

"At once," the Frenchman replied, but his attention remained fixed on the earl. He bowed and said, "I must warn you, sir, Michelaine Sully is no ordinary girl. She does not cower easily."

Braden continued to smile. "But, monsieur, I am no ordinary man."

While Pichon was gone, Stephen concerned himself with finalizing the details of his purchase. He signed papers appointing Pritchard his agent in residence and suggested that an officer be sent to Grand Pré to survey the best of the available lands.

Finally the girl was brought in. Evidently she'd given Pichon some resistance. Her hands were bound before her, secured tightly by a rough, hempen rope. Tall and slender, oddly dressed in men's buckskins, with her long brown hair plaited and tied with a strip of linen, she glared sullenly at Pichon.

Pichon nodded when the colonel asked if she spoke English and then was ordered to leave. "Her resentment of you is obvious."

Chelaine acknowledged the traitor's dismissal with a brief smile before her withdrawn, sullen expression returned. She would not tell the fat, pompous officer any more than Pichon had sought. In her resentment, she had failed to note the colonel's use of the plural.

"Young woman, I am aware of your association with the renegade Le Loutre. By your attire, 'tis clear enough you've stayed with the resistance." Pritchard rose and circled the desk, pausing before her, hands clasped behind his back. "I propose this—that you be allowed to remain in Nova Scotia. When we capture the

Otter," the girl smirked at the presumption, "your brother, should he still be with the rebels, will receive a full pardon. What I desire now is information about this Raven fellow, Corbeau. What he looks like, where he rendezvous with the resistance." She looked up, not bothering to conceal her contempt for the man or his offer. Pritchard scowled. "Should you maintain this silence, deportation awaits. Eventually, you'll be forced to serve a number of years in bond. I cannot say how kind or harsh your master shall be." He paused, to let the threat sink in. "How much better you would fare in your birthplace."

"How generous. What good does it serve to remain in a land overrun by scum? Your troops have burned my home."

The colonel colored at the insult but held his temper. "Then, wherever your village is, you'll be granted a small plot—"

"You waste your time—and mine," she insisted, and straightened with an air of haughty defiance. There was a rustle of movement behind and slightly to her right. Chelaine turned her head as an elegantly clad man rose from his seat by the hearth. He was very tall, his weight proportionate to his height and . . . breathtakingly handsome. His gaze raked down her figure and sent a shiver rippling down her spine; then, with an unusual, animallike grace, he strolled toward her.

It was difficult to take her eyes from his face. At once she was both frightened and fascinated. Pichon was no threat and the colonel only spoke of a fate to which she had already resigned herself. Without a word, this man intimidated her. It was his eyes, she thought. They looked so cool, an ice blue framed by long, almost black lashes. He had paused near her. Now he took a step back, studying her with a sardonic expression. Instantly, she hated him. In contrast to his impeccable, rich clothing, she was made aware of how drab and unfeminine she looked.

The earl moved away, ignoring her for the moment, addressing the colonel as if she weren't present. "None of your promises will secure the information we seek. See that she's sent to my ship. If you've a quill and paper handy, I'll pen a note to my manservant."

Chelaine stared at the man's broad shoulders as he leaned over to write the note. She had no idea who he was . . . or why he meant to take her aboard his ship. His bold appraisal had brought a memory of the colonial scout to mind, but there wasn't a hint of desire in this stranger's eyes. The colonel was fawningly deferential, eager to oblige his slightest wish.

"I will tell you nothing," she insisted.

Braden dusted the note with a sprinkle of sand, shook it, and folded the paper in half before he deigned to turn. "That remains to be seen, mademoiselle." Pritchard called for his aide, and when the man appeared, handed over the note with an order that she be escorted to the earl's ship and left with a guard.

"That won't be necessary," Stephen said.

"You're sure, m'Lord?"

"Quite. In fact, I've ordered my man to see she's untied once she's in my cabin. You give her too much credit, sir. She may look like a savage, even fancy herself resourceful, but she is, after all, only a female."

Chelaine glared, galled by the insulting summation, but she was seized by the arm and drawn toward the door before she had a chance to refute his arrogant claims.

Chapter Three

IN THE HOUR OR MORE OF HER CONFINEMENT TO THE BRIG'S main cabin, Chelaine had paced, raged, battled despair —and explored the spacious quarters. She had never seen such magnificence. The English lord had spared no expense in making the room as comfortable as possible. A wide, deep berth lay in a curtained alcove opposite the door.

To the left of the door, there was a heavy rectangular desk of some rich, reddish wood, its glossy, polished surface clear save for a candle lamp bolted to one corner. A thick, sea green carpet stretched before it, running from the portal to the berth and covering an open area to the edge of a pair of wing chairs separated by a round table. A tall, handsomely carved armoire stood beside the door, so deep it formed a private niche with, of all things, a deep, enameled bathtub!

She tried the bed and found the mattress softer than any she had known. Covering it was a thick, green quilt and beneath the blankets, sheets of linen so fine she wondered at the skill with which they'd been woven. A half hour after he'd untied her, the earl's manservant, Samuel, returned to light several lanterns. When he set out towels, a cake of soap, and a nightshirt on a shelf above the tub, she bluntly inquired as to what he was doing.

"Plain enough to see, missy. I'm preparin' a bath, as His Lordship ordered," he answered curtly. She didn't at all like the crusty old goat but the feeling was mutual. "'Tis for you, before you ask. Though God knows you need one, I can't see why he should allow you the luxury."

"You waste your time, old man. I will not bathe."

Such impudence shocked Samuel, deepening his disapproving frown. "You'll be learnin' to mind as you're told. No one disobeys Lord Stephen."

"What can he do if I refuse?" she mused aloud. "I am not afraid of him as you are."

"Fear has nothing to do with my obedience. I respect the earl. Known him long enough to follow orders no matter what he wants. You'll learn."

Tentatively she questioned, "He beats those who disobey?"

"He don't have to. Never known Himself to lay a hand on any who serve him." He flashed a malicious grin. "Yet."

"I am no servant. I am . . ." It wasn't clear to her what she was doing here but certainly she was *not* a servant. "When does he return?"

"When he pleases," Samuel groused and added, "Any time, though, for he sent word not a quarter-hour past, sayin' he'd be back soon."

Chelaine paced again, following a track she had made in the deep pile of the carpet. Finally she settled in the chair nearest the berth, facing the door, worrying at her bottom lip as she tried to think of some way to escape. Even if she slipped past the crabby Samuel, the crew on deck would stop her. The windows were too small to wiggle through and besides, the bay was icy cold. If she made shore, she would only be caught again. There seemed no way out of it.

At any other time she would have welcomed a bath, especially the novelty of soaking in the deep, scoop-backed tub. But with *his* return imminent, the thought of shedding her clothes in his presence made her skin raise goosebumps. Perhaps he would stay above deck . . . no, she remembered his eyes and knew he would not allow her privacy. The cabin was his, he would not leave it merely to satisfy her modesty.

If Henri could see her now, he would forget his anger and somehow save her. Leaving the dead scout behind, she had ridden northeast, and though the gelding was tired, she could have made the rendezvous easily—if she had not stopped to speak with the band of women and children wandering lost in the wooded meadow. They seemed so confused and helpless, she had directed them north and assured them they would be welcomed by the Louisbourg commandant.

Out of the circling woods, mounted soldiers suddenly appeared. She had bolted, but the gelding was no match for their fresher mounts. With the others, this time stripped of her knife, she was herded to the capital and held in a house at the garrison. Deportation was bad enough, but Pichon had brought her to the attention of this dark-haired, cold-eyed noble, and now she was thoroughly confused by what lay ahead.

Even as she considered searching for some kind of weapon, the door opened again. Expecting to see Samuel, she found herself staring at his master. The earl paused long enough to locate her, then strolled to the desk, laying his hat and gloves on it. On his heels, the old man returned. Setting down the two buckets of steaming water, he moved quickly to assist the earl from his greatcoat, hanging it carefully in the armoire before returning to his task.

"Have you fed her?"

Samuel paused as he poured water into the tub. "No, sire. You didn't say nothin'—"

"I know. When you've finished with the bathwater, see to a meal." The cool, blue gaze shifted to her. "I trust you're hungry, mademoiselle?" Chelaine shook her head, refusing, though her stomach rumbled at the mention of food. "Ah, well, I must dine alone. For one, then, Samuel. And do make sure the water isn't too hot. We don't want the young . . . lady scalded, just clean."

"Aye and that might take a second washin'," he grumbled, before retrieving the empty buckets and cocking a brow. "If you'll pardon me askin', the hold's cleaned out, ready for them other women. Shouldn't *she* be there?"

"No, Samuel, she'll be staying with me," Braden said with just the barest hint of censure in his downward glance. "No more grumbling from you, now, or I'll forget how long you've served me and . . ." He left off. They both knew he would never punish him, no matter the reason. "Go on with you, then. I'm hungry."

When Samuel muttered his way out of the cabin, Stephen nudged the door shut with his heel and took a quick survey. There wasn't much Michelaine could have bothered, but unless he'd misjudged her, she had explored the cabin. He crossed to the berth and found the covers disturbed, tempting a smile. He knew full well that the materials and thick, down mattress must seem a luxury to an Acadian farm girl.

The chair was only a few feet away; he moved to it and stood before her. Purposely ignoring him, she stared down at her clenched hands. He reached and caught her wrist, pulling her firmly to her feet, though she tried to wrest free. Examining her wrist, catching at the other, he stared at the reddened marks left by the rope. "It's a shame they bound you—but then I suppose you gave them cause. I've some ointment that should heal these abrasions."

Her eyes widened, wary and distrustful. "Why do you care?"

"Because I always see to the condition of my possessions. You'll soon find that I'm a man of habit. I prefer cleanliness, hence the preparations for your bath. I like order as well, so you will assist Samuel in keeping the cabin straightened. I expect you'll be rebellious at first but that won't last."

He had released one wrist but held the other. Chelaine jerked free and tipped up her chin defiantly. "I do not wash and he, your man, will clean for you. I am no serv—" Suddenly, with an awful clarity, it sank in. He had referred to her as a possession. "You think I tell you of Corbeau by threat of indenture?" She smirked at the idea. "It will not—"

"I've already seen to that." Stephen slipped his hand within his waistcoat and produced a paper which he unfolded. "I don't suppose you can read but you may recognize your name." Chelaine peered at the official-looking document, sealed at the bottom with a splotch of impressed red wax. Indeed, there was her name, and next to it a large X. Above her name, his name and titles were printed in a neat, legible hand. Stephen

36

Andrew Christopher Harte, earl of Braden, Viscount Reredun. "Your period of servitude is one year," he went on, "though, of course, time may be added if you're foolish enough to attempt an escape."

It wasn't legal. "I never sign this paper," she protested. "It means nothing." Still, she made a quick grab for it, and anticipating the action, Stephen stretched his arm, holding it beyond her reach. "I did not sign," she repeated, and made one more attempt to snatch the paper that said she was his bondservant. Finally she gave up; his arm was long, and he seemed to derive some enjoyment from her frustration. "You think this makes you my master . . . it does not," she asserted with a spite that gritted her teeth.

"It bears witness by an officer and gentleman."

"You are no gentleman."

The earl chuckled. "I referred to Pritchard. At any rate, I am, by this paper, your master . . . to do with as I please. Should you continue to rebel against my commands after a day's grace, I will be pleased to show you that my will is the only law aboard this vessel."

"I am not afraid of you. Samuel, he said you have never struck a servant."

"Samuel is growing old and rattles on like gossipy crone. In your case, I may amend my attitude. I don't intend to quarrel each time I make a request. If you choose to obey, my temper will remain checked."

Samuel appeared following a tap at the door, lugging two more buckets of water. "Seen to your supper, I have. Cook should have it ready by the time that one's in the tub."

"'That one' will not be in the tub," Chelaine insisted, and started to sit down. A hand closed on her forearm, keeping her afoot.

"She will." Stephen's tone brooked no further display of rebellion. "Are you done, Samuel?"

"Aye, m'Lord."

"Good, then you may leave." When they were alone, he turned his attention to the girl. Her mouth was set in a thin line as she glared at his hand. "Time to bathe, Michelaine." Her eyes raised, catching the glow from one of the lanterns, a luminous gold-brown that reminded him of a lioness he'd once hunted.

He spoke as if she were a troublesome child. She glanced past him at the vapour rising from the tub, then met his chilling blue eyes, faltering under their gaze, feeling helpless and trapped. "You only want me to bathe so you can leer," she accused. "You . . . lecher!"

A sudden warmth melted the chill, turning his eyes a liquid blue. He started to chuckle, and the sound evolved into a deep rumbling laughter that mocked the claim. Chelaine's cheeks burned, and she longed to slap him but wisely chose not to.

Still holding her arm, Stephen took off for the armoire, pulling her after him. Opening one of the doors, he revealed a full-length, beveled mirror. He positioned her before it, and taking a stance behind her, watched as she stared at her reflection. Wispy curls framed her blushing face, a streak of dirt crossed one cheek. She looked like a homeless waif.

"Still think I'm a lecher?" he asked, and raised a hand to wipe at the streak. She'd had no chance to bathe during her internment. Clean, her brown hair promised a lighter shade. "I assure you my tastes run to women with full curves. If you persist in refusing to eat, come morning, I'll see you force fed."

Chelaine wrinkled her nose, as much at her reflection

as the threat. "If you find me ugly and thin, then I will starve myself."

"Did I say you were ugly? *Au contraire, petite.*" Her eyes widened at his smooth, fluent French. "Somewhere beneath that outlandish outfit, you are more than passingly pretty. Perhaps even beautiful." Their eyes met in the reflection, the gold of France, the blue of England, clashing. "And you will not starve. I won't permit it."

"You are afraid of loosing your property?"

"Losing," he corrected.

"Losing, then. It would be a way to cheat you of my service." She turned and glanced over her shoulder. "I hate you."

"That's clear enough. I see we'll have to work on your grammar." His brow arched, his shoulder lifted and then fell in a careless shrug. "I can live with your hate—for as long as it lasts."

Chelaine clenched her teeth. How smug he was even to imply that she would ever cease to despise him! For now she would hold her tongue and do as he asked. "If you leave me be, I will wash."

He stepped back, and the mirror reflected a mocking, half bow. "I shall be at my desk, dining, 'm'lady' . . . and if you feel ill at ease, leave the door as it is. I shan't see a thing, even if I wished to."

Another knock sounded at the door. It was Samuel with the supper meal. Chelaine slipped around the armoire door and leaned against the corner formed by the angle of the chest and the wall. He had made it quite clear that she wasn't worth a look. Even while it pleased and reassured her, she felt . . . well, he needn't have made her feel as if she were a boy because of the breeches and shirt. She sighed and quickly began to strip, anxious to settle in the water before he changed his mind. He was so . . . enigmatic, so damnably assumptive, so . . . attractive. About to step in the tub, his voice suddenly startled her, though it came from across the room.

"Toss those . . . things around the door," Stephen ordered. "You won't be needing them." He could almost see her mouth round with shock and those gold eyes glitter in defiance.

Not needing them? What on earth was she to do without her clothing? And he had claimed to have no designs on her! "I have nothing else," she complained. "What am I to wear?"

"Samuel laid out one of my nightshirts. It will do for the present."

She dared not refuse. Chelaine bent, retrieving her shirt and breeches and tossing them over the top of the door. Her boots sailed farther, with the hope of landing amidst his meal, but fell far short of the mark. Scowling, she put a foot in the water. Far from cool, it was still very hot. If she voiced a complaint, it would only bring Samuel with cool water, and she had nothing to hide her nudity.

Gritting her teeth, she set the other foot in and slowly sank into the water. It came to the hollowed V at the base of her throat. At the bottom of the slippery enameled surface, she touched something squishy and startled. Then, bravely, she grasped it and raised her hand. A sponge. Nearby, on the shelf, lay the soap. She had to stretch to reach it. When she lathered it against the sponge, a wildflower scent arose, and with it her curiosity. It was not his. The earl smelled of musk and tobacco. Perhaps his wife. He was certainly old enough

40

to be wed. "Are you married?" she asked, unable to contain her curiosity.

Stephen looked up, swallowing a bite of stewed chicken, choking a bit in surprise, drinking from his wine glass before he answered. "No lady has had the honor of becoming my countess." He took another sip and canted his head. "Why would you ask?"

"Because you do not seem the type who washes with such pretty soap." Behind the screen of the door, Chelaine raised the sponge and slid the lather over her shoulders and throat, relaxing now, contented . . . for the moment. "Someone traveled with you. Your mistress?"

He was tempted to let her believe it, but with a smile at her continued curiosity, he revealed that the soap was his sister's. "She's about your age . . . and very much a lady." The smile deepened to a grin as he added a jibe, "Lucy would never dream of donning breeches. She'd rather die—"

"Then in our icy Acadian winters, your Lucy would freeze her—" Chelaine stopped just short of indecency. Again, he had made her aware of the difference between herself and the females in his world. For two years, the Otter's cause had been hers. She had carried messages for him, easily passing the enemy lines, even flirting when it was necessary, deceiving the simpletons when a man would have been stopped and searched. She had received her share of proposals, as well, but only one man held her affections, and he was not even aware of her love. If he had been, it would have made no difference.

Corbeau, the same man this arrogant, cold-hearted aristocrat had sworn to capture, this was her love. Closing her eyes, she leaned her head back, remembering. She had only followed her brother for a glimpse of the Raven. And when one of his men had discovered her hiding in the bushes, she had been dragged forth like an errant child, humiliated before her hero. The night was dark, Corbeau no more than a tall, shadowy figure who had soothed Henri's anger and gallantly touched his lips to her hand. Then she had done the unthinkable. Impulsively she had thrown her arms about his neck and kissed him. Henri was mortified, Corbeau surprised, and later she had paid for the incident with a spanking. Long after the punishment faded, the memory remained. Even now, she could feel the warmth of his lips, the tickle of his mustache brushing her mouth. But he was married . . . and she had vowed to remain unwed.

"I don't hear any sounds of scrubbing, Michelaine. You've soaked long enough. Wash your hair."

Brought back to reality by the cool, even-toned commands, Chelaine scowled in the direction of the desk. She had meant to wash it but now decided not to, just to thwart His Wonderfulness. "I am finished washing," she called. "The water grows cold. I will do my hair another time."

Stephen sighed and shook his head, pushing back his plate. He'd met his share of strong-willed females, but this one was the worst of them all. *"Now, Michelaine."*

"If I do, I will catch my death of cold. You will lose your 'servant.'"

"The room is warm, and there is an abundance of towels to dry you." he replied. For sheer drama, there was scarcely an actress who could match the girl. "I'll not ask again," he warned.

Holding the sponge between her hands, Chelaine squeezed, pretending her fingers were about the devil's throat. She dropped it with a splash and pulled at her braid, unwinding the plait. She couldn't refuse, and yet it rankled her pride to give in. The room was silent, then there was a loud scrape, the sound of the chair legs against the deck. Heels clicked against the wood, muffled across the carpet. She quickly soaked the sponge and shook her hair loose, dabbing at it.

Suddenly the armoire door swung shut. The earl seemed composed, though there was a tension in his stance. "The water isn't cold," he observed. This much was true; steam still hung over the tub, wreathing it like a low-lying cloud. Chelaine raised the sponge and sank lower. "My dear, you're trying my patience. I don't like being tested."

"You are not as awesome as you think," she said. "I will not let you frighten me." Her chin tipped up, her lashes lowered. "I have met men worse than you."

The earl lifted a brow. "Have you, now? Then permit me to step lower in your esteem." He moved around to the side of the tub and held out his hand. "Give me the sponge." Now her eyes widened in alarm; she seemed to waver between rebellion and submission. Sensing victory, Stephen smiled.

It was the smile that decided her. In a fit of temper, she drew back the sopping sponge and threw it. His reflexes were amazingly quick. Catching it in midair, he was still drenched by the water that squirted from it. Earlier he had removed his waistcoat and vest. Now he held the sponge in one hand, pulling the front of his soaked shirt away from his chest.

Chelaine panicked, regretting the rash act. She was trapped. As his hand moved toward her, she twisted, grabbing for the edge of the tub. The sponge came down on her crown, his hand pushing her under the water. Swallowing gulps of soapy water, she choked and came up sputtering and coughing, only to find the lathered sponge applied to the heavy mass of drenched hair. Soap dribbled down into her eyes and she blindly batted at him, to no avail. He scrubbed hard, working his fingers through the tangles, heedless of the curses she laid on his head.

Although a good deal of her hair was piled atop her crown, some of the wet locks hung over her shoulders and coiled in ringlets across her breasts. Stephen worked steadily at the scrubbing, but as she floundered, he was distracted by a display of firm, rounded flesh. She was slender rather than thin. The shapeless shirt had hidden much of her alluring curves. With a frown, he dunked her again, rinsing away the suds.

This time Chelaine had taken a breath and held it, keeping her mouth shut. Her tormentor, for she could think of him in no other terms, pulled her upright, and just when she had cleared her eyes of water, the sponge came down again, sluicing streams of water down her face. She recovered enough to swear at him, this time in French.

The earl was laughing again as she dragged the wet tendrils away and glared balefully at him. "Beast, am I? You might think so now, but a good week's sail lies ahead. I'll have your respect by the time we dock in Boston, or one of us will be worn for the effort." The confidence in his eyes left little doubt as to whom that would be. "Now, towel dry and be quick about it. Or must I assist in that as well?" His brief bow was mocking as he added, "I'll wager I'd derive more pleasure from it than you."

"Bastard!" The epithet was out before she thought.

Expecting some retaliation, she tensed, but he only stared, one corner of a long, sensual mouth indented.

"You are obviously intelligent, though unfortunately given to fits of unrestrained temper," Stephen observed. "I've shown you I can master you by strength, though I mean to see you brought to heel by willpower alone. I've never fancied meek women. Spirit is all well and fine, provided it's tempered by common sense. I would rather see you bend than break." His eyes were icy once more. "Do I make myself clear?"

Chelaine was too worn to do more than nod. *"Oui . . .* yes."

"Yes, m'Lord. From this point forward, you will address me thus." She stared fixedly at the water, struggling for self-control, finally managing a very soft, but mocking, "Yes, m'Lord."

"I didn't quite catch that."

Chelaine's head came up, her voice overloud and indignant as she repeated her answer. "That's an improvement, though we'll have to work on respect." Stephen reached for a sheet towel and held it out. "Do dry quickly," he urged, "before you catch your 'death of cold.'" With that reminder of her earlier claim, he turned on his heels and left her, opening the door to pull out a fresh shirt. The hour was late and he changed his mind, reaching for a nightshirt instead. On the other side of the door, water sloshed as Chelaine rose. He would give her time to dress and call Samuel to empty the water and clear away the tray.

It was clear that he was changing clothes. Chelaine dried herself hastily, and still damp, reached for the nightshirt. It suddenly occurred to her that the berth was wide and comfortable, yet it was the only sleeping

45

arrangement in the room. The earl had made his opinion of her lacking charms quite clear. He would not be put out of his own berth for the sake of her modesty. She could only assume that he meant her to share the bed. She rubbed at the dripping mass of her hair, unnerved by the thought.

"You're dressed?" The question startled her, but she remembered to phrase her reply with the required 'm'Lord.' "Good, then I'll send for Samuel. If you're shy of having him see you in my nightshirt, slip into the berth and draw the curtains."

The door shut and the two stared at each other. She was shocked to find he wore nothing but a similar nightshirt. On him, it came to his knees, showing a pair of muscular calves covered lightly with wiry hair. The V neckline was open to midchest, revealing more dark curls.

For his part, Stephen found her enchantingly appealing, waiflike, and lost in the folds of material that ended near her slim ankles. She'd dried a good bit of her hair, and free of dirt, it curled in a cloud of layers over her back and shoulders. Though she'd rolled back the cuffs, her hands were hidden, and only the tips of her fingers stretched beyond the white lawn sleeves. Reaching out, he rolled them back farther. "Come over in the light," he said. She hesitated, unsure of his intentions, and he gently caught her elbow, drawing her toward the pool of light cast by a lantern affixed to the cabin's center beam.

In the mellow light, her hair coiled in damp ringlets around a face whose even contours approached an almost ideal beauty. He reached out, drawn to the texture that looked silken. Shining and clean, her warm brown shade glinted with streaks of burnished gold.

She stepped back, wary of the examination, and his gaze left her face, traveling downward. She seemed lost in the shirt, but here and there it clung to a spot still damp, enhancing rather than hiding the swell of her breasts.

Embarrassed, Chelaine dropped the towel and fumbled at the row of buttons, starting at the bottom, meaning to secure them all. The last gave her trouble. The earl's fingers brushed hers aside, deftly fastening the button. Irritated by the unasked-for assistance, she glanced up to find him regarding her with a hooded gaze.

Stephen drew his fingers away. "I'll call Samuel."

Chelaine nodded, then blinked, sure she had imagined a thaw in his eyes. Yet, how could those winter-chill orbs ever look warm? Oddly disconcerted, she watched him cross the room. Acadians had never honored titles. The early seigneuries were extinct now, and though Quebec had its share of noble visitors from Old France, Acadia never saw them. Whatever their nationalities, this man would stand head and shoulders above any assembly of aristocrats. On him, even the simple nightshirt took on an elegance. Her blush deepened as she scurried for the berth, rings rattling along the bar as she jerked the curtains closed.

Crossing her legs Indian-style, elbows resting on her knees, she propped her chin on her hands. The darkness of the alcove led her thoughts to a future that seemed shadowy and vague. When the ship sailed, she would leave a life that, if simple, was comfortingly familiar. Shunning Elise's attempts to domesticize her, Chelaine had been as disorderly as Henri and her two older nephews. She'd tagged after the boys, trying to best Louis, always surpassing André.

Climbing trees, running free, riding, all had given her a heady sense of freedom. Henri had seemed proud of her skills. Still, what place would these talents have in a world where women were expected to dote on men, to fawn over them, to play docile and demure? Lost in her brooding reverie, Chelaine had not heard Samuel come and go, nor bid his master a good night's rest.

As Stephen parted the curtains, she looked up, startled. Lost in the folds of material, Michelaine looked like a child. He frowned. Her moods were so mercurial—and he felt more easy with the untamed rebel than this wide-eyed, vulnerable innocent. "I'm tired, Michelaine. You must be as well. By habit, I rise with the sun."

Chelaine sighed in resignation. "I suppose I must sleep on the rug," she said, and asked if he had a spare blanket. The floor boards were hard but she had camped on harder ground. Unfolding her legs, she set her hands at the mattress edge and scooted forward. The earl was frowning still, though she could not think what she had done now. He reached, catching her beneath her arms, lifting, to set her on her feet. The strength and warmth of his hands made her aware of how little protection the nightshirt afforded.

"There's no need for that. I—" The air of soft vulnerability vanished, replaced by a defiance that had grown familiar. Her hand rose to brush at his. Once free, she primly straightened the shirt, insisting the deck would be fine. "I am a servant, only. This is proper, yes? For the help to find a place lower than—"

"Your manner borders on insolence," Stephen complained crossly, annoyed that she had prodded his usual tightly reined self control. "*I* decide where—"

"You wish me to sleep in the hold? Samuel says it is where I belong."

"Like yourself, he's only a servant." Because she expected a scowl, he smiled. "You'll hold your tongue when I'm speaking. These constant interruptions are unseemly, improper if you better understand the term." He stepped closer, intimidating by his size as well as his tone. "The berth is wide enough for two and—" she opened her mouth, but at a stern look closed it. "—and I shall be gracious enough to share it."

Michelaine colored, a deep rose suffusing her prominent cheekbones. "You show an uncommon modesty for a girl who parades about in tight, revealing breeches." She glared, but he continued. "You'll not sleep on the carpet. The only other choice is there." He pointed to his right, where a hammock had been slung between the wall and a beam. Her decision was obvious, but he couldn't resist a last jibe. "Your virtue is safe in either case, though I'm sure you'll find the berth more steady."

"I will manage." The sling looked awkward, but the alternative was unthinkable. She moved toward it, but the earl stood so close she could not pass without brushing against him. Even as she raised her head to excuse herself, he moved back. Sensing his gaze on her, no doubt waiting for her to struggle with the unfamiliar object, she straightened her back and examined the hammock. A blanket lay folded at one end. Determined to show him up, she unfolded it and, turning, settled in the widest folds of canvas. Not so difficult after all. Smiling with insincere sweetness, she wished him a good night.

Stephen waited. If she thought that was all there was

to it, the girl would find it took a certain skill to maneuver one's self without tumbling out. Shaking out the blanket, she covered herself and clutched the edges of canvas. So far, she was managing better than expected. He turned, lowering the lantern wick, and slipped into the berth.

More confident now, Chelaine swung one leg up and stretched it, then the other. His Lordship was in bed, probably irked by the ease with which she'd adapted. With a smile, she wriggled, adjusting her weight. The movement set the sling swaying, giving her pause to wonder how well it would serve when the ship was at sea. She closed her eyes. By then, she would have mastered it.

The room had grown more chill, and though the blanket was warm, her feet poked out. Still cold from the bath, they felt like ice. Raising an ankle, she tried pushing the woollen hem over her toes but only succeeded in loosening it. Now a part of her calf lay uncovered. Sure of her balance, Chelaine sat up, reaching for the hem. As she caught hold and tossed it toward her feet, the hammock swung, and instinctively she grasped for a hold.

The movement abruptly spun the sling, and with a hard thud Chelaine landed on her back, catching the brunt of the fall on her elbows and derrière. She gasped at the pain that jolted down her arms and sat up, rubbing a hand over her bottom. For three weeks, she had suffered one shock after another, one humiliation piled atop the next. This last raised a well of tears that spilled over her lashes. She rolled onto her knees and bent her head, covering her face with both hands, shoulders shaking with muffled sobs.

At the sound of the fall, Stephen had thrown back

the covers. He hesitated. If she'd broken something, he'd have heard a scream. In the dim light he saw her assess her injuries and settle back on her heels. She was weeping, more from embarrassment than hurt.

He slid his feet to the deck. It had been ridiculous to offer her a choice. He should have ordered her into the berth, heedless of any protests. Now he padded toward her and paused, wondering if he should let her cry it out before he helped her rise.

Her tears slowed to a trickle. Wiping at her eyes, she saw the earl's legs, then followed them upward, expecting to see him gloating over her tumble. She wasn't sure which was worse—the fall, or letting him see her cry. She bent her head again.

Going down on one knee, Stephen reached out and caught her chin, tilting it up, wiping at a tear rolling down her cheek. With a sigh he slipped his right arm around her back, raised her and caught her knees, lifting her with him as he stood. She wiggled and made a feeble attempt to push at his chest, then gave up with a sniffle. He carried her to the bed, set her down and sat beside her. Raising one sleeve past her elbow, he checked for any pain that might indicate a fracture.

Though his fingers pressed gently, then slid higher, probing her upper arm, Chelaine winced as he touched her elbow. He raised the arm, bending it before he turned his attention to the other. She wondered if he meant to examine her derrière as well. She resented the examination and pulled away. Unable to stop herself, she glared. "Your property is not broken. Let me—"

"Your vanity is more damaged than anything else," Stephen said. When she asked him to let her by, he shook his head. "You'll sleep here, against the wall if you prefer." An obstinate look narrowed her eyes, but before she could protest, he pushed her back and leaned across her, a hand planted on either side of her shoulders. "I don't intend to let you interfere with my sleep. Aren't you bruised enough? You'd only fall again—and likely break your silly, stubborn neck." Raising back, he nudged her shoulder with a hand. "Now, roll over."

Chelaine stiffened in resistance, but he seemed in no mood to brook any defiance. Doing as he ordered, she shifted as close to the wall as she could, turning her back on him and dragging at the blanket.

The berth creaked as he settled his full weight on it and covered himself as well. He could have offered her his pillow, but one look at her stiff back banished the thought. Tucking an arm beneath his head, Stephen stared up, considering how long his patience would last. She had a spirit to vex the most saintly of men, and he was far from that. On the morrow, he would set her a number of tasks that would leave her so exhausted she'd have no more strength than to crawl into bed at the day's end.

I wish I were dead. Chelaine repeated the thought several times and amended it. She wished *he* were dead. If he thought he could turn her into some timid, frightened servant, he would find that she was more strong-willed than himself. Some way, somehow, she would make him sorry he'd brought her aboard. Beside her, he turned onto his stomach, and she pressed closer still to the wall. For moments she held her breath as he wrestled with the pillow and stretched out, then settled down. Just as she exhaled, relaxing, he moved again, crooking his arm.

When, after a while, his breathing came evenly, she turned onto her back and peeked. Despite the chances

52

he'd had, the earl had made no attempt to force her. Even with inches separating them, warmth radiated from his body. They were both naked, only the thin nightshirts covering their bodies. She remembered the strong, corded muscles that had lifted and carried her so easily. It seemed she was safe from an assault like that which she'd endured in the woods. He'd emphasized the kind of women he preferred. She was only a girl, a thin girl. At least that kept him from desiring her. Still, she wondered why others had wanted her while this attractive and virile man did not.

Chapter Four

CHELAINE LEANED AGAINST THE BOW RAIL, ARMS RESTING on the wood, studying the scenery as the brigantine skirted the coast of southern New Brunswick. "This rocky land, it looks very like Acadia," she said softly, a fleeting hint of wistful longing fading her smile. A breeze astern floated forward to stir her bright curls, and she brushed at a silky tendril that tangled across her lashes. Turning slightly, gazing up at her companion, she smiled once more. "It does not seem so different. Will Boston be as this, with hills and many trees?"

James Avery returned her smile, entranced by the tawny eyes that gazed up at him. It was hard to believe she was the same girl who'd been brought aboard in Halifax, bound and looking like a sullen, resentful lad. The pale yellow gown clung to her curves, and though a lace shawl modestly draped her shoulders and covered the lace-edged bodice, it enhanced rather than hid an enchanting display of cleavage. He blinked, swallowing hard, trying to remember her query. "Boston? Oh, 'tis hilly, miss, but trees like those, they're long gone. Still, there's some fine elms planted along the Common and—"

"And the young woman shall see the city soon enough for herself," interjected a voice that brought the mate stiffly to attention. His ruddy face, topped by a thatch of carrot red hair streaked blond from the sun, colored with embarrassment. "I issued an order for a starboard course change, Mister Avery," Braden stated, ignoring Chelaine as he scowled at his officer.

"I . . . I thought I told the helmsman, m'Lord," Avery stuttered. "I'm sure—"

"Apparently you were too distracted to relay the information, sir," Braden said tersely. "I've seen to it myself. Were I you, I'd hie myself below to consider the punishment for neglect of duty."

"Aye, m'Lord." Avery saluted smartly, his conversation forgotten in the wake of the reprimand. "Begging your pardon, sir, I—" He broke off; there was no excuse, and any further explanations would only incur the earl's wrath. With another salute, he slipped past Chelaine and toward the aft hatch.

Stephen's lips pursed as he studied Chelaine's profile. Her fair brows were troubled, evidencing dismay as she watched the mate's hasty retreat. Beneath her straight, pert nose, her lips were parted slightly, a hint of color dusted her cheeks. Traveling downward, past the slim, straight column of her throat, his eyes widened at the rounded swell of ivory flesh that showed above the low neckline of Lucy's gown. Her breasts appeared more prominent for the tight, gathered bodice and the small span of a waist that narrowed without the corset she had refused to don. He reached out, caught hold of her upper arm, and jerked her about to face him, missing the flare of anger at his unnecessary roughness as he firmly adjusted the shawl over her bodice and turned her toward the rail, away from the crew's watchful eyes.

Chelaine pulled away, and the shawl fell open again, but she was too upset to concern herself with propriety. For a few minutes she stared out across the waters, seething, then glanced sideways. The earl's stern scowl had disappeared, replaced by his usual cool composure. "I suppose you blame me—"

"Avery knows his duties. You didn't drag him bodily from the sterncastle. Still, the man owes his confinement to quarters to your indiscreet presence. You were told to stay below."

The accusation stung. She had been allowed a half-hour's exercise in the morning, and the earl had promised her another spell of freedom from the stuffy cabin if she mended the shirts he had set out. "You promised—"

"I didn't forget," he interrupted curtly, annoyed by her lack of concern over the décolletage once more displayed. "You had no right leaving the cabin without my permission. I said I would come for you—"

"When the ship's bell rang six times." The sun was lowering to the west, and the watch had just changed with the chiming of eight bells. She turned on him, arms crossed beneath her breasts, unaware that the act only curved her full breasts higher. "You let the other women stay above for an hour each morning and afternoon. Why am I not given the same exercise?"

Stephen's eyes raked down her, purposely fixing on her chest. The fifty or so refugees in the hold needed fresh air and sunlight—and none of them was as beautiful nor displayed herself as enticingly as

Chelaine. "Those poor damsels are wearing proper attire, while you . . ."

A blush spread over her from toe to head, warming Chelaine despite the cool, rising wind that tugged at her curls. *"I* did not choose *this,"* she retorted. "You took my clothing—"

"Which only revealed a different, equally distracting portion of your anatomy. I do believe you enjoy the crew's attentions more than the exercise."

Her mouth rounded into an exasperated O of indignation, Chelaine glared sideways with a narrowed, spiteful look. "If I am a bother, put me in the hold," she insisted. "One of the matrons will spare me a blouse, another a—"

Stephen's lips quirked at the suggestion. "And have you inciting them into some sort of rebellion? If not happy with their lot, the women have resigned themselves. No, my dear, you'll remain with me, where I can keep a watch over your activities."

Above them gulls wheeled and dove, echoing raucous cries. She glanced up, watching, then her gaze studied the coast. A small fishing sloop was sailing to their stern, headed northeast. "Your colonial fishermen aren't as cautious as our Acadians," she said. "It will storm before nightfall."

The wind came from the north and the ship's sails billowed, propelling the brig forward with a following sea. There wasn't a cloud in the sky. Stephen pointed this out with a gesture and scoffed. "So much for your predictions. I know when the weather's turning foul."

She sighed. Hadn't she lived with the sea all of her life? Chelaine smiled to herself, smugly confident that her intuition would prove out. Even as she closed her eyes, tipping her face to catch the slanted rays of the sun, a gust of eastward wind tugged at the waves drawn back at her temples, secured by two tortoise shell combs. She could smell the moisture in the air, not the tang of salt spume but fresh water. The seagulls were more aware of the coming change than the man who fancied himself so able a sea captain.

Once again, Stephen caught her shoulder, firmly turning her from the railing. "You've done enough damage for today," he insisted. "I want you down below." A flicker of color caught his eye, and he raised his gaze to the rigging to find one of the crew openly oggling Chelaine. "I'd see to my work, Bowden," he warned, "before your gaping lands you in the brine." Then to his errant charge, who resisted his grip, he added, "Need I say more? Get below. *Now.*"

"No!" It never failed—each time he addressed her in that arrogant, assumptive tone of authority, she wanted nothing more than to thwart his desires. She faced the railing again, pretending he didn't exist.

"Have it your way, then." Before she had a chance to provoke him with an open show of defiance in front of the crew, Stephen circled her shoulders, swept an arm down beneath her legs and lifted. He moved so swiftly, without warning, that for a few moments she was still, shocked into silence. Recovering quickly though, she pushed at his chest and wriggled, kicking with her legs. He only banded her more tightly and, well aware that his crewmen were smiling, stalked purposefully toward the companionway hatch.

"*Put me down,*" Chelaine growled through tightly clenched teeth. She, too, had a glimpse of the open amusement among the men, a wink exchanged, a nudge of an elbow as one man prodded another's ribs. The earl ignored her, carrying her effortlessly, despite the volume of material made up of dress and several layers of petticoats. She felt as if she were the captive of some pirate; it wasn't enough to have everyone aboard thinking she was his mistress . . . the accursed devil had to sweep her off like a prize. Despite her twisting, wiggling bid for freedom, he managed the stairs with uncommon ease. Once at the cabin door, he bent, lifted the latch, and entered, setting her on her feet so abruptly she almost toppled.

Rage supplanted caution. She could almost hear the crew snickering and the smug expression on His Lordship's face only added to the humiliation. She swung without thinking, smacking his right cheek with an open palm. They were both equally stunned by the action, and fast on the heels of satisfaction, Chelaine was shaken by the consequences of such defiance.

The imprint of her fingers showed clearly, a reddened outline on the smooth bronze of his cheek. As he recovered, his eyes glittered like ice chips, pinning her with a half-hooded fury that excelled her own. Not even sure why, Chelaine reached up, gently laying her cool fingers over the spot she had struck. Her mind was a battleground of confused thoughts, indignation warring with a belated temperance. His arrogance deserved such a dressing down . . . why, then, did she feel remorse?

Stephen's first instinct was retaliation. Though Chelaine had acted out of rage, the audacity of striking him couldn't go unpunished. In the wide-stretched topaz eyes something intriguing had supplanted horror. She seemed more remorseful than afraid, bringing her hand back to his cheek with a tender soothing touch.

Their eyes remained locked as he caught her wrist and tugged. Whatever she thought of his intentions, there was no resistance when he drew her close, cradled the back of her head, and lowered his mouth to hers. His lips brushed hers and found them soft, pliant, yielding. Stephen slid his hand down her back, pressing her closer still as he teased her with kisses. She made some sound, not a protest, nor a whimper, but a sigh that vibrated as if he had touched some chord of music within her. His fingers tangled in the silken waves. For the moment, there was nothing of the rancor or pitched battle of wills, only the stirring pleasure of her mouth surrendering to his.

Some powerful emotion swept through Chelaine, banishing everything but a compelling desire to remain within his arms. There was a reined strength in his hold, giving her the feeling that she was safe from everything that might hurt her. Unlike the bruising assault of the scout's kisses, the earl moved his lips so tenderly that a curl of pleasure left her lightheaded, spreading a warmth throughout her body that made her feel as weak as a kitten.

It was Stephen who broke the embrace, reluctantly drawing back to stare at the pouting curve of her lips before he firmly grasped her shoulders and set her away. She opened her eyes, dazed and almost puzzled by the parting. Her breath came and went in an artlessly tantalizing rise and fall that strained the bodice, almost tempting him to draw her close again.

Chelaine stared up at the man she had sworn to hate, her captor, her tormentor, and for moments that seemed stretched by time, she felt nothing but a sense of loss. Blinking several times to clear her head, she was surprised when the flutter of her lashes sent a spill of tears coursing down her cheeks. Nothing he had done, no arrogant commands, no cutting insults had stirred her to cry. She had no use for tears, they were a feminine wile, a weakness . . . yet this gentle embrace had brought them rising from her. She blushed and looked away, biting at her bottom lip. "Do you . . . always kiss the women who slap you?"

Stephen reached out, lightly closing his fingers about her chin to turn her face back to him. He saw the tears but dismissed them as remnants of the rage that had passed. "I've never had one dare, little one," he mused. She glanced up, her lashes spiked and damp, eyes glistening with some indiscernible emotion. "I admit, carrying you off was a little overdramatic."

"I . . . I should not be on deck without your permission."

The admission was as close to an apology as pride would permit. "You're used to your freedom. And I've deprived you of it."

Chelaine felt a smile tug at her mouth as she wiped at the dampness beneath her eyes. Each of them seemed bent on accepting the blame. They were fighting again —but themselves this time. "I chose a course that deprived me of that," she admitted honestly. "If I must be subject to someone, there are worse men than you."

"And better . . . like Corbeau?" It was something he said without thinking and regretted as soon as the words were out. Chelaine was suddenly wary, the gentle mood between them vanished like smoke.

Though the earl had questioned her about Corbeau, he had not pushed for answers as Pichon had done. It had never entered her mind that he had any other reason to pursue the smuggler than for the personal satisfaction of besting him. The idea that he might be jealous was ridiculous. "Corbeau?" Her mouth tipped up in a hint of irony. "He is more spirit than man, more a legend than reality. And," she couldn't help the envy in her voice, "he is married."

"But you wouldn't mind if he were in my place?"

He seemed bent on pursuing the subject whether she wanted to discuss Corbeau or not. She lifted her shoulders and let them fall. "I do not know him, only of him . . . as all Acadians do. Still, I think he would not keep me bound to him by some paper, against my will."

"As you said, you don't know him." Stephen stared past her, scowling at nothing in particular. "Perhaps when I bring him to ground, you can meet this hero of yours. In the light of day, with his hands bound, he may lose some of his appeal."

"He is not *my* hero," Chelaine snapped, then turned abruptly and crossed to the corner wing chair, pausing, drawing the shawl about her as a sudden shiver swept over her skin. She looked back, puzzled. "What he did, firing on your ship . . . is this reason enough to hunt him? Why can you not let it be? If he is as reckless and vain as you claim, he will eventually be caught. Or perhaps now that Acadia has been conquered, he will simply fade from sight."

"I could be persuaded to do that if—"

Chelaine heard nothing but an eery echo of the scout's threat. He, too, had wanted something in return for her cooperation. Though the earl had not tried to take advantage of her, this kiss had revealed a latent desire. The other time she had killed to save her honor. This time, she had no weapon and, too, she was oddly drawn to this "master" of hers. "I am keeping you from more important work, m'Lord," she said, and turned about to sink onto the chair and lay her head back. "Do what you will to find Corbeau."

"His capture no longer matters?" Stephen questioned. Something had shifted her mood again. She looked very tired and withdrawn, beset by brooding thoughts. "Or perhaps you think I'm no match for this dauntless devil?"

"I think the better man will win out." She gazed at him and sighed in exasperation, wishing he would let her alone. "Men do as they please. I cannot stop you any more than I could Corbeau." Her eyes closed. "Always, it is the women who suffer."

The earl felt strangely uneasy with her melancholy air. He'd seen her defiant, raging, frustrated at his commands, sullen, even smiling as she had the morning she had liberally salted his breakfast eggs. "Have you suffered so terribly?" he probed. "Any woman in the hold would trade places with you."

The deliberate taunt had its desired effect. Chelaine stirred, straightening stiffly, her eyes snapping with challenge. "Find one who is willing to flatter your vanity then. I didn't ask to be here. Torment someone else. I endured your kiss—"

"Endured?" Stephen's jaw dropped. "You impudent little minx! *I* drew back. If I hadn't, you'd be on your back now and—"

"Conceited beast! Do you forget your arms were holding me close?"

"For all the resistance you put forth, I could have held them at my sides. Endured, indeed—believe what you want. We both know what passed between us was mutual desire."

"You pulled me close, I . . ." She could say no more,

for she hadn't resisted. "I hate you! You vain, pompous . . ." Chelaine sputtered. She had already called him everything despicable, in two languages. "Go away," she wailed. "Go join your crew and laugh over—"

"Shut up!" Any moment now, he expected a flood of tears to come pouring forth. "I'll have Samuel prepare a bath. At least a half tubful. Your tears should fill it the rest of the way." With that he turned, jerked open the door, and left, slamming it so hard the door shuddered on its hinges.

Even before the wood stopped reverberating, Chelaine was out of the chair, wildly searching for something, any handy object to launch across the room, preferably something breakable. There was nothing available, and by the time she'd made a circuit of the room, her anger was dissipating and the idea seemed silly.

Though he hadn't abused her, Stephen Harte was as cruel in his own way as the colonial soldier who'd attacked her. The other had been blunt about his needs and bruised her body in an attempt to possess her. This bastard of an English lord wanted her as well, but he meant to strip her of every shred of dignity and leave her not even a chance to claim she'd been used. One had used his body as a weapon, the other his willpower.

She had adapted to his orders, but that wasn't enough. The earl had shown her a few minutes of warmth and sympathy and she, fool that she was, had responded with a trust that was crushed when he ceased his game-playing. That was what it amounted to—he was a master at the art of manipulating people as he wished. Dropping into the chair once more, she leaned her forehead against one of the wings and vowed to guard her emotions more closely. He would not win . . . she wouldn't let him.

The bath *had* helped to soothe her ruffled feelings. As the afternoon wore on to dusk, the seas became rough, and Stephen had grudgingly admitted she was right. The winds had shifted, sending dark, roiling storm clouds from the shore out to sea. He had spent his time on deck, issuing orders to secure the ship and making sure the women and children were given extra blankets.

Now, after supper, the brig was pitching heavily, rolling as each strong surge of waves hit her starboard. Dressed in Lucy's silk, lace-trimmed nightgown, Chelaine moved to clear away the supper dishes, stacking them on a tray to carry to the door. They'd spoken very few words during the meal and she had only picked at her food. It was just as well—with the storm tossing the ship about, she would feel less queasy on an empty stomach.

As she leaned over to lift the tray, Chelaine found the earl beside her. "Allow me," he said with a polite, reserved consideration that brought her eyes up in wary distrust.

"I can manage," she insisted, but even as she did, the deck swayed heavily to port, and it seemed wiser to let him take the tray. She had a difficult time staying afoot. With the tray of china dishes, she wouldn't have made it to the door without a crash. Sure-footed, he shifted his weight, matching his balance to each shift of the deck, easily crossing to the door to set the tray outside and call for Samuel.

With cautious, tiny steps, Chelaine headed for her favorite chair. Halfway across the room, she lost her balance, but the earl was there, righting her, supporting her arm as he led her to the chair, despite the tension that stiffened her at his touch. Once she was settled, he bent and took two glasses from the cabinet beneath the table, set them next to a brandy decanter, and poured himself a drink.

"May I get you some wine?" he asked, glancing across the room at the liquor cabinet to the right of his desk. "There's port and madeira, possibly even a burgundy."

"I will have brandy," she answered, more to shock him than out of a desire for the stronger drink. The request brought a skeptically raised brow.

Since he'd come below, Chelaine had maintained a frosty distance, answering his few questions with a simple yes or no. Though her temper had cooled, he sensed a challenge in the request, decided to call her on it, and poured the other glass full of the liquor. "It would seem that you learned more of men's ways with the rebels than the mere wearing of masculine attire," he commented drily. "Exactly who taught you to drink liquor?"

Chelaine allowed herself a tiny, pleased smile, accepting the glass and taking a sip. "The same trapper who taught me your tongue," she admitted as he settled into the other chair. "He dared me to join him at one of the taverns at . . ." She had almost said Louisbourg and silently chided herself for the near slip. "I accepted the dare, and though the drink was rye, I did well."

"This happened on more than one occasion?" Stephen swallowed a large gulp of his own drink and studied her with a puzzled air. "I would have thought your brother guarded you too closely for such brazen ventures."

With a shrug, Chelaine took another sip, determined to show him she was not to be intimidated by their earlier encounter or by his condemnation of her way of life. "My brother was often absent." She smiled, recalling that that first drink had nearly choked her. There had been two other times, again on dares, and the last a wager for money. She had managed to down three drinks before Henri suddenly appeared, infuriated by her presence among the tavern girls and his fellow rebels. He had slugged poor John Denton, sending the trapper sprawling, before he had hauled her home and taken a birch rod to her bottom.

"So . . . you think you can match a man drink for drink, eh?" By the look on her face, she was proud of herself. "This brandy is older than you, my dear, far more potent than any home-brewed rye whiskey." The statement only made her drink again, more than a sip. This time her rather jaunty smile was for him. "What else did you get away with while your absent brother left you to your own exploits? I imagine your 'friend' had more in mind than a lesson in tippling."

Chelaine frowned at the insinuation. "John Denton was old enough to be a grandfather, m'Lord. If you think he—"

"Come, Michelaine, a girl of your vast experience should know that a man's passions aren't dimmed by age. My own grandfather was chasing after the housemaids well into his seventies. The man must have made—"

"Never!" Denton had more or less adopted her, taking pleasure in teaching her English. She, in turn, had often mended his buckskins and seen him to his lodgings when he overindulged. "The trapper, he had a wife at the fort, a Meti girl—"

"Ah, there—you see. Old enough to be a grandfather and young enough to take an Indian wife, a girl, you said. I imagine he sired a brood and it wasn't his first."

Chelaine stared into her drink and raised it, determined to ignore the goading. Denton had only watched over her in Henri's absence. If he had any faults, it was his fondness for drink, and after a hard life trapping in the forests, that was excusable. "He was my friend," she replied defensively.

"I can't, for the life of me, understand why you were with your brother in the first place. Your parents must have been mad to let you go off—"

"I am an . . . how do you say? . . . an orphan."

"You had no one but this brother?" Stephen swirled the liquid in his glass. "I can see now why you grew up so wild."

"My sister and her husband raised us. After papa left."

"You said you were orphaned."

"Mama died hours after I was born. Papa left our farm to Elise and . . . went away. He might as well be dead."

"You mean he abandoned a newborn and a . . . how old is this brother of yours?"

"Henri is five years older." Chelaine never liked to think of her father. To her, he was as dead as her mother. "Papa was never meant to farm. He was a sailor. After she died, there was no reason for him to stay." She shrugged and raised her glass, drinking again. "The farm thrived under my brother-in-law's care. After he died, it went to his son André."

"There were no other girls in the family?"

She shook her head. "Why? Why do you concern

yourself with my history? I have not your
. . . pedigree. I am no one."

"You're awfully proud for a little nobody." He
glanced at her glass, surprised to find she had almost
drained it. If anything, she looked alert and bright
eyed, certainly not tipsy. "Well, mademoiselle, you do
seem to be able to hold your liquor. Or is one your
limit?"

Though she had said as much herself, it was galling
to have this regal lord call her a nobody. She straightened, her back stiff as she held out her glass. "I can
match you drink for drink," she insisted. He had not
even finished his, and she allowed herself a snide
smile at the observation, "Unless you intend to nurse
yours."

"Far be it from me to refuse a challenge
. . . especially from a slip of a wayward rebel. I only
considered your tender years. I don't generally ply
females—or children—with strong drink."

"I am no child. You are, perhaps, afraid that I might
best you?"

The earl smiled, a smile as cool as the blue of his
eyes. "It never entered my head that you could." He
tossed off the rest of his brandy and set the glass down,
uncapping the decanter to refill both, pouring hers only
half full. "It's only fair," he replied in answer to her
arched brow. "By my size alone, I have an advantage."
She shook her head and insisted that the match be
equal. When he handed her the glass, it was as full as
his. He raised his own in a toast. "To your pride,
mademoiselle . . . in the hope that it goeth not before
a bruising fall."

"That alone would keep me afoot, if I . . . *when* I
outdrink you."

Stephen watched her. Michelaine did, indeed, seem to have an acquired capacity for drink. She appeared no more affected than before the first taste. All he felt was a slight relaxation, an easing of the reserve that had followed on their earlier disagreement. "I wonder, girl, if—"

The thought was left unfinished as Samuel popped his head in following a rap at the door. "Avery wants your opinion of a course change, m'Lord," he said, and gaped at the sight of the girl with a glass of his master's fine, aged brandy in hand. "'Tis gettin' nastier by the minute, and he thinks . . ." He refused to go further, preferring to discuss the matter with Lord Stephen. "I told 'im you'd be up. 'Tis rainin' to beat the devil, though. I'll get your slicker."

Stephen sighed. The mate could handle any changes necessary. Still, the *Lucinda* was his ship. He tipped back his head, swallowing successively until he'd drained the brandy. Samuel waited, holding out the oilcloth overcoat and a pair of loose, oiled-leather boots. Shrugging into the coat, discarding his shoes to wedge his feet into the boots, he glanced back at Michelaine. "Unless you've given up . . ."

Her chin tipped up, a pleased smile playing at her lips. "I will wait."

Once the earl was out the door, the smile dissolved. Chelaine stared at her glass, then glanced around the cabin. Everything had a slight, warm haze. She was content with her stamina thus far, but if he returned and pushed the match further, she wasn't sure she would win. If she finished her drink, it was a draw. A draw was not a loss. Already lightheaded, she raised the glass, and rather than prolong it, swallowed until the last drop was gone. Wiping delicately at a drop that wet the corner of her mouth, she set the glass down with a satisfied clink, then came to her feet.

She exhaled a deep breath, dizzy, and for a second disoriented. It was the storm of course, setting the room to swaying. Aiming for the berth, she took slow, careful steps, unaware they seemed exaggerated. Gaining the edge of the mattress, she sat, kicked her legs high and rolled. She was feeling the liquor, but with any luck, His Greatness, Lord of Everything, would not notice. Lying back, she gazed at the polished boards above the berth. Somewhere up above, Stephen . . . she giggled at the daring of using his given name, even in the privacy of her own thoughts, *he* was battling the cold rain of a storm *she* had predicted, while she was safe and dry, warm and cozy . . . and not a little sleepy. She rolled onto her stomach and tugged the pillow beneath her chest and face. It smelled of Stephen. A nice smell, spice, musk, something in the bottle he splashed on after shaving. He was terribly attractive when he shaved, standing before the armoire mirror, bare from the waist up, the muscles along his back and shoulders rippling as he moved an arm, as he . . . Chelaine smiled, her lashes drifting closed, all warm and cozy . . . safe from the storm.

Chapter Five

GRIPPING THE ROPE RAILING, STEPHEN CAUTIOUSLY DE-
scended the stairs, water sluicing from his slicker. On
the last step, he slid, righting himself with a loud,
resounding oath. As he moved along the dimly lighted
companionway, his boots squished. His shirt was plas-
tered to his chest, cold water trickled down his neck.
For all the protection it provided, he might as well have
gone on deck without the slicker. More galling than the
clammy feel of his clothing was the memory that
Michelaine had predicted this weather—and he had
scoffed.

The storm had come from the land, heading due east.
The worst seemed to have passed, though while he was
above, waves had broken over the rails and a hard,
driving rain made it nigh impossible to see. The wind
broke a spar, but otherwise the ship was secure. He'd
ordered a hard starboard turn, angling the bow to ride
the waves instead of wallowing in their troughs. Ahead
lay open sea and no danger of running aground on the
rock-bound coast.

Balancing a hand against the wall, he pried off the boots, irritably kicking them aside. Another curse brought Samuel scurrying forth from the small room where he slept. The old man took one look at him and swore himself, hurrying to take the slicker Stephen shrugged off and retrieve the waterlogged boots.

"A bloody tempest, to be sure, m'Lord!" he exclaimed, and tsked over the sodden shirt and hose. "You'd best change and dry off. I'll come and—"

Stephen raised a hand. "No need, Samuel," he insisted, glancing at the cabin door. "I've Michelaine to help me, if need be."

"Aye—if she don't take it to mind to refuse. She's an odd one, all right. All the airs of a lady, none of the graces." He frowned at the water puddling the boards, reminding himself to have a cabin boy mop it up. "Can I be bringin' you something warm—a toddy or perhaps some tea?"

"I've more a mind for brandy, thank you all the same." Pulling at the riband that tied back his hair, he shook his head and a shower of droplets flew. "No need to stay up and fuss. I'm for bed, and so should you be."

"Ah . . . a good night to you, then, sire—such as the weather permits."

"And to you. It seems the worst of it's passed."

More from habit than requirement, the servant bowed and watched his master pause at the cabin door, already pulling at his shirttails. The Acadian lass was a handful, sadly lacking in proper respect for her betters. Yet, if she refused to do Stephen's bidding, 'twould be her voice that issued forth. His Lordship never raised his voice above the well-modulated tones of the noble gentleman he was.

Inside, the room was quiet. Michelaine had disappeared. Though the bed curtains were half drawn, she couldn't have missed the noise in the hall. The brandy must have gone to her head. "Michelaine?" A muffled "Hmm . . ." answered his call as Stephen pulled off his stock and tossed it aside, then stripped off his sodden hose and shirt. Reaching around the armoire, he grabbed a towel and headed for the table. Her glass was empty. Filling his own again, he chugged back several draughts, paused, and drank again until it was gone.

This time he bellowed loud enough to wake the dead. "Rouse yourself, girl! I need you." The warmth of the liquor flowed through him, dispelling some of the chill as he cocked a backward glance at the berth. A pair of shapely legs appeared before, too quickly, a slim, tapered hand adjusted the gown. Michelaine's feet touched the cold deck, toes wriggling. Finally she appeared, both hands brushing back her tousled waves from a drowsy face, the delicate lines of her mouth set in a slight pout.

"What is it . . ." She took in his appearance, and her eyes widened. A small hand covered the hint of a smile. "You look . . . drowned."

"A most astute observation." He gestured at her empty glass. "I thought we were set for a match."

The thick, brown-black waves at his temples were soaked, and a flow of water dribbled from the longer waves at his nape. "I was tired. Of waiting," she fibbed, then shrugged. "Neither won, we both had two—"

"I had another while you were lying abed." She frowned at the news and started to rise, wavered, and sat back. "So much for your tolerance, girl. Two drinks and you're tipsy."

"I am not!"

He crossed to the berth and caught her chin, raising

it. Her eyes looked sleepy, but it was the brandy. "Move aside. If you stood, I'd only have to catch you." As he pushed the curtains open, she raised her legs and scooted back. Stephen sat and tossed her the towel. "If you're not, then, make yourself useful."

Chelaine blinked away the feeling of lassitude, inhaling deeply to clear the fog muddling her thoughts. "I could have another drink and still not lose," she insisted as she bunched the towel and dabbed at his shoulders. He turned with a smirk that mocked the claim. Irritation sobered her further and she scrubbed hard at his chest and upper arms. In vain, though, for rivulets of water continued to course from his hair. *"I could."*

"Is winning so important?"

"To you, it is." She sat back and with a petulant look, thrust the towel at him. "Dry yourself."

Stephen shook his head. Something devilish in him, perhaps the drink, brought an obstinate refusal. "You've forgotten who's the master, who's the servant." For the sport of it, he wagged his head, sprinkling her gown with drops of water, then handing her the towel. "My hair needs drying. See to it." With that, he made himself comfortable, swinging his legs up, crooking his right knee as he leaned his head against it.

Chelaine glared, though the look was lost on the damp curls at his crown. She seized the towel and furiously bent to the task, scrubbing briskly with both hands. A muffled complaint only increased the vigorous mopping. Suddenly he raised up, caught the towel ends and looped the material about her shoulders. The damp chill penetrated the thin silk, stirring a shiver . . . or perhaps it was the dark intensity in his gaze as he slowly gathered the ends taut. Her hands pushed at his chest, but he continued pulling until she was next to him.

In a velvet-toned voice, he commented, "You weren't very gentle, Michelaine."

"I . . ." She wriggled, aware of the warmth radiating from him despite the dampness of his skin, aware that a very thin layer of silk was all that lay between her breasts and the hard muscles of his chest. His leg shifted sideways and her knees gave way, leaving her trapped and helpless, banded close by the towel. *"You* are the one who cannot hold—"

A tug on the towel and an arching of his neck cut off the claim. Stephen's mouth sought hers, one hand tossing the towel aside. The other swept through the long, silken curls to cradle the back of her head. She stirred, her nails pressing his shoulders, a brief resistance that fled even as his tongue delved within the soft warmth in a teasing exploration. He had meant to chastize her, to bend her to his will, but that was forgotten with the supple feel of her silk-clad body molded to his, her nipples firming to stab at his chest. He rolled, and she was on her back, his arms encircling her. For what seemed a very long time, they stared at each other. The magic of their first kiss was back, arcing between them like some invisible, drawing force.

Chelaine gazed up in fear and fascination, with the feeling of a trapped creature facing its predator. He was the hunter, she the quarry, and yet . . . the hunter's eyes held no threat, only a burning blue warmth before they slid lower to fix on her mouth as he kissed her again. She should be struggling. That was rational thought, yet her heart and senses delighted in the stirring brush of his lips, and in Chelaine those two forces were stronger than reason. That feeling had returned, the security found in his strength, and if she remembered at all that a sense of betrayal had followed on the earlier embrace, she was past caring.

A soft moan rose from her . . . or was it her? Chelaine was, at once, deeply moved, her body trembling as his fingers gently stroked her temples, and detached. Surely it was some other girl who willingly yielded up her mouth, whose lips responded to the light pressure. It couldn't be her, for she lay in the arms of an Englishman, and the English were her sworn enemies. With his hands caressing her so tenderly and his warm breath brushing her throat in a nibbling kiss, he was just a virile, impossibly attractive man. Nothing else mattered.

Stephen raised his head, sure he was dreaming. Michelaine lay still, her long lashes casting spiky shadows over her cheeks. A wild tangle of honey brown waves surrounded her, spread across the white sheets, coiling in silken ringlets over her breasts. Her lips were slightly parted, touched by the same rose that blushed her cheeks. His mouth lowered, touching the soft hollow at the base of her throat. A scent of wildflowers lingered on her skin, still sweet and clean from her bath. Whether it was the brandy or the soft pliancy of her body, the effect was intoxicating, luring him to run a hand along the contours of her firm, high breasts. She stirred restlessly, but not in resistance, as his fingers trailed across her ribs, tracing the inward curve of a waist narrow and almost fragile in its slenderness.

With a stifled groan, he rolled away, lying on his back, staring up, though he saw nothing. Beside him Michelaine stirred, half raising to lay her hand on his chest with a hesitant, tentative touch.

Having given herself up to the pleasure his tender

caresses called forth, Chelaine could not understand what had come between them. She felt the thudding beat of his heart beneath her fingers, the heat that radiated from the taut, corded muscles. She gazed at him in wonder, puzzled by the tension that clenched his jaw. A pulse ticked at the edge, inches from his firm, set chin. She placed a fingertip to it, and he stiffened, facing her, catching her fingers to bring them to his lips. His eyes were heavy lidded with desire but glinting with a frustration that seemed foreign to his cool, imperturbable nature.

Suddenly, in a moment of insight, she realized that his need for her made him vulnerable. In many ways they were alike . . . both stubborn, proud, unbending. Though she had surrendered to his strength, he still fought the passion that would banish his self-control. For the present, the yearning made them equals, and she wanted that as much as the delight of his strong hands gentle on her skin. He still held her fingers. She raised them now, touching his cheek, stretching to plant a shy kiss at the corner of his mouth.

Shock rippled through Stephen. Chelaine wanted him, the action said as much without words, and he . . . he was too aroused to let the mood slip away. He reached back, behind his head, fumbling for a silk-braided cord, tugging on it to draw the curtains closed. In the darkness, he drew her close, and she seemed to melt against him. His hunger was tactile, and though she shivered, her body stirred in answer as his hands roamed freely over the firm flesh whose proportions seemed as near perfection as he had ever known. Thought and reason fled before a ravening need that sent his spirit soaring. If she trembled, it was innocence awakening, and she had offered it up, freely, an unexpected blessing, one he would have been mad to refuse.

Glad that he had drawn the curtains, Chelaine snuggled close, and though a tiny fear niggled at the back of her mind, she felt safe. Strength and gentleness in the same man were rare. She closed her eyes, and the darkness enveloped her. For minutes he held her, pressing light kisses at her temples, teasing her skin with the feathery brush of his lips, stirring a coil of pleasure deep within when his warm breath at her ear preceded a nibbling just below it. She could almost believe he loved her, so tenderly did he seek to arouse her with his hands and mouth.

Every part of her had an allure all its own, the silk of her hair was more fine than that of the gown, the texture of her skin as soft as velvet. He tugged at the nightgown, drawing it upward until it lay in folds across her thigh. She trembled at the exposure, but his mouth sought and found hers, stilling any apprehension with gentle, reassuring kisses. Her lips parted willingly, and he explored the sweet warmth, the swirl of his tongue eliciting a sigh.

He pulled the gown higher. Imagining the ivory flesh stretched taut across her belly caught his breath as much as the sight would have. His own body seemed to fascinate Michelaine. Her fingers traced the muscles of his shoulders and arms, following the rise and slope of each with the tips of her fingernails. "Christ! You're so lovely," he whispered hoarsely, "so beautiful. You've no idea how much torture it was . . . to lie beside you each night and not reach out . . . to want you and—"

"I had no defense," she answered, awed by the admission. "How often you said I was your property, to do with—"

"I'd never have forced you." His head lowered, nuzzling at the swell of her breasts with his cheek. "But you must have known that." The gown was soft, but he longed to feel the still softer beauty it veiled. Rising, he brought her up with him, still pressing brief, hungry kisses at the corners of her mouth as he caught the material, dragged the folds free of her arms and tossed the gown aside. Her fingers timidly crept about his neck, twining together as he pulled her close. Michelaine quivered at the contact and sought refuge in a kiss. Twisting, he rolled back and briefly lingered at her lips before shifting lower, eager for the sweet taste of the proud, firm nipples crowning her breasts.

Chelaine gasped as his tongue flicked lightly, then an even more startled cry tore from her as the moist heat of his mouth engulfed the peak of her breast. His every move was suave and confident, sending ripples of delight racing along her skin, curling her toes as his tongue swirled circles, its rough texture driving her wild. Her hands touched his damp waves, splaying through the short, layered hair at his temples, a primitive instinct arching her shoulders back.

His name echoed in a soft whisper as Stephen continued the teasing assault on her senses. Chelaine stirred, aware of a building tension, centered low, at the base of her belly. His hands seemed everywhere at once, caressing her breasts, trailing lower to explore every curve and hollow, toying with the curls between her thighs. His palm pressed her thigh back, and with an ease that shocked her, his fingers gently parted the soft fold of flesh below the curls. A haunting memory rose, the rough, crude trespass of her attacker. She stiffened, expecting pain, but Stephen's touch was feather light, so soft she relaxed.

The small bud of flesh responded to his stroking like a flower blossoming under the sun's warm caress. He longed to take her now, to make her his, but his own desire came second to a stronger need. This first time, he meant to arouse her to a fever pitch, to give her pleasure before she knew the tearing pain that preceded the loss of her maidenhood.

Suddenly his warm breath caressed the tender spot, a moment later the liquid heat of his mouth worked the same magic that had left her nipples aching. She rose up, shocked anew at the bold intimacy, but he pressed her back with the flat of his hand, managing to translate his own enjoyment. Chelaine lay still, eyes closed as the delight of the movements brought her fist against her mouth, stifling a whimper.

Stephen went on, stirring her to a wild abandon. Soft moans and whispered cries spoke of her intense pleasure. Her thighs tensed, she arched suddenly and quivered, shaking in the throes of an impassioned release. Finally, when her restless twisting calmed, he sat back, pleased. She held her arms out and he slid forward. They were both flushed, heated by the same fires, their mouths meeting in a breathless, lingering kiss.

The languor that had spread through her limbs was with her still, and the eagerness of her kiss seemed to surprise him. He drew away, but she clung, gripped by an insatiable hunger for yet another branding kiss. If she had regrets, they would come later; now she wanted him as she had never wanted anything in all of her young life. "Such bliss . . . I never thought . . ." The expression of her feelings came forth in disjointed phrases. Suddenly, dispelling the dreamy fog of contentment, she felt the hard length of his manhood trapped between their bodies. Again, a flicker of remembered terror shook her. Stephen would hurt her; even if his possession was gentle, the probing of that muscle would make her arch in pain. She could not voice her fears, not when he had given her such pleasure. For his sake, she would endure it and grit her teeth before she cried out.

Sensing her apprehension, Stephen held her tightly, renewing the kisses that had soothed her before. She was shaking, desperately afraid, and there was little he could do to ease her fears. "Chelaine, sweetheart, I can't lie," he said softly. "You know so little of lovemaking. I would not hurt you, but there will be—"

Chelaine set her fingertips against his mouth. "I will not cry. I know . . ." She could not put words to her understanding, "Make me yours."

Once more his lips came down on hers, brushing lightly, then more stirringly. Chelaine's spirit was underscored by a courage few women possessed. She was willing to give herself—all of her honor—and the offering humbled him. "You're mine already," he assured her, and then considered how that sounded in the light of her indenture. "Because I want you. The paper is worthless, a means of keeping you for myself. Selfish . . . isn't it? You may choose to run from me, but I'd follow. To protect you." He didn't voice a troublesome thought—who would protect her from him?

"You are less selfish than you pretend." Chelaine laid her palm against his cheek, sighing. The talk had intruded on the magic of the interlude, raising worries she would rather set aside. Another sigh whispered from her, and Stephen turned, kissing the center of her palm. "Hold me close yet," she asked. "No more explanations . . . only hold me."

He gathered her in his arms, awkward with her as he had not been with any woman in so many years. If she knew what a fumbling schoolboy he felt, if she guessed at his feelings, there would be no peace in the morning's light. He rested his cheek against her silken tresses, eyes closed, oddly enough drawing on her strength. Michelaine Sully faced the world with a heart for any fate. His own mother had been much like her, a survivor. Without thinking, he sighed himself.

Chelaine heard the sound, and a greater fear than the pain that would come with possession set her heart thumping erratically. He desired her, he had given her pleasure, and this weakness of hers took the edge from the pleasure he was due in return. Even now, did he regret the physical longing that had turned a struggle of wills into passion? Something in her sought to hold him with this new-found power that came of his need. She raised her hand, stroking the damp waves at his temples, then sliding her fingers along his nape to massage his shoulder. Closing her fingers on his shoulder, she tipped her head up and kissed his brow.

In an artless way, Chelaine made him aware of her willingness. Stephen touched her cheek, seeking her lips, finding them soft and yearning. This time the gentle kisses renewed the heat of passion. He moved down, lingering a second over the sweet taste of her breasts, running his tongue along her ribs before he raised up, to kneel between her thighs. Swiftly then, before her fears built anew, he stretched, his weight balanced on his arms as he set himself to the soft, velvet cleft. She stiffened at the contact, then arched her hips to receive him. He pushed forward in a thrust, expecting a muffled outcry, then lunged hard and entered her.

Tensed for pain, Chelaine felt only a slight resistance, and that eased as she relaxed. The hard, swollen muscle filled her, and its animate throbbing set her nerves tingling. A sense of wonder followed and she held her breath, sure there would be some hurt in the act. Stephen leaned over her and drew his hips back, then slid forward, repeating the motion in slow strokes. No pain, only a wondrous pleasure. She was sure it was his practiced skill and the gentle way he had led her to the consummation.

Only briefly did the ease of his entry puzzle Stephen. He drove against her, rocking his hips in a rhythmic probing, urged on as she twisted in the throes of abandoned response. Chelaine moved with him, meeting each thrust with her hips, digging her nails into his shoulders, flexing and digging again.

Rolling on his side, he raised her thigh and held it, slowly revolving his hips, pushing deep, lost in the building surge of power that steadily spiraled to an exhilarating peak. They were both breathless, he panting, she moaning softly, almost keening an echo of the wild wind that tore through the masts.

Nothing mattered but the raw strength buffeting her parted thighs. This delirious sense of fulfillment surpassed the dreamy languor of her earlier pleasure. Suddenly she was on her back again, her knees pressed to her belly as Stephen buried himself in her, pounding at her with a pace that set her nerves raw, aching for something that seemed just beyond her reach. Then it came, a sudden, exquisite feeling, a wash of power that sent her soaring free, as free as one of heaven's winged birds, floating on a current among the clouds. Distantly, she felt her lover tense and plunge forward, arching back, groaning.

Stephen poised, straining for the last remnants of his climax, then, still tumescent and buried in her softness, he fell forward, his head coming to rest on the cushioned pillow of her breasts. For an endless time Chelaine was lost in a void, some misted place beyond her earthbound, breathless body. She came back slowly, reluctantly, to find tears trickling from the corners of her eyes. Her hair was wet and tangled, curling tightly in damp ringlets at her temples and forehead, her skin slick with sweat.

Though he recovered first, Stephen lay exhausted, contentedly listening to the rapid flutter of Chelaine's heartbeat. Finally he rolled his weight from her, but she moved with him, clinging with a tenacity that spoke eloquently of a longing to be close. Oddly, in the wake of his spent passions, he wanted her again, though his body was too tired to obey the call of desire.

For a while they lay nestled together. His arm circled her and Chelaine rested her palm against his chest, secure in the strong, steady beating of his heart. Stephen said little, his lips pressed to her forehead, occasionally nuzzling her hair with his cheek. She wanted something more, an endearment that would keep him as tender and loving as he had been.

"What are you thinking?"

His answer was a sigh, followed by an unnerving silence. Finally he turned and glanced down, pressing a light, careless kiss on the tip of her nose. "Nothing, really." Then he set her arm away and rose, swinging his long legs aside to sit at the edge of the mattress, pushing the curtains apart. The light illuminated his profile as he dragged a hand back through his hair.

Chelaine raised up, supporting herself on an elbow, puzzling over his mood. He came to his feet and stretched, then walked away, disappearing from sight. She lay back again, alarmed by the distance that seemed to have sprung up between them.

Stephen crossed to the armoire and drew out a nightshirt, then went to the wash basin on a shelf above the bathtub, wetting a towel to wipe away the sweat and cleanse himself before he donned the shirt. His expression was brooding, his eyes creased with a slight frown. Wetting a fresh towel, he started for the berth, pausing to pour himself a small amount of brandy, tossing it back before he continued.

Chelaine lay on her side facing him, an arm beneath her head. In the light, her figure was perfect, the white contours of her waist and shapely hips alluring. He stared a minute, then sat. Her expression was troubled, apprehensive. With her breasts so full and prominent above the flat of her ribs and stomach, she tempted him to take her into his arms again. Instead, he managed a smile and gently prodded her onto her back, using the towel to cleanse the sticky fluid from her thighs.

The act embarrassed her even as she found some hope in the tender concern. When he finished, he sat back, stared at the towel, and leaned his head against the wall, eyes closed.

"Something worries you, yes?" she probed. "Tell me, please?" He seemed so different, so aloof, that she wondered if all men were like this . . . warm and tender in pursuit of their needs, diffident once they were satisfied.

Stephen's eyes opened. She looked tense, anxious even. "I'm . . . disappointed, Michelaine." Shock widened her eyes before she reached for the sheet, dragging it up, holding the material before her. He glanced away, staring across the room. "I can't understand why you had to pretend—"

Pretend? She had no idea what he meant. "I did not," she protested.

"I wouldn't have been angry," he insisted. "You could have told me."

"Told you? But what?"

His eyes met hers, and he frowned, disturbed by the seemingly real confusion that gripped her. "That you weren't a virgin."

Chelaine had never imagined such a reason for his withdrawn air of brooding. Her cheeks burned, more in anger than embarrassment. With a trembling hand, she brushed her hair back over a shoulder. "Why would you say this . . . this—"

"Calm down," he insisted. "I said I wasn't angry." She had gone from languor to apprehension, and now her golden eyes flashed with indignant fury. "I'll get you a drink."

"No! That was what led to this . . . seduction."

Irritated now, he grimaced. "I wouldn't have pressed you if you hadn't wanted me. There's no pride gained in force." He showed her the towel. "D'you think I don't know the signs? There's no blood on this. And there wasn't any pain. You were tense, but I took it for innocence." He tossed the towel away, suddenly angry himself, his eyes narrowing in suspicion. "Someone forced you. You were raped. Who was it?"

Chelaine stared down at her hands, stiff and tense as she clutched at the sheet. A fall of waves obscured her expression as she shook her head. "No one raped me." Yes, she had expected pain, and she knew enough to understand that there was always blood on the bridal sheets. Pain and blood . . . her eyes closed, a terrible ache in her throat made swallowing difficult. The man who had attacked her . . . he had hurt her and she had bled. For days the soreness between her thighs had not eased. He had robbed her of her maidenhood . . . but not possessed her.

Finally Chelaine glanced up, her eyes so wounded and full of hurt Stephen reached out, wanting nothing more than to comfort her. She saw him move and recoiled, covering herself, using the sheets as if they were a protective shield.

Even after his death, the man haunted her. How could she tell Stephen—with this estrangement between them, she could not think of him by that name—how could she tell the earl that she had killed a soldier, an Englishman, though he had been colonial? His attitude intimated a desire for revenge. What more could be done to avenge the man's assault? In a toneless voice, she asked why it mattered to him.

"Why?" Stephen questioned incredulously. "You've no reason for shame if some bloody bastard attacked you. Good Lord, Michelaine, if you were alone and helpless . . ." Suddenly his features hardened. "Perhaps there was no rape after all." He shook his head, puzzling over her attitude now and the fears that had beset her before they'd made love. "You blush so easily . . . these past days and nights, your modesty and want of privacy," he gazed at her and puzzled aloud, "Everything indicated—"

"Honor?" she supplied, bitterly resentful of the "disappointment" he had mentioned. A part of her wanted to confide, to tell him what had happened by the stream, but she could not. To think of that terrifying ordeal was difficult. To speak of it, impossible.

"Honor, yes . . . and virtue. If you weren't a virgin, you knew there'd be no pain." Relentlessly, Stephen pressed for an excuse, though each question distressed her more. "Michelaine, I was gentle. I didn't hurt you—and you wanted me."

Her mouth curled in an ironic smile. "You care so that I did not bleed for you? Perhaps you feel cheated?" He had hurt her deeply with the persistent insinuations; she wanted to hurt him in return. She rubbed at her temple, throbbing now with the onset of a headache. He suspected a lover . . . perhaps she should invent one. "I see no need to talk of this. You must live with your disappointment." Her eyes met his, mocking his frustration. "You are not alone."

That taunt stung. The gall of pretending he had left her unfulfilled. Suddenly he tossed out a baited query. "You're in love with Corbeau?" His smile was mirthless, more a smirk. "How gallant of him . . . to take advantage of your infatuation, your naîveté. And you claimed to know so little of him."

Of any man he might have thought of for her lover, Corbeau would irritate him the most. Chelaine stared, then lowered her lids as if he had guessed. Let him squirm with the thought that she and the smuggler he sought had been intimate.

"Your brother should have guarded you—"

Chelaine's eyelashes rose, revealing a glittering triumph. "My brother, I told you he was often absent. I love Corbeau. We belong together."

"Even though he's married? Was this an affair, or only one night of passion?"

Her head came up, defiant. "That is my concern." A corner of her mouth indented. His pride was pricked, and that pleased her. "Does it bother you?"

"Only if you were thinking of him while you twisted and moaned in my arms."

Chelaine's smile came on the heels of a shrug. "Would you believe me if I say I was not? You were satisfied."

"And you. Your response was no pretense."

"You are attractive. I thought you desired me. It was no more than lust."

The earl scowled. "I admit I was taken in. You're a natural actress. So accomplished, in fact, you could have persuaded me to give up the quest for Corbeau."

"With my body?" Chelaine was incensed. "Trade myself for a promise you would never honor? That makes me a whore. I am not . . . not yours or anyone's."

"Not anyone's? Hardly true if you slept with—"

"I love him. Do what you will with me."

"And if he dies for this love of yours? The poor fool won't even know why he was doomed."

"You are too confident. Corbeau will elude you."

Stephen arched a brow that doubted the claim. "I might have let him be if you hadn't held him in such esteem. You would have forgotten him. Why long for a man who doesn't care when you have one who does?"

"You?" Chelaine scoffed. "You pretended to. In the darkness, you forgot that I was your servant. If you care so, then free me."

"And lose you?" He shook his head, refusing. "You needn't worry over my desire. I restrained it before. I'll wait on the pleasure of bringing this hero of yours to justice. In the light of day, with his hands bound, he will seem far less desirable."

What had she done? Chelaine was suddenly alarmed, shaken by the consequences of her lie. She caught at her bottom lip with her teeth, biting hard. She must tell the earl the truth now. Perhaps he would even give up his idea of revenge. Swallowing hard, she glanced up at him. "I lied about Corbeau." The dark brows rose, clearly doubting. "It is true. I was . . . assaulted, in the woods, a day before I was captured with the other women."

"And you're claiming this assailant raped you?"

She shook her head. The story came out, in halting phrases, how he had trapped her, hurt her before she could reach her knife and strike at him. Finally, shaken by the recounting, she stared at Braden, a film of tears glistening in her eyes. "So . . . you see, there is no need to go after Corbeau because of me."

Her tears were real enough and, too, the pain and distress. Stephen frowned, then looked away. "A very valiant effort to protect Corbeau, Michelaine. The scoundrel doesn't deserve such loyalty."

He didn't believe her. The tears spilled over, coursing down her cheeks. "It is true!" she protested, reaching out to lay her hand on his arm. At the contact, his eyes came back to hers, once again, cold and icy. "If I . . ." Beneath the cool tears, her cheeks burned with a feverish blush born of shame. "If I become your . . . mistress—"

"You said you'd be no man's whore, Michelaine. I'll make you mine again when Corbeau has met his end. I can wait."

Stunned by such ruthless determination, Chelaine jerked back her hand, wiping at tears that seemed to flow from a deep spring of misery. "How I hate you!" she stormed. The earl was worse than her attacker. That man's intentions had been clear from the first; this one wanted the same, but he had covered his passion with that cool veneer of civilized restraint, seduced her with a pretense of tenderness. One man, brutally direct, the other deceptive, but both determined to use her for their own satisfaction. "By all I hold dear, I swear I will make you sorry for this night." Tears blurred his image, she swiped at them. "You cruel, heartless bastard!"

"My dear, you've already called me every conceivable epithet," he replied. "After a while, they lose their effect." He reached for and caught up the nightgown, offering it to her. "We're both exhausted. Morning will see your distress eased by more rational thoughts. Like the storm, this will pass."

With a trembling hand, Chelaine wiped at the moisture pooled beneath her eyes. She clutched at the gown, wishing she had some way to strike out at his impenetrable composure, a way to hurt him. "If I had a knife now—"

"But you don't," he said, and for a moment, just an instant, he looked unguarded, as if he'd accepted his guilt and saw himself as she did. "You'll find other, less fatal, less physical ways to avenge yourself," he observed. "There's a thought to ease your weeping. I shield my feelings, but all men have weaknesses." A sigh rasped from his throat as he turned away and whispered low, "Perhaps, I've met mine."

Chapter Six

CHELAINE HAD FINALLY SLEPT, WORN BY EMOTION, HER tears ebbing in exhaustion. Stephen was the one who couldn't close his eyes. He spent the night in the wing chair, soothing his troubled conscience with drink, wondering why destiny had matched him with the one girl who had the power to awaken a heart that had resisted involvement for years. Her spirit and strength were a match for his own. Perhaps, he even thought, she was stronger than he. Many women had tried to lure him into commitment, all had failed because he knew their ambitions, their aspirations. It was no conceit to admit they found his wealth and rank worth pursuing. Some swore those attributes meant nothing. Some claimed they would have desired him if he'd been common and penniless. He took his pleasure and left them satisfied, but none could affect his resolve to remain free.

He was gone in the morning, leaving Chelaine to sleep on. For her sake as well as his, he kept his distance the remainder of the voyage. If she wondered why he rigged the hammock and slept in it, she said nothing. Chelaine had retreated behind a mien of stubborn silence. He no longer issued commands. She stayed in the cabin, he spent his hours above deck, his temperament irascible when he wasn't at the railing, lost in brooding reverie. Even Samuel kept a low profile, aware that something had altered his master's relationship with the girl who shared his cabin.

Once they docked in Boston, the women and children who'd spent the voyage in the hold were sent to an internment area. The earl retired to his town house, settled Chelaine in a spare bedroom, and sent for a seamstress favored by his sister. While the woman fitted Chelaine with a proper wardrobe, Stephen spent his days attending to business; nights he was absent, out with friends while Chelaine dined alone and kept to her room.

Their one confrontation was sparked by Stephen's decision to keep her indenture a secret. He had chosen to represent her as a distant cousin, an orphan related to his French mother. She was his ward, he her guardian. To that effect, he'd written Lucy, apprising her of the homeless girl whom he had by chance discovered and saved from the uncertain fate of her fellow Acadians.

Chelaine could see no reason for the ruse. In her distrust, she questioned his motives. "You may be legally bound to me, but I see no reason to use that bond to make a menial servant of you," he'd explained with a patience she found condescending. "As a member of the family, you'll pass the winter in the comfort of my country estate. You'll have nothing to do but take your ease. My sister will welcome your company. You may even find some desire to emulate her bearing. She'll be pleased to help you adjust to our customs and manners."

Why she would care to make herself the model of an English lady left Chelaine speechless. If he hoped to see her change into someone more suited to his way of life, then she would resist whatever "graces" his half sister attempted to teach her. She had no choice but to accept this whim of his, but unless he resumed his arrogant commanding, he couldn't bend her to his will without revealing something of the bondage in which he held her.

Once her wardrobe had been completed, Stephen had her trunks packed, and they set off for the home called Hartehill. What she had seen of Boston awed Chelaine. No rural Acadian village could compare with a bustling seaport, its streets lined with tall, stately homes and shops whose stock provided Bostonians with luxuries both colonial and imported from England.

Now, as the elegant coach bearing the earl's crest carried them west across the narrow spit of land that connected the small peninsula of Boston proper with the mainland, Chelaine sat huddled in a corner of the coach's interior, watching as the houses became less crowded together, the cobbled streets turning into a road that led toward a village called Roxbury. Somewhere before that village lay Hartehill.

Unsure what to expect of a sister to so haughty an aristocrat, Chelaine hid her apprehension behind a mask of indifference. She continued to gaze at the snow-covered landscape long after the monotonous mantle of white became boring. However dull the view, she preferred it to facing His Lordship, who had settled in a corner of the opposite bench, at an angle to her. The interior of the coach was warm. He had removed his muffler and loosened his greatcoat, set aside the hat he carried more out of habit than utility.

Bored by the scenery he had viewed in every season, Stephen's attention was fixed on Chelaine. If she had looked charming in Lucy's somewhat ill-fitting summer frock, she now appeared to be what he had made of her . . . the fashionably attired young girl whom everyone would accept as his ward. A pale blue woollen cape covered a sprigged muslin dress that showed her slender figure to advantage. The fur-trimmed hood lay about her shoulders, a matching white muff hid her slim, tapering hands. Lucy would approve. If she found Chelaine lacking etiquette, the lack of it would be accounted to her upbringing in a land whose populace were simple farmers and fishermen. Chelaine was adaptable, a quick study. Soon enough she would acquire the airs of a lady.

As the coach slowed and drew to the side of the road to allow passage of another vehicle, Stephen took advantage of the moment to slide along the padded leather bench and sit directly across from her. Her only reaction was a flickering glance, devoid of curiosity, before she turned her attention back to the window view.

"Chelaine, you're ignoring me purposely," he ventured in an affected, lazy drawl.

There was some pleasure in the knowledge that her indifference had begun to wear on him. She glanced up, lashes lifting in a guise of innocence as she puzzled over the claim. "Ignoring you, m'Lord?" She shook her head. "No . . . it is only that I find the countryside so interesting."

The innuendo was clear enough. Chelaine set her muff aside, folding her hands in her lap, gazing off again, the barest hint of self-satisfaction evident in a soft, upward curve of her lips. Stephen sighed, leaned forward to rest his elbows on his knees, and reached out to catch her hands and enfold them in his own. Resistance tensed her fingers, she frowned at the action, then looked up, questioning him with an arched brow.

"Forgive me, do," he said with a beseeching expression no more sincere than her earlier protest of ignoring him without intent. "I can't help but wonder why the sight of snow fascinates you. 'Tis the same stuff which abounds in Acadia."

"Yes, m'Lord."

"You must remember to address me as Stephen," he reminded her. "There's no need for such formality between cousins. The servants would remark on it."

"You care what they think?" It wasn't like him to deign to notice the opinions of those who served him.

"I care to see that no rumors are bandied about that might discredit your position. The servants ofttimes meet with their peers. Such idle gossip has ruined more reputations than you might guess." Toying with her fingers, watching her, he noted a wince. A close examination showed several cuticles bitten. Her thumb in particular looked raw and sore. "You've no call to feel nervous, Chelaine," he assured her. "By now, Lucy has your room prepared, a fire blazing in the hearth, a warm meal set to welcome you."

"I am not nervous."

He touched the sore thumb again, saw her wince and held the finger forth for her to see. "If not, then why—"

97

"You have the right to question me. My feelings are my own . . . all I own. If I choose to worry at my thumb, you suffer nothing."

"A lady cares for her hands as much as her person."

Chelaine smirked at the reference. "You cannot make a lady of me."

"No," he admitted, and flashed a quick grin. "I can't. But you've the makings of one. Only you can decide if the position appeals."

His light eyes, all the more notable for the dark thick lashes that framed them, bore a challenge. It was almost as if he dared her to become what she disdained.

"You are nervous. Perhaps your fears are for Corbeau?"

He was so confident, so cocky, she couldn't help but mock his intention to find and bring Corbeau to justice. "You will never capture him," she asserted, smiling for the pleasure of provoking Stephen.

"My dear, I've never entertained the idea of failure." His answering smile was smug, complacent. "I don't pursue anything I want without a great deal of forethought. I've an advantage over the fellow—he has no idea I'm after him . . . or why."

"Neither do I. What little damage he did to your ship has been repaired. He is not your enemy."

Stephen's lips curled in disdain. "He damned well isn't my friend. You're curious over my motives? I don't usually explain myself to anyone . . . but for you," he paused, and his gaze swept over her, an unnerving survey that made Chelaine stir restlessly, "for you, I'll make an exception."

She checked a sarcastic retort that would have mocked the "privilege" accorded her. This man was accountable to no one, and yet she *did* want to know what drove him in this obsessive quest for Corbeau.

"I like a challenge. The renegade you've idealized thinks he's invulnerable, exempt from capture." He bent his head slightly, acknowledging, "Not without reason. Despite a heavy patrolling of Acadian waters, our navy's failed to bring him in. The Admiralty is mired in convention, wallowing in regulations that hamper independent thought. Corbeau, on the other hand, answers only to himself. The hunters have misunderstood the nature of their quarry."

"But *you* understand him."

Stephen nodded. "I do. Aside from his sympathies with the French, he exacts not a little delight in making fools of his enemies. Corbeau's in it for the risks, the high adventure. He's in his element at sea, on land the Acadians have been his allies. The game is his, the rules set by him . . . what chance had the naval corvettes against such odds?"

At first, Chelaine had scoffed at the earl's superior air of presumption. Now, though, she had to admit his observations made sense. There was more to him than a suave aristocrat, boasting of his prowess. "So, you think you are the one man who can bring about an end to the smuggler's exploits? All this, when no one knows who he is, where he lives . . . what he looks like."

"If anyone can, 'tis me. The key lies in trapping, not hunting him. I've not yet decided what bait might prove irresistible to such a cautious scoundrel, but every man has his weakness." He smiled, more to himself, as if he envisioned Corbeau cornered, then as he turned his attention back to Chelaine, his smile broadened, the even white of his teeth setting off the sun-burnished color of his skin. "Actually," he admitted, "I admire his daring. Meeting face to face should prove quite interesting."

"And possibly fatal . . . to you, Stephen. As you say, each man has some weakness. Or are *you* exempt from such human frailties?"

"I may seem so, but yes, I've my own weak spots." His eyes crinkled with humor at the confession. "If ever I have failed at what I set my mind upon accomplishing, 'twas some miscalculation on my part. In this instance, there'll be no errors."

It was the most humble statement she had heard from him. To say as much to her was a wonder in itself. "Then you seek him to show you are his equal?"

"His *better*, sweet. In a match such as this, there can only be one winner." He lifted a shoulder and let it drop. "I've other reasons—"

"Your honor?" Chelaine ventured. He had given his word to leave her be and had kept it. "It is something you value, yes?" Stephen nodded. "How honorable were you to spend your lust on me that night?"

His mouth thinned in a line. The query had caught him by surprise. "Ah . . . well, that *was* a slip of character. Regrettable. The brandy had some effect on my self-control. I'd much preferred to have won you by charm alone."

"What conceit!" Chelaine forgot caution, bristling over the man's gall. "The drink only showed how little—"

Stephen wagged his head in chagrin. "Lust, my innocent, was not what we shared."

"It was not love."

"Passion, then," he conceded. "Lust is such a crude term."

"Call it what you will, this passion made you want Corbeau for more than any challenge." Chelaine knew a certain guilt for ever having brought Corbeau into their argument, but nothing could alter that now.

The flare of emotion in Chelaine's eyes showed in other ways. Her fingers had curled, forming tensed fists, not threatening so much as containing her anger. Stephen pried them open and raised her hands to press a kiss on her palms, his expression enigmatic as he gazed over them to meet her startled eyes. "What I feel for you is more than mere passion," he confessed, "less than love. I don't love easily."

Chelaine tried to free her hands, but he held them firmly captive. "Have you ever?" she asked. For such a cold, reserved man to feel love seemed impossible.

"Once. Just once."

Her mouth curled in scorn. "You know nothing of love."

Stephen sighed, puzzling aloud, "What brought us to discuss such a subject?" Again he did a quick survey of her fresh, youthful features before he asked, "Have *you* ever known love?"

"No . . ." Chelaine admitted she had not. "But I am not as old—"

"Old?" The assessment stunned him, a frown drew his brows together. It was a saucy judgment, unjust, for he was in his prime. "I do suppose to a child of your inexperience—"

"Was it a child you held and caressed that night?" With a tug, she wrested her hands free and clasped them together in her lap. Her eyes narrowed in a glare, her chin rose with regal hauteur. "I have such reasons to hate you—"

"—but you don't," Stephen asserted smugly. "Despite your indignation, you find me attractive. That night you discovered a desire that made you a woman. It's your heart—or mind—that rejects what your senses found so pleasurable."

"My mind? How can you presume to guess my thoughts when your own are confused?" Chelaine threw up her hands in exasperation. "First I am a child, then a woman . . . know yourself before you judge me."

"You're both, Chelaine. Desire rules your body, emotions you can scarcely control hold sway over your thoughts." Stephen's lashes lowered, his gaze unnerving as a smile played at his full, sensual mouth. "When you can discipline your feelings, you'll be an enchanting creature."

"I hope not to be here if that comes to pass."

"'Twill sooner than you might think. I've no doubt you can rein your passion . . . 'tis newborn and just stirring. The other . . . if you can let reason rule that wild, irreverent nature of yours, anything you wish will be yours."

"Anything?"

His lips quirked as he guessed her thoughts. "Almost anything. You could have any man you wanted. That's a thought to dwell upon while I'm away."

"You are leaving so soon?"

"Why, Chelaine . . . is that dismay I hear? If you'd rather I stay—"

Chelaine wrinkled her nose at him. "I would rather you go to—" she stopped just shy of sending him to the devil. "If you cannot tell delight from dismay, you should hone your own senses. What makes you so confident I will be here when . . . *if* you return?"

Stephen flashed a crooked, engaging grin. "I'll return. I'm too accursed obstinate to go out before my time. As for you, Samuel is staying behind. Only he knows of your indenture. 'Twill remain so unless you choose, unwisely, to run off. Then, my lovely little rebel, you'd be found . . . and found out. I shouldn't like Lucy to know of our deception."

"Your deception. I do not care what your sister thinks of me. We are strangers."

"You won't be for long. Lucy has a way of making friends with anyone she meets."

Chelaine grimaced. If the girl was anything like her arrogant brother, they'd have nothing in common. "If she knew—"

"But she won't. I trust you'll keep silent . . . for your sake more than mine."

Retrieving her muff, Chelaine tucked her hands within it and turned her attention back to the window. The conversation had only fueled her resentment of a situation over which she had no control. She was powerless, but oh, how she would have liked to take the wind from his sails! Nothing she could do would make a dent in his composure. He admitted he had weaknesses, but she had no idea what they might be. Like the man he sought, he set the rules. As long as it was his game, neither she nor any other had a chance to bring him down.

As she stared out at the rolling hills blanketed in snow, she considered what sort of weakness he'd alluded to. To be a bachelor, at his age . . . he was immune to the charms of women. Eyes closed, she remembered the skilled caresses that had stirred moans from her. His mouth, his hands, the virile strength of his lean body; Stephen Harte was no novice at the art of seduction. Could it be that desire was his weakness?

Rage, resentment, curses only amused him. Despite his vow, he wanted her still. Why else treat her so benevolently when he could have made her a maidservant, used her at his leisure until he tired of her? A tiny smile touched her mouth. If he wanted her, perhaps because she had so clearly shown her disregard for him, that might be a weapon to use against him.

No, she was deceiving herself. She might be a novelty to a jaded appetite, but his interest would fail soon enough. If ladies of quality, who had the advantages of breeding and the graces he found admirable, had not managed to capture his affections, what chance did she have?

The coach slowed almost to a halt. Stephen, who had fallen silent himself, answered her questioning look by gesturing out the window. Before the driver turned the horses to the right onto the drive that led up a slope, she caught a glimpse of a three-story mansion. Snow crusted the rose brick exterior, drifts of it covered two gabled windows. In the fading afternoon light, the lower floor windows gave off a warm, mellow glow.

"Hartehill," Stephen announced with a measure of pride in his voice. As the coach began a slow climb toward the house, his gaze returned to her. "Your home, Chelaine, and mine. I don't doubt Lucy's stationed herself by the door, eagerly awaiting a glimpse of our French cousin."

Chelaine settled back with a sigh. She *was* nervous, and to hide the sudden trembling that shook her, she bent her head, resting her chin against the raised muff. "She will not like me," she whispered against the downy soft fur, "I know—"

"There you're mistaken," Stephen insisted, reaching across to lower the fur piece Chelaine held like a defensive shield. His fingers stretched, lightly following her jaw to curve beneath her chin and tip it up. Wide, wary eyes gazed back, resentment temporarily banished by anxiety. He gave her a reassuring smile before settling back. "My sister is sweet and good-natured. She's very different from me."

Whether it was true or not, the admission brightened Chelaine's spirits. Unable to resist one last barb, she smiled back at Stephen and with a honeyed tone of voice retorted, "If that is so, then I *know* I will like her."

"Indeed?" Stephen flashed a crooked grin, if only to show her the comment had no effect. "You share a common bond—"

"You?" Chelaine tilted her head high, ready to mock such arrogance.

He nodded, still grinning. "That as well, but before you chose to interrupt, I was about to say that you are both orphans. I brought Lucy here after my father and stepmother were killed in a coach accident. She came a stranger, like you . . . so you can see, her sympathies are with you even before you meet."

"I have never thought of myself as an orphan. And our circumstances are not alike. Your sister is among her own kind here—and she has a powerful, influential protector in you."

"As do you," Stephen reminded her. "Unless you slip . . . or choose to reveal our secret, you'll find a great many benefits in my guardianship." The coach slowed, and a glance out the window revealed they had pulled beneath the portico extended over the drive. Gesturing with his hand, Stephen drew her attention to the wide, heavy oaken door set above a semicircle of stone steps. "Welcome home, cousin. Before you enter, begin to think of yourself as such. It will ease your transition immensely."

Chelaine quieted, suppressing a feeling of impotence. She had to play along in this charade, as much as she desired to reveal the truth. Stephen climbed down the coach step and turned; she had to endure his closeness as he reached back to catch her waist and swing her to the ground. Very briefly their eyes met, his crinkled in amusement, hers narrowed in frustrated spite, then the front door opened, and a bright spill of light flooded the porch. Stephen's hands, still on her waist, tightened in a warning before he released her, tucked her hand in the crook of his arm and turned. By then, he was smiling; Chelaine's resentment simmered beneath a mask of reserve.

She saw Samuel first. He'd gone ahead that morning with her trunks and his master's baggage. The man stood back holding the door handle, and then Lucy appeared. Chelaine had a few moments to study the girl before they climbed the steps. She was petite and dainty, with fine delicate features set in a round face. Shorter than Chelaine by some three inches, with the remnants of baby fat still plumping her figure, Stephen's sister looked the ideal of a fair, blue-eyed, blond English lady. Her countenance *was* sweet, even more so when her bowed mouth curved in a delighted smile at the sight of Stephen.

Once they were within the foyer and the door had shut out the winter chill, Lucy enveloped Stephen in a hug, then stretched to kiss him, her eyes sparkling as she took a step back to study him. "You're away far too often," she chided, softening her words with a hand laid gently against his cheek. "You *are* staying this time? Of course, you are. It would be rude to go off soon after you'd brought your cousin home." She stepped back again, to allow Stephen to shrug off his greatcoat and hand it, along with his muffler and gloves, to a hovering Samuel.

Chelaine stood slightly behind Stephen, gazing about, vaguely aware of Lucy's one-sided conversation while she surveyed the opulence of the entry hall. The town house had impressed her, but this . . . the walls were papered in a pale gold, watered silk, there were half-tables set against them with silver candlesticks flickering, their light reflected in several ornate, gilded mirrors. If the rest of the house were as grand, it seemed she had come to live in a palace. Samuel had taken her muff at the door; as she stood there, awe-stricken, one hand absently worked at the frog closure fastening her cape.

A sudden soft squeal startled her, she found her hands caught and warmly squeezed, there was a second to focus on Lucy's smiling face before she was drawn close, kissed on both cheeks, and then hugged with the same ebullience Lucy had accorded her brother. The rush of affection widened her eyes, she caught a glimpse of wry amusement in Stephen's, and then Lucy proceeded to run on in a flurry of questions that tripped from her tongue so rapidly Chelaine hadn't time to form an answer to one before the next tumbled forth.

"Oh . . . I never expected you to be so lovely!" Lucy glanced at her brother briefly in a mild reproach before her eyes, close in color to Stephen's, but warm and fringed by pale brown-blond lashes, returned to Chelaine. "All Stephen wrote was a short note inform-ing me he'd found you alone and helpless, almost subject to deportation. How awful for you, dear, thank Heaven Stephen recognized your name on the list of refugees! I shudder to think . . . well, that's all behind you now. You're safe here; of course, everything must seem strange, but you'll settle in and we shall soon be fast friends."

"Enough, chatterbox!" Stephen interjected before Lucy went on any longer. "There's time aplenty to become acquainted." It was a firm directive, but Stephen's affection for Lucy showed in an indulgent smile as he caught her wrist and gently tugged her back to his side. "At least let Samuel take her cape."

"Oh, my . . . here I am, overwhelming you with queries, and you must be chilled to the bone, tired and unsettled! Forgive me, Michelaine, I—"

"Chelaine."

Lucy's fair brows met in puzzlement at her brother's correction. "Chelaine? Is that how you prefer to be called?"

"It is all I am known by."

"What a pretty sound it has, so soft and feminine! Well, do forgive me for rambling on. Stephen says it's a trait I must correct, a fault—"

"Just about your only one, Lucy," Stephen asserted. Samuel had taken Chelaine's cape, and she stood quite still, less tense than when they'd entered, but still taken aback by his sister's irrepressible curiosity and the strangeness of her surroundings. "On the way, I assured Chelaine you'd have her room prepared and a meal ready. I hope . . ." he paused and left the answer to Lucy, stretched out his hand to Chelaine, and offered a smile that beseeched her cooperation. After a short hesitation, she accepted and let him draw her toward him.

"Cook has a leek and potato soup simmering. That

should warm us all. And for an entrée, roasted guinea hen with sage dressing, an onion—"

Stephen exchanged a look with Chelaine and held up a hand. "My mouth is watering already. Why don't you show Chelaine to her room, allow her to freshen a bit, and acquaint her with the amenities? Which bedroom did you—"

"The green room, across from your suite, next to my own." Lucy smiled at Chelaine, held out a hand, and Stephen relinquished her with a raised brow that warned Lucy to check her impulsive barrage of questions. In acknowledgment, she wrinkled a short, pert nose and caught Chelaine's hand, tucked it in the crook of her arm, and gave her a soothing pat. "I promise to give you at least a *few* moments to answer before I pose another question, dear," she confided in a droll tone designed to poke fun at herself as well as her brother's admonishment.

Stephen watched the two stroll toward the staircase. Chelaine would soon adjust to Lucy's somewhat overwhelming personality. In comparison, she seemed subdued and introverted, but once she relaxed, Chelaine's spirits would rebound. He had no doubt his departure would be a relief. She needed the time and distance his voyage would put between them . . . for that matter, so did he.

Chapter Seven

CHELAINE SAT BEFORE HER DRESSING TABLE BRUSHING out the wealth of tawny, burnished curls that trailed halfway down her back. Across from her, Lucy perched on the end of the bed, resting a cheek against the corner post, watching her. For once, Lucy was quiet, her mood reflective as she considered the vast changes Chelaine had undergone in a relatively short six weeks. Within a day of her arrival, her reserve had melted away—oddly enough, coincident with Stephen's departure for Boston and the return voyage to Acadia he'd insisted was necessary.

Looking back, Lucy decided that, as much as she adored her brother, to someone unaccustomed to his commanding presence, he could well seem intimidating. At any rate, Chelaine had quickly warmed to a friendship that was so close now, it almost seemed they were sisters. Chelaine confided her concern that she would embarrass herself and them by her ignorance of social graces. Raised on a farm, with no knowledge of the greater world beyond her simple Acadian village, she found herself abruptly transported to an elevated status, floundering with the customs and mores of an elite and foreign culture. She wanted very much to be a part of the circles in which Stephen and Lucy moved.

Lucy's heart had gone out to her. She quickly moved into a daily routine of lessons, everything from table etiquette to the forms of address and courtesies due the varying ranks of the social gentry. Fortunately, the colonies lacked the multitude of nobles that permeated the upper classes of England. There were always visiting dignitaries, some members of privilege such as the Royal Provincial governor and other Crown appointees, but Stephen held as high a title as any to be found. The most distinguished citizens of Boston were members of its founding families, and others, who'd settled and won their fortunes in trade, joined the widening set of acceptable gentry.

Lucy interrupted her reverie to glance over, catch Chelaine's eye in the mirror, and smile. "You carried yourself like a duchess this evening," she commented, and Chelaine's cheeks, still suffused with a remnant of excitement, blushed with a deeper shade of rose. "Stephen will be stunned by your transformation. I would be as well if I hadn't seen your progress day by day." Her eyes were thoughtful and distant a few moments before her hand rose to cover a giggle. "Jason Trimble lost his composure each time you glanced at him. He could barely speak a sentence without stuttering, and he gaped so—" she broke off to affect a perfect imitation of the boy whose sixteenth birthday fete they'd attended, "his father had to poke him once or twice."

It wasn't like Lucy to make fun of anyone, but the observation was accurate, her portrayal of his awkward, fixed gaze so close, Chelaine dissolved into giggles herself and finally laid the brush aside, her eyes tearing from the uninhibited, shared laughter. She stood, crossed to the bed, and sank down next to Lucy, still wiping at her eyes. All it took was one look between them and the laughter bubbled forth anew, trickling to chuckles after a short while.

"Burke was even worse off," Lucy added. He was the older of the last two sons who still lived with their parents. At eighteen, he was more worldly, far more handsome, and engaged to be married in May. He'd sat glumly through supper, ignoring his fiancée, a sulky brooding darkening his face, alternately casting admiring glances at Chelaine and frowning over his gawking brother. "I'll warrant Sally had a word or two with him after we left."

Chelaine had found the two young men amusing, but the idea of causing a rift between Burke and his betrothed left her uneasy. "You don't think they'll—"

Lucy guessed her thoughts and finished, "No, I don't. She might have smarted at the lack of attention, but Sally Potter would never risk losing Burke. She's not that pretty to begin with, and he's a fine catch." She leaned back against the post and sighed, a little worn by the gales of laughter, and finally winding down from the delight of an evening out. The Trimbles were their closest neighbors. They'd invited Chelaine and herself for Christmas, and Lucy had returned their hospitality a week later with a dinner on New Year's Day. "Remember how nervous you were at Christmas?" Chelaine nodded. "Well, after the last two evenings you can't have any doubts about your charm. Of course the Trimbles afforded you the chance to try your wings, but by the time of my début ball in early May, I predict

with utter confidence that you'll be the talk of Boston."
She smiled, a little wistfully, happy for Chelaine, but
sure she would have every eligible bachelor paying her
suit.

"The début is *your* special evening, Lucy." Intuitively, Chelaine sensed distress and knew she was the
source. "You know I cannot even dance well yet. I
don't believe I'll ever master that grace without tangling my feet in my skirts."

"Oh, but you will! Master Kinmont will be coming as
usual, at least through mid-April. He told me you're
doing remarkably well." Adrian Kinmont made his
living tutoring young ladies in dance. Twice a week,
barring any weather that made the road from Boston
impassable, he came and spent two hours of an afternoon showing them the latest dances, practicing with
each. It *was* the one skill that gave Chelaine any
trouble, but she had months to practice. "Stephen will
help out once he returns. He's unusually graceful for a
man his height." Lucy felt a yawn coming and tried to
stifle it, failed, and politely covered her mouth.

"You do not seem worried," Chelaine observed. She
was tired, too, but once Stephen's name rose, her
interest was piqued. "It's a very bad time of year for
him to be sailing Acadian waters."

"Stephen's at home on the sea. And he's off so
much, I rarely think of any danger." Again, Lucy
yawned, her eyelids growing heavy. "I'm sorry, love—
it isn't the company but the hour. Stephen should be
home in another week or so."

"Ah . . . then I will give up worrying as well." She
leaned forward, curled an arm about Lucy's shoulder,
and kissed her cheek. "Go to sleep. Before you fall
asleep sitting there." Lucy nodded, with a wry smile,

admitting she might. She slipped off the bed, stretched, and leaned close for a last hug.

"Have a good night's rest, Chelaine. And don't give Stephen another thought. He's likely homebound right now."

"Good night, Lucy." Chelaine watched her friend drag toward the door and called out to her. Lucy glanced back, brows raised. "I just . . . I wanted to say thank you, for everything you have done."

Lucy raised a smile, an effort as she grew sleepier. "There's no need to thank me, love. You were the one who worked so very hard. Stephen has no idea what a wonderful surprise awaits him." She waved a hand then and yawned once more before she left.

Chelaine sat back on her bed, plumped her pillow, and leaned against it, a troubled sigh escaping as she closed her eyes and envisioned Lucy's sweet, trusting face. The plan to avenge the wrong done her by Stephen, just a seed of an idea planted on the afternoon of her arrival had, before she spent her first night sleeping here, sprouted, nurtured by an anger that ignored all else he'd done. She had more than a chance of success, and this evening had only bolstered her confidence. Stephen would be surprised, so much so she hoped, the desire he'd felt for her two months before would pale in comparison. She would be cool to him, polite but distant, then seem to be drawn irresistibly by his virility, caught up in an attraction against her own volition. Yes . . . that would definitely appeal to his overgrown conceit!

She had no qualms about Stephen. If she won his affection and left him broken-hearted, it was a fate he richly deserved. Lucy was the one who set her conscience nagging. She would have helped Chelaine adapt to living here, by her own decision, sooner or later. Lucy was the innocent, caught between them. And she could never understand Chelaine's reasoning. How could she, when she'd known nothing but kindness and loving consideration from Stephen? When Chelaine left—it would surely be before the grand ball to be held at Hartehill—she wouldn't be able to bid Lucy farewell. She wasn't even sure how she'd make an escape, only that once Stephen was well caught in her trap, she would vanish.

He'd warned her not to try and escape, told her exactly what would happen. She'd be caught, brought back, revealed as nothing more than a bondservant. Then, the warning made sense. He'd have suffered nothing, perhaps been admired for his benevolence, his generosity. Now, though, because he'd afforded her the time and chance to adapt to his world, there was an additional measure of fortune to her planned revenge. She had already proven she could move among his peers, had acquired a self-assurance that could be stretched to appear to be aristocratic hauteur. The element of surprise, the timing of her departure, everything seemed to work to her advantage. She could be off on a coach, bound for the territory of Maine, an extension of the Bay Colony. Maine bordered on New Brunswick . . . so lately French held and still sparsely populated enough to work northward, through woodlands, on to Île Royale and Henri, at Fortress Louisbourg. So far to go, a risk-laden journey, but to be free, with her own kind! . . . A sudden wave of homesickness assailed her. She hadn't thought of Henri for so long, and Acadia seemed forever lost.

Before she gave in to senseless weeping, Chelaine stubbornly banished Stephen and her plans for him from her mind, set aside thoughts of home, and slipped beneath the comforter, settling in after several attempts to find a spot that suited her. For a while her mind was active, refusing to relinquish an excitement in anticipation of Stephen's return. Finally, giving in to a pleasant imagery of the satisfaction that would eventually be hers, Chelaine drifted off.

Lost in a contented dream, Chelaine snuggled beneath the blankets. A restless sleeper, she shifted positions time and again and now, turned onto her side, stirred a moment, sighed, flipped over onto her back. The dream fragmented, losing continuity, and she unconsciously struggled to catch at it.

Across the room, near the door, a shadowy figure emerged from the dark, padding silently toward the bed. A man stood beside the bed, ears keen for any unusual sounds. Chelaine's breath came and went with even regularity. Moving quickly, he settled beside her and bent forward, closing his palm over her mouth. Startled awake, disoriented, she went stiff with shock, instinctively striking out with her hand, a scream forming, rising, muffled as the hand pressed more firmly. Her fingers scraped the man's cheek, eliciting a low curse, followed by a sharp, impatient command to be still.

It wasn't the command or fear that finally ceased her struggling. The voice, sure and authoritative, spoke in French; reason enough, even dulled by the vestiges of sleep, to pause and question who had entered her room so late, who would come to her and address her in her native tongue. The hand smelled faintly of tobacco, yet another impression that reinforced a dawning suspicion that whoever he was, he could well be Acadian. How often had she filled and prepared a pipe bowl for her sister's husband, or done the same for Henri?

Still in French, low and husky, the voice out of the darkness was less strident. "I am a friend . . . sent by your brother, Henri, to find you. You believe this?" Chelaine found it difficult to believe she wasn't dreaming, but the voice was real, the pressure of the hand easing slightly as if its owner were still wary of releasing her. "How else do I know you are Chelaine Sully? You wish proof . . . I do not blame you." He moved his free hand, juggled something, and then told her to open her right palm. On it he placed a heavy, round object, indiscernible in the darkness, but as she closed her fingers, shock rippled along Chelaine's spine. Just by the feel, she knew and recognized her father's ring. It could only have come from Henri. "Now you believe, eh?" She nodded, and satisfied she would not cry out, he drew his hand from her mouth.

Chelaine struggled to rise, and as the man moved back, his hand closed on her arm, helping her to sit up. Still stunned, as much from the stealthy intrusion as the slow, dawning realization that this faceless, unknown man had contact with her brother, she tried to organize her thoughts. He hadn't identified himself . . . yet as her fingers brushed his cheek, she'd felt the bristled hairs of a mustache. Henri had been due to rendezvous with Corbeau, Corbeau wore a mustache . . . it seemed impossible, but she couldn't help wonder aloud. "Corbeau?"

"Yes, it is I. When you failed to return from your impulsive search, Henri charged me with the task of finding and rescuing you." He heard her begin a question and set a finger to her lips. "You have many questions, as have I. The answers will wait. For now, you must dress, quickly. We must be away before anyone hears."

Chelaine nodded, still groggy, then shook her head to clear a fog of muddled thoughts. "Wait! There are things you do not know. I cannot leave, not yet." A heavy silence followed the statement. She sighed, searching for words to explain. "If you had come a month ago . . . How did you find me? How did you manage to enter the—"

"Does it matter? Why can you not come?"

"I . . . I must wait until the master of this house returns." It sounded inane to refuse such a chance to escape, a chance she might not have again if she refused. She was so close to achieving her goal, a consuming desire that had driven her so hard for nearly two months. "Oh . . . I cannot explain."

"What hold does this man have on you?"

"I am indentured to him. But you see I am not treated as a servant." Suddenly she realized how that sounded. Bonded, yet living in luxury. What conclusion could Corbeau reach other than to think she was Stephen's mistress?

"You are not in love with him?"

"No!" The denial came out almost vehemently. "But I must stay . . . to settle something . . ." How could she, though? She might win at her game, see Stephen humbled, but Corbeau offered an immediate return to Henri. "Of course, I must go. You cannot risk—"

"This is so important?" She nodded, then affirmed it in words. "And you are safe?"

"Yes."

"Then I will give you time to settle this matter. I winter in the area." He gave her a street address in Boston, the number of a house. "You have the ring;

send it there and I will come. You are sure of this decision?"

Chelaine sat quietly, still tempted by the chance to flee and be done with Stephen Harte forever. She imagined his reaction, finding her gone, vanished, with no way to trace her. That would frustrate him, but no, she'd come this far, she would see the end to her game and then exercise the option Corbeau had granted. "I am sure," she replied, and more to affirm her decision to herself, added, "very sure." Her fingers closed tightly over the ring. "How was Henri? Did he seem—"

"Angry? Yes, that and worried—with good reason."

"Then when I do return with you, I must face his anger." The idea of humbling herself, admitting her caprice had brought grief to him as well as to her, sent a shiver across her skin.

"You will not have that chance, Chelaine. Henri wants you safe, but you are not to return. Ever." He heard her sharp intake of breath and went on before she could protest. "When we leave this place, I will take you to one of our island possessions in the Caribbean. Your brother wishes this and more . . . I am to see you married and settled. You will have some choice in the bridegroom, but it is time for you to understand your place is with a husband and children."

Stiff with shock, unable to believe the decree that banished her from her homeland, from seeing Henri once more, Chelaine bowed her head, some bit of dignity bracing her against the threat of tears. Corbeau was only delivering her brother's message, acting on Henri's desires out of loyalty. She recalled that night— now it seemed ages ago—when she had kissed him. He was married, Henri had said so. If not, she would have found happiness as his wife. They were alike; if Stephen

119

found her desirable, would Corbeau not have? "*Are you married?*" she questioned, and even before a chuckle followed a brief silence, she turned crimson at the brazen inquiry. Fortunately, the darkness hid the warm flush that swept her from head to toes. "I was only curious," she said in an attempt to cover the embarrassing moment. Once again, she'd made a fool of herself before the one man she admired. "Henri said so."

"Has Henri ever lied to you?"

"No." Nothing more needed to be said. Chelaine experienced a few seconds of intense jealousy for the woman who had won Corbeau's heart. She still believed she could have made him love her, but he'd likely been wed already when she first felt the stirrings of something more than an idealized fascination. She couldn't change what was, only accept it and conceal her feelings.

"Then I will be off. Whatever holds you—"

"No, wait!" Chelaine had suddenly remembered Stephen, his purpose in returning to Acadia. "You know whose home this is? Of course, you must . . ." He'd managed somehow to find her, scout out the location. Corbeau had to have watched, studied the comings and goings of the occupants and servants of Hartehill. "He is a powerful man, wealthy, influential —Corbeau, you have made an enemy of him."

"How did I manage this?"

"In early November, you fired a shot at a brigantine, south of Halifax. It was his ship, Stephen Harte's—"

He nodded, acknowledging the incident. "I recall it now. For this reason he is determined to see me run to ground, eh? He must be very vain. The damage was so slight."

"He *is* vain, and the damage was more to his pride than the timbers of his ship. Even now, he's been gone six weeks, searching the coastline and, no doubt, questioning any of our people still detained."

"This incident in November, it is all that sends him on such a quest?"

"You cannot know how stubborn he is. Stephen sees it as a challenge, not only to his pride. He finds adventure in this hunt . . . a chance to relieve his boredom. And because you seem invincible, it would be all the more gratifying for him to be the one to bring you to 'justice.'" She reached out, touching his shoulder, eager to impress Corbeau with the very real danger Stephen posed. "Do not underestimate him."

"He'll learn nothing from any Acadian. As for his search, you see how fruitless it is. He is there, while I—" amusement shaded his voice, enough so that Chelaine could imagine his confident grin, "am here, in *his* home. Have no fears for me, little one. I have not survived this long only to be cornered by some indolent Englishman who fancies himself my equal."

"He is not just *any* man. He is an earl, but there is nothing of the mincing dandy in him. Stephen is sharp-witted, determined, an opponent to be wary of."

"I am always cautious," he assured her. "And I will not return to Acadian waters until spring. Chelaine? Answer me this . . . why would you stay with such a man?"

"I . . ." The explanation involved so many details, some too personal to admit to Corbeau. "He does not frighten me. And if, by chance, he does learn something, I will warn you." She hadn't justified her reasons for remaining with Stephen, but the last assurance seemed enough motive to stay, if only as a source of information. The idea gave her an extra measure of satisfaction, to be a spy for Corbeau, to foil Stephen by turning any advantage to a disadvantage.

"You seem very cool-headed for all that Henri raged over your uncontrollable, impulsive nature. Perhaps, you are growing from a girl into a woman."

Chelaine blushed again. "The earl is a man who masters his emotions. It may be I have learned from him," she admitted. Corbeau sighed, reached out, and cradled the back of her head with one hand, bending forward to kiss her brow lightly. A frown tugged at her lips. The kiss was paternal, like that of a father bidding his child a fond farewell. He drew back, stood, and despite the darkness, she could make out a vague, tall shape. "Corbeau?"

"Yes? You have not changed your mind?"

"No. But I wanted to thank you for searching for me. You took a great risk, coming here." The shadowy shape bent in a gallant bow that brought a smile to her lips.

"For you, the risks are as nothing." He turned away and then glanced back. "I thrive on them, Chelaine. Like the wolf who snatches a sheep from the fold, I am away before the shepherd learns of his loss. And the wolf, he enjoys such challenges as much as his meal."

"Perhaps you should have taken the wolf's name in place of the raven."

A low, brief chuckle followed. "Corbeau had the sound that appealed," he admitted. "I, too, am vain. How dashing can a smuggler be, known as Loup?" A faint, silvery ripple of laughter acknowledged his choice had more élan. "You see, even a renegade has his conceits. Now sleep, I go as I came, a shadow."

Chelaine lay back, listened as the door opened, and

only then thought to glance toward it, hoping to catch a glimpse of Corbeau in the dim light of the one lamp left burning in the hall. Too late. He was gone. He had urged her to sleep—but who could sleep after such a startling encounter? Now her anticipation of Stephen's return grew. How long would it take until his desire for her had turned into an obsession? He'd kept his vow, his honor was important. She would be treading a very fine line, luring him on, yet somehow the desire would have to become second, surplanted by affection, love, a yearning more than physical. She would know just the moment, perhaps let him declare his feelings . . . she wouldn't spurn him or suddenly flaunt her deception. No, he mustn't have any hint that she was anything but flattered.

Rolling onto her stomach, Chelaine hugged the pillow and smiled to herself. She had managed so much in six weeks, could another six see that moment arrive? It was too much to hope for. As soon as Stephen found it impossible to live without her, she would send the ring to Corbeau, summon him to a rendezvous, and be off . . . leaving His Lordship, the earl of Braden, Viscount Reredun, alone to struggle and suffer with his unrequited love. It would be clear soon enough exactly what she'd done, humbled a man whose pride, honor and vanity had too long gone unchallenged, whose arrogance had finally been pricked. Her only regret would be the fact that she would be unable to see his downfall.

Chapter Eight

"You're quite satisfied with my proposition, then? I mean, I shouldn't like to think you're only acting out of indulgence for a relative's whims."

Stephen had been staring out the coach window, absorbed in his thoughts. The closer they came to Hartehill, the more he wished he might have arrived home without his cousin in tow. Not that Edward wasn't welcome. Lucy would be overjoyed to see him after nearly a year since his last visit. Chelaine was his concern. He wasn't sure she was ready to meet a member of the family—or, for that matter, whether Edward was ready for her. He didn't doubt she'd changed, but how much . . . enough to feel at ease with a gentleman, a stranger?

"You presented the matter well, cousin," he replied with a slight smile as he nodded his assurance. "From any other man, I might have questioned the worth of such a venture, but I see nothing but profit to be gained in expanding the trade to Virginia, for both of us. I only wonder no one's come up with the suggestion before.

It's time our exports were handled here. Why should the Bristol or London merchants wax fat on colonial efforts when we can handle the tobacco shipments and charge less of a commission for the service? And who better to manage the consignments than a man who has the planters' trust—as well as mine? Yes, I am satisfied."

"Good. I wanted to be sure you considered it a sound investment." Edward was even more pleased than he appeared. If Stephen hadn't approved the idea of setting up a branch warehouse in Richmond, he'd have had to face the humiliation of requesting another loan. His home and fields were mortgaged twice over, the profits from a good crop the previous year barely keeping his creditors from foreclosing. Now he could count on a steady, quite generous stipend and look forward to a percentage of the fees for arranging transport of this year's crops. "You know I'll work twice as hard for you as I would for myself—to see your trust in me justified."

"I never doubted you would. How soon can you return with the signed agreements?"

"It won't take long at all. With the tariffs, customs, and taxes, not to mention the exorbitant fees charged by the British merchants, the planters I spoke to were all too eager to deal with a reputable firm here in the colonies. I've their full cooperation—it shouldn't take more than three weeks, perhaps a month before I come back here with the notarized contracts for Harte Mercantile. All we'll need then is your signature."

"Lucy will be delighted you'll be living in Boston through the spring. You know her début is May the third? You'll be here for that occasion and then be able to set up the offices in Richmond."

"Lord, I can't believe how the years have passed! Lucy, all grown and of an age to be wed." He wagged his head and sighed. "You've your work cut out, just sorting through the rakes and youngbloods who'll find so pretty and well-connected a lady a match eagerly sought."

"I know, it's been on my mind the past year. Suddenly, I am cast in the role of the overprotective guardian when I've had call to find such fathers and brothers a nuisance in the past."

"Far in the past, cousin," Edward reminded him. "It's been many a year since you wisely chose to devote your attentions to mature young widows who meet your needs without the indignant intervention of a parent demanding your intentions."

"It wouldn't hurt you to remarry. The début should afford you a chance to find some agreeable young lady with a plump dower. God knows, there are enough of them to choose from."

"I may avail myself of the opportunity." Edward considered how his fortunes might increase by a suitable match, this time with a girl he found attractive. "Tell me more about this ward of yours," he asked. Shifting to make himself more comfortable, he propped a leg on the opposite bench and raised a sandy brown eyebrow in curiosity. He hadn't been as surprised by Stephen's generous offer to take in the orphaned girl as he had been to learn she was a distant cousin, a French relative.

"You'll have the chance to judge her yourself," Stephen glanced out the window and noted how close they were to home, "very soon. She's a sweet girl, not shy, but I expect you'll find her quiet and subdued. Chelaine's barely had time to settle in. The land and language are foreign to her, and she's living in far better circumstances than life in Acadia afforded." Stephen stared down at his gloved hands, a hint of amusement tipping the corners of his mouth, his reflective mien eliciting Edward's interest.

"Is she pretty, then?"

"Pretty?" Stephen nodded, his lips curving in a full smile as he glanced at his cousin. "More than pretty. But I'll not bias your opinion. You can wait just a while longer and make your own appraisal." He quirked a brow and mused, "I'm curious myself to see how she's adapted. Our acquaintance was brief. I found her, brought the girl back, and left her in Lucy's care."

"And how long were you away?"

"Seven weeks. And near another since I returned to Boston. So you see, Edward, I'm as anxious to greet her as you."

In her bedroom at Hartehill, the subject of such interest was seated before her dressing table, trying very hard to quell her uneasy nerves as Lucy's maid finished the task of pinning Chelaine's willful curls into a neat arrangement atop the crown of her head. "There, miss," Bess said with a relieved sigh as she smoothed the thick ringlets that fell from the coif of curls, "all done—and with enough pins to be sure none of them springy curls comes free." It seemed there was no ease in dressing either girl's hair. Her Ladyship's fine, blond tresses were so straight they required a nightly rolling with linen strips. Miss Chelaine's natural curl was hard to contain, did as it pleased almost as if each silky lock had a mind of its own. Thankfully, she preferred to wear it loose. Only for His Lordship's homecoming had she given into Lucinda's urging to let

Bess work it into a more elegant style. Now she handed a looking glass to Chelaine, stood back, and admired her efforts, waiting for approval.

Chelaine examined her profile critically, not so much in judgment of the maid's skills as a reflection of her desire to look perfect, as perfect as possible, when Stephen and his cousin arrived. She'd had eight weeks to improve everything from her accent to her walk, and despite repeated assurances from Lucy, she still wished for another eight to add to her self-confidence. Bess cleared her throat, and Chelaine set down the looking glass to face the maid with a beaming smile. "You've done so much. I'm very pleased, Bess. But I will not put you through such an ordeal again. You must ache from standing there so long." She did herself, not only from keeping her head still and erect, but her scalp hurt from the pressure of so many hairpins. The effect lent her a more mature look, but if not for the occasion she would have worn her hair brushed down—and comfortable.

"'Twasn't no trouble, miss," Bess answered, fudging a bit over the trying experience. "Lady Lucinda thought you might like these," she stepped to Chelaine's right and picked up two small combs wired with pale blue silk flowers so artfully crafted they seemed real. She tried one on either side of the capped curls, met Chelaine's questioning gaze in the mirror, and smiled. "They match your gown, miss, and add a pretty touch." Chelaine nodded, and the maid positioned them, stepped back and grinned, then fussed a moment more, using a hairpin to draw out a soft halo of dark gold wisps and tendrils, just enough to frame Chelaine's face and draw attention to her wide, lovely eyes. "If I can say so, you look . . . very beautiful. Ah, wait 'til Lord Braden sees you!"

"You're too kind, Bess. Thank you, again. Do you know where Lucy could—"

Before she finished, there was a tap at the door, and Lucy poked her head in, gave a near shriek of delight, and tripped forward in that energetic, springy gait that only she could manage without looking like a frisky colt. "Oh, Bess! You've outdone yourself. Chelaine, I feel like a mouse beside you." She nodded a dismissal at her maid and waited until she'd left before catching at Chelaine's hands to bring her to her feet. "Do a turn," she pleaded, and after Chelaine had revolved once, clapped her hands in glee. "My Lord, I can't wait until they arrive! What a moment that'll be—I'd be willing to wager Stephen gapes at his first sight of you. And Edward, well, he'll *adore* you."

Though she was as excited as Lucy, Chelaine's was more of a long-awaited anticipation. She'd had to face this day sooner or later, but now that it was upon her, she trembled slightly, wished there was some magical potion that would calm her apprehension. Her appearance satisfied her . . . it should have, for ever since Lucy had gleefully shaken her awake early this morning, with a note from Stephen indicating the time of his arrival and mentioning a visit from a cousin, the entire morning and a good bit of the afternoon had been spent in preparation. A warm, scented bath, the washing of her mass of thick waves, the selection of a gown . . . they'd gone through her entire wardrobe before deciding on the pale blue-gray dimity shot with silver thread. The same thread embroidered the elbow ruffles and the layer of stiff lace that edged the low-scooped neckline. They'd eaten lightly, in between the many tasks, but Chelaine was glad of it for the unsettled fluttering of her stomach.

It was enough to face Stephen, but seeing him for the first time along with this cousin of theirs from one of the southern colonies added an extra measure of anxiety. Lucy had given her a sketchy account of Edward Harte. He was the only male cousin on their father's side of the family, the others being the five daughters of an aunt who still resided in England. He lived near a town called Richmond and raised tobacco . . . Chelaine had the impression he was something like a country squire, a gentleman who lived off his estate.

"Lucy? Do I *look* as nervous as I feel?"

"You look very poised and confident, just as you should," she answered. "Chelaine, it's only Stephen. As for Edward, he's very polite and even-tempered. You'll like him." With a twinkle in her eyes, she added, "He's not near as imposing as Stephen. Relax, darling!" Chelaine looked a little pale, and Lucy reached up, chafing her cheeks with the flat of her thumbs, raising a touch of color. "They should be here any time. After the first few moments, you'll forget all about your fears." Chelaine nodded, but her glance was dubious. Lucy caught her hand and gave it a squeeze. "I'll be there with you all the time." At that assurance, Chelaine smiled and resolved to banish any trepidations. She *had* to appear tranquil. "Why don't we go down and have tea in—"

Following a tap at the door, Bess called out that the coach was coming up the drive. Chelaine stiffened, but even before Lucy had time to bolster her confidence again, she inhaled deeply, slowly breathed out, and took a last glance in the mirror, practicing a smile that did look poised. "I am ready," she announced, and as Lucy surveyed her regal posture and composed mien, she nodded in agreement.

Lucy was first down the stairs, managing to speed down them without tangling her feet among her skirts and petticoats. The door was already opened by Samuel as she reached the bottom step and swept forward. Chelaine took them slowly, head high, one hand trailing on the banister, her skirts caught up slightly with the other, in a graceful descent she'd practiced arduously until it became second nature. She paused halfway down, arrested by the sight of Stephen. She had forgotten how handsome he was, and for a half-second she experienced a lurch of unbidden desire that caught her breath. His cousin stood beside him, a sandy-haired, attractive man, wiry rather than muscular, several inches shorter than Stephen, and eclipsed by his suave self-possession as well as by his physique.

Affectionate hugs and kisses were exchanged, Edward held Lucy at arm's length, exclaiming over how pretty she looked, what a refined young lady she'd grown to be. In the meantime, Samuel had taken Stephen's outerwear and stood by, waiting to do the same for Edward. Lucy turned back to her brother and hugged him once more.

"You almost had *me* worried," she chided. "As it was, I had to reassure Chelaine you hadn't been shipwrecked!" That confidence raised a skeptical brow.

"If she worried so, I'm surprised she isn't here to greet me," Stephen observed.

"But I am," Chelaine said. Stephen's head came up, his gaze swept up the staircase, taking in her appearance before his eyes finally met hers. The stunned shock that stretched his eyes wide, the utter astonishment that parted his lips and slowly gave way to a smile, the gleam of approval, all were more gratifying than anything Chelaine had imagined. "I thought Lucy deserved a moment to welcome you before I interrupted your reunion." She was vaguely aware of Lucy's delighted grin, of Edward's attention fixed on her, aping his cousin's surprise and admiration. "And I did worry, before Lucy confided you were a master mariner, able to deal with any foul weather."

"A biased opinion, to be sure," Stephen insisted, watching as Chelaine continued her descent with a serene expression and a carriage so noble she gave one the impression of a princess about to grace them with her presence. Not hauteur, but a confidence so strong, if he hadn't known her fears when he'd left, he would never have known her poise was acquired. A side glance at Edward confirmed that. He'd expected a reserved, rustic girl, intimidated by her surroundings, and stood gaping at a beauty any man would have been proud to present at court. "I've no need to ask how well you've adjusted to Hartehill." Without looking, he could feel Lucy nearly gloating over his reaction. It was immediately clear that she and Chelaine had become more than friends; they were allies, and the flicker of a look she exchanged with his sister spoke of a feminine conspiracy that jangled his nerve ends in a cautionary warning.

Chelaine strolled forward, extending her hands to Stephen, so bouyed by success she felt as if she were floating. He caught them, and despite her thorough self-command, she experienced something of a tingle, like a static shock, at the contact with his skin. Even aware that they played roles before an entranced audience of two, she was unsettled a moment as he drew her close and bent his head to kiss her cheek. He'd recovered quickly. The kiss was meant to be a show of fondness for his ward, but he held her captive moments longer than necessary, until Edward cleared his throat in a discreet attempt to rush an introduction.

"You'll excuse me, Edward," Stephen commented, a wry amusement crinkling the outer corners of his eyes as he noted just a hint of wariness in Chelaine's gaze. He held her right hand high, led her the few steps that separated them from his cousin, and presented her. "My ward, Michelaine Sully. My dear, our cousin, Edward Harte, of Virginia."

"But we all call her Chelaine," Lucy piped up, watching as Edward accepted Chelaine's hand and granted her a deep, formal bow before he kissed her fingertips. Stephen shot her a quick look that said volumes, transmitting both admiration for her part in Chelaine's transformation and awareness of the bond between herself and Chelaine. She returned the glance smugly, justly proud for Chelaine.

"The pleasure is mine," Edward managed to state without showing the stupification that threatened to knot his tongue. "Stephen was unusually reticent in describing you for me. I vow, I'd not appear so dull-witted if he'd apprised me of your beauty." Chelaine inclined her head, acknowledging the flattery graciously before she dazzled him further with a smile and the full attention of a pair of liquid, topaz eyes fringed by long, feathery lashes of dark golden brown.

"I merely said I'd allow you to judge Chelaine without my influence affecting your observations," Stephen remarked. "And 'tis obvious I couldn't have done her justice in words."

"Well, why don't we all retire to the drawing room?"

Lucy suggested. "We've plenty of time for conversation before supper." She moved closer, suppressing a giggle at her cousin's undisguised enchantment with Chelaine. "Edward?" She stood by, anxious to pry him away from Chelaine so he might escort her and allow Chelaine a few minutes to revel in Stephen's equal, if more contained, fascination. He seemed not to hear, and she repeated his name. As Chelaine gently withdrew her hand from his, he blinked, coming out of a trancelike stare with a visible effort to shake off his fixation. Chelaine retreated and Lucy offered him her hand, tucking it within the crook of his arm. "We'll be far more comfortable seated near the drawing room hearth, darling. I want to hear all you've been doing and what brought you for this unexpected, but delightful visit."

Edward found himself led along, a captive to Lucy's flurry of inquiries. He offered up a weak smile and tried to pay attention, but he couldn't keep his mind from Stephen's entrancing French cousin. Finally, with an effort, he managed an intelligent answer, briefly going over the purpose that brought him north, as they settled on one of a matched pair of sofas facing each other angled out from the fireplace.

"You seem to have made one more conquest," Stephen observed drily.

Chelaine's brows lifted in feigned innocence. "One more? Surely you don't count yourself . . ." He moved nearer, and a part of her was alert to that spark of attraction again, even though she showed no sign of any agitation. Stephen regarded her with a bemused look, more at his own expense than hers, offered her his arm, and flashed a grin that was, at once, wickedly teasing and engaging.

"Perhaps I should rephrase that. I'd never admit to being any woman's conquest. I prefer to be the conqueror. However, in due justice to your startling transformation, I will say that if any woman had a chance at such a feat, you would be the one. I may amend my own rules and allow you to make me your conquest."

"Whatever gave you the impression," Chelaine replied in a honeyed tone of voice, "that I would care to try?"

Stephen had started to lead her toward the drawing room. He paused for a minute, did a slow, lazy appraisal of Chelaine from head to toe before he met her eyes. "Oddly enough, I find myself unable to think of any other reason for such drastic, though bewitching, alterations. Before you protest, it isn't conceit that leads me to this conclusion." Her head tilted, dubious of the disclaimer. "Conceit suggests an exaggerated estimation of one's worth. I am quite realistic when it comes to self-appraisal. I am worth your efforts. Whether you care to pursue them is entirely your decision." He caught the flare of indignation in Chelaine's suddenly narrowed gaze but continued to smile with an annoying congeniality. Gesturing to the room, he reminded her to affect the fondness she'd shown him in her greeting. "Otherwise, my dear, Edward will wonder over your sudden change of mood. We must keep up appearances, mustn't we?"

Though he divided his attention equally, with no obvious deference to Chelaine, Stephen spent the afternoon and the supper hour observing changes other than the incredible poise she'd acquired. Her table manners were above reproach, she listened attentively to the recounting of the business venture he and

Edward had entered into, seemed pleased it would mean a long stay in Boston for him, asked questions that flattered even as they revealed a keen understanding of the profits to be made.

Lucy was more subdued than usual; Stephen suspected she was sitting back proudly watching over Chelaine like a mother hen, letting her chick make its way but ready to come to her aid if any trouble arose. As it turned out, there was no occasion for intervention. Chelaine acquitted herself so well through the meal and afterwards, for a brief spell in the drawing room, that once Lucy and she had retired, he had to endure a half-hour of effusive, flattering comments on her deportment, her beauty, and grace. While he wholeheartedly agreed on Chelaine's charms, Stephen didn't need an accounting. He finished his brandy, covered a yawn, and suggested he and Edward should follow the ladies' lead and get some sleep themselves.

Now, having shed his stock, coat, and vest, unbuttoned his shirtfront, and rolled back his cuffs, Stephen sat in one of the two chairs in his sitting area that faced the back of the house and his bed. His feet were stretched full length, crossed at the ankle, a half-full glass of brandy in hand. He closed his eyes, absently swirling the amber liquor, reviewing his homecoming from the moment Chelaine had drawn his attention to her presence on the stairs. His mouth stretched in a smile as he tried to imagine how *he* had looked from her vantage.

A tap sounded at his door, so faint he dismissed it as imaginary, but after a moment, it came again, a touch louder, persistent enough to lure him from his musings. He rose, crossed to the door, and opened it a crack, then wider as he found Chelaine standing there, clearly anxious about the chance of being discovered near his bedroom. Though she'd gone to her room three-quarters of an hour before, she still wore her blue gown. Her hair was unpinned, brushed out in fluffy layers about her shoulders. "What a pleasant surprise," he drawled, then crooked his head at an impatient hushing gesture as she set a finger to her lips. In a lower voice, he invited her within. She stared past him briefly, as if his suite were something to be avoided at any cost.

"Come out," Chelaine whispered. Stephen bent his head, glancing up through his lashes, considering her request. "Please?"

Just to sate his curiosity, he settled against the doorjamb, assumed a patient attitude, and waited to hear what was so urgent she'd risked possible embarrassment to come to him. "Well?"

Earlier, Lucy had asked him about his quest for Corbeau. The subject piqued Edward's interest and afforded him some amusement when Stephen explained his reason for hunting the smuggler. Edward had thought the venture "jolly good fun," and while she'd struggled to restrain her own curiosity, Stephen had dropped a hint he had learned something of value. "You know nothing more about Corbeau than when you left," she insisted now.

Stephen tipped back his head, smiling. If not for the necessity of maintaining quiet, the assertion would have brought a laugh. "You ventured out at this hour, just to inform me—" Down the hall a door latch clinked and he straightened. Chelaine froze, unable to decide whether to run for her room, or whether it was too late for such a retreat. Stephen decided for her. He seized her wrist, dragged her into his suite, and stepped into the hall, closing the door all but a crack.

Edward emerged from his room, dressed for bed in a borrowed nightshirt and robe. He saw Stephen and hailed him with a wave, then padded toward him in a pair of oversized slippers. "You're still awake, too? I thought I heard a noise in the hall and came out to investigate."

"I heard the same." Stephen covered a yawn and stretched. "Likely one of the maids on her way to the servants' loft. I shouldn't give it much thought. The servants are always up and finishing their duties after we've retired. I'm going back to bed. It's been too long a day."

"Hmm . . . I s'pose you're right. Well, if you're too tired to talk any longer, I shan't keep you. 'Night, Stephen."

"Sleep well. And if you hear any more sounds, don't bother checking. Sometimes the house creaks and settles, especially if your ears are keen for any noises."

Edward nodded and turned, retracing his steps. Stephen waited until he'd disappeared into his bedroom, with the door firmly shut, before he swung open his own door and entered, softly easing it closed, leaning back against it to consider the close call. He could have come up with some excuse if Edward had sighted Chelaine, but it might have left his cousin suspicious.

Chelaine stood across the room, warming her hands by the hearth, gazing upward at the family portrait that hung above the mantel. He couldn't judge whether she was purposely ignoring him or truly interested in the painting. For the moment, he was content just to study her. The red-orange glow from the smouldering split of hickory caught the highlights in the cascade of rippling curls and waves spread over her shoulders and down her back. Again, his first sight of her came to mind, and a stir of desire flared, quickly suppressed. He approached her, and while she stiffened at the click of his heels, her gaze remained on the portrait.

"You look very like your father," Chelaine observed without turning. He did, they might have been twins, except the older man lacked his son's commanding presence. In the grouping, he stood behind a high-backed, ornately carved, upholstered chair, just a portion of his right side showing, his left arm draped over the top of the chair, a hand curved about the shoulder of his wife. She looked sweet, gentle and loving. Her hair was a rich wavy auburn. Chelaine couldn't make out her eyes, but she imagined they suited her fair, milky skin and complemented her coloring with either a green or hazel shade. Stephen sat on a low footstool to her left, his upper body half turned, his features in profile as he gazed up. "How old were you then?"

"Ten. It was painted the year she died."

His love for his mother was still alive; there was a residue of pain left at her loss after so many years. And, too, it showed in his posture, as he leaned slightly toward her. He was handsome even then, lacking the arrogance he'd acquired with maturity. Something in his expression troubled Chelaine. She grasped the mantel for balance and stretched on tiptoe. It was resentment. She suddenly realized his gaze was directed past his mother, at the possessive hand that touched her shoulder. She settled back on her heels, glanced about to find Stephen studying the painting as well. "You disliked your father." It was a statement rather than a question.

His eyes lowered to meet hers, disconcerted by the

observation. "Is it that evident?" he asked, and then, before she answered, went on. "All we had in common vanished with her death. She died in childbirth and his child with her."

It was an odd way of phrasing the cause of her demise. Stephen not only blamed his father for the pregnancy, but he spoke as if the baby wouldn't have been a full brother or sister. "His child," it sounded so detached. "Lucy told me of this portrait, how sweet your mother looked. I agree. You must have—"

"What else did Lucy tell you?"

He was irritated, but she wasn't sure whether it was his old feelings for his father or the fact she'd discussed him with his sister. "Only that your father never recovered his grief, and her mother was too busy to bother with her, that you gave her the love they denied her."

"That was true. He married again six months after my mother died. It was a . . . necessary arrangement. I didn't give a damn for either one but Lucy . . . she was as alone as I."

"I don't wonder she adores you so."

"And you did nothing to alter her opinion?"

Chelaine canted her head, surprised by the accusing question. Irritated now herself, she retorted, "Why should she know what you're like?"

Stephen reached out, brushing the waves back over her shoulder before he cupped her chin and tipped her head up. "You're so sure you know what I'm like?"

The question needed no answer, but she spoke her mind. "I know of traits she's never seen."

"Just as I know much of you that would dismay her. I suggest we keep our faults from her . . . since we both care for Lucy." Stephen moved beside her, resting his forearm on the mantel. "Much as I hate to disrupt our pleasantries with a mention of your renegade hero, I believe you came to me to learn what I know of him."

"You know nothing! You were baiting me and—"

"It appears you took the bait. As it happens, the bait was not a fanciful lie but the truth. I do know the place where the man makes his rendezvous with your rebels." Doubt battled with a desire to test his assertion. With a toss of her head, she strolled away from him, studied the massive, carved posts of his canopied bed, then turned and glanced back at him, trying to cover her interest with an air of nonchalance. "You could not. No Acadian would betray Corbeau. And the British know nothing."

"Then when I return after the spring thaw, Corbeau should run no risk in anchoring at Baie Cristal."

She tensed, her mouth went dry, but to her credit, Chelaine recovered her shock at the name so quickly there was just a hint of wariness in her eyes, and that was covered by a wide-eyed curiosity. "Baie Cristal? I have never heard of such a place."

"An admirable comeback, Chelaine. The more I see of this 'new' you, the more there is to admire. But you've forgotten whom you're dealing with. I was the one who cautioned you to acquire the skill of masking your feelings. There are other signs beside your expression. I can read them."

"Oh?" Chelaine lifted a shoulder and let it fall. "And what do they tell you?"

"That you're lying. Of course, I'd not have expected anything less."

"If you believe this, then by all means, go. Spend the spring and most of the summer watching for him. There must be better uses for your time."

"You mean you wouldn't be delighted to see me waste my days in this 'foolish' watch for him?"

"All that would delight me is to return to my room."

"Ah . . . but Edward may still be awake. You don't want to disillusion him by a stealthy retreat from my room to yours."

"The alternative is more risky."

Stephen came toward her. She stared at him, measuring his intent, but stood her ground. He paused beside her, reaching overhead to rest a hand on the thick bedpost. "You know you're safe with me."

She allowed herself a self-satisfied smirk. "I do. Your honor is the only trait I admire in you. You've kept your vow . . . and will keep it."

"You place more faith in it than I. You intend to make me sorry I swore it, though? Somewhere beneath that sweet face lies a cruel streak few could rival."

"I can think of one who rivals it at this moment." She smiled, for the sheer pleasure of mocking him. "Stephen, I think you were sorry even as the words left your lips."

"My dear, you've not only blossomed, your success has gone to your head. By contrast, my 'conceit' smacks of humility."

"Hah! Humility, indeed. Your temper is tried by envy of Edward."

Stephen scoffed at the idea, chuckling at the claim. "*Edward?* He doesn't know you as I do. And he hasn't seen you parade about in breeches."

Chelaine's complexion paled, emphasizing the angry color staining her cheeks. She set her hands at her waist and scowled. "Nor in your nightshirt!"

"I found you most appealing without a stitch on. *That* I remember very clearly."

"Then let your memories console you!" Chelaine started for the door, but Stephen easily outdistanced her, with enough time to spare to lean back against it, cross his arms and smile. "Let me pass," she demanded.

Stephen wagged his head. "Not yet." She reached past him and tugged at the handle, grimacing at her inability to budge the door. She straightened with a deep breath and faced him, a stubborn set to her features as she, too, crossed her arms. "You don't hate me anymore, do you?" he asserted. "If you ever did. In fact, you're fighting your attraction to me."

Chelaine caught at her bottom lip, lowered her lashes, and tried valiantly to control her temper, seething with frustration. Finally she met his amused gaze, found his grin insufferable, and fumed, "And you dare call *me* conceited! I . . . I could slap you for—"

His tongue clicked against the roof of his mouth, chiding her. "Have you forgotten what followed the last slap?"

"How could I? I have forgotten nothing of that *miserable* voyage. Now, let me out!"

Taking in the flush of color that brightened her high cheekbones, the sparkle that glinted from between her narrowed lashes, Stephen lifted a brow as if contemplating her request. At last, his head bent, fixing her with a heavy-lidded, obstinate look. "For a kiss."

"Oh! You . . ." She sputtered helplessly before her mouth rounded into an indignant, exasperated O, and her chin firmed with a familiar obstinacy. "Your vow—"

"—was to refrain from making love to you until I'd achieved my goal." He shrugged off her outrage. "One kiss can hardly lead to more . . . unless—"

"Unless *what?*"

His mouth twitched with a lazy humor. "I'm more than willing to let *you* take advantage of *me.*"

"This is not amusing." Chelaine reached for the handle again, but with his weight against the door escape was impossible. "Let me out of here or . . . or I'll scream." Even as the threat left her, she knew it for an empty, desperate challenge.

"You wouldn't."

His confidence grated on her frayed nerves. "Try me." He'd pushed her past the point of self-control, she no longer cared what she said. "I will," she warned.

"No, Chelaine. Any such sound would alert the entire household."

"You don't want to ruin my reputation," she reminded him. "Not after all the trouble you took to see—"

"Come now. A kiss is such a small price to pay. If I were found in your room, it might look the worse for me . . . but that isn't the case. Lucy would be shocked and Edward . . ." Stephen shook his head. "It's hardly worth the trouble to refuse so simple a request."

He had her just where he pleased, bending to his will again. She wanted nothing more than to strike out, deliver a swift, painful kick to his shins, anything to wipe the smug content from his handsome features. For a while she'd been in control—how had he turned it about to his advantage? He was right about the scene, she'd be humiliated, not he, and that made the matter all the more galling. It was her own fault for allowing him this chance. With a disgruntled sigh, she gave in, glancing up warily. "*One* kiss?"

"Just one."

He seemed to think she would swoon at the touch of

his lips, and it amused him vastly to have her cornered. Still, if it would gain her release . . . "I have no choice."

"It seems not."

"Then take your kiss and be done." Stoicly resigned, she closed her eyes, waiting.

Stephen studied her with a barely checked amusement. She'd given in but grudgingly. "You'd have made a fine Christian martyr, Chelaine," he reflected. "Have you forgotten your response to our first kiss?"

Her lids flew open at that taunt, then narrowed spitefully. He couldn't simply kiss her. "Must you make an ordeal of this? Yes, I have put that memory away."

Stephen's glance mocked the claim, his attitude patently indulgent, as if he were dealing with a recalcitrant child. "You have not . . . and neither have I."

Chelaine thought she'd scream, damn the consequences, if she had to endure another minute with him. "Either kiss me or let me leave," she insisted.

"You're the one who wants out. I should think it more suitable if you kissed me."

She stared in disbelief, then whirled about, throwing up her hands in frustration. "What sin did I commit, to be punished so?" she questioned aloud in anguished wonder. "This isn't real. I have died, and for my sins, you are to torment me!"

"How dramatic," he observed. "You're quite alive, and it's a matter for conjecture, *who* is tormenting *whom*. You've cast me in the role of a Lucifer—"

Chelaine abruptly turned about, head high, eyes glittering. "A role that suits you well. Lucifer was the most handsome of the angels . . . until his vanity banished him from Heaven."

"At least you haven't depicted me with scales and a

145

forked tail," he commented sardonically. He was wearying of the argument himself, but something, perhaps it was a devilish pride, would not allow him to relent. "This isn't Heaven, Chelaine—nor is it Hell. We are earthbound . . ." his lips quirked in a mirthless smile, "until one of us does the other in. Kiss me now and you can go."

In anger and frustration, to be done with it, she almost flung herself at him. Instead, with a deep breath to calm her, she stepped close, set her hands against his chest, and stretched, lightly touching her mouth to his. Suddenly, without seeming to move, his hand cradled the back of her head, his arm slipped about her waist, drawing her close. Chelaine stiffened, but her protest, muffled by the light, teasing pressure of his lips, came out a helpless whimper. Beneath her hands, the muscles of his chest flexed, radiating a heat through the thin, cambric shirt that stirred unwelcome, bittersweet memories.

Just as suddenly as she was seized, Chelaine was freed. She wavered a few moments, blinking back a wave of feeling that blurred her vision. Stephen's gaze was enigmatic, his thoughts indiscernible as he steadied her with a hand at each shoulder and then released her.

"Was that so awful? *I* found it a pleasure." Without looking, he found the latch, closed his fingers about it, but before he turned it, canted his head, a vaguely puzzled smile curving his lips. "Why is it, I wonder, that a simple kiss between us never fails to turn your eyes misty?"

Chelaine stared, shaken by the embrace and frightened by her response. He had easily, quickly aroused her and then casually set her away, seemingly unmoved. "I think nothing between us is, or ever will be, simple," she admitted.

"True. A most astute observation. I must give it some consideration," he said as he swung the door open. His hand rose to cover a yawn. "In the morning, perhaps. Rest well, Chelaine."

Struggling for a measure of dignity in the face of such a callous dismissal, Chelaine gathered her skirts and swept past him, pausing a second to check the hall before she hurried across to her own door.

In his room, Stephen leaned a shoulder against the closed door, lost in thought. The scent of her lingered in the room, remaining to haunt his senses though she had fled. Then, as he pushed away from the door and crossed to the bed, a bitterly self-mocking smile curled his mouth. One hand closed tightly about the newel post in a grip that whitened his knuckles. He gazed at the wide, comfortable bed, imagining Chelaine lying there in his arms . . . where she belonged, and where, by his own decree, he could not have her.

Chapter Nine

SEQUESTERED IN HIS STUDY, SEATED AT THE DESK, STE-
phen tried to concentrate on the verse from a poetry
volume he'd drawn from his shelves. His thoughts kept
drifting to Chelaine. Throughout the past fortnight,
since he'd come home, she'd taken great delight in
taunting him, flirting subtly in a cat-and-mouse game,
never again allowing herself to be caught alone with
him, as she had that first night.

Soft chords of a melody played on the spinet came
drifting down the hall, just audible enough to further
distract him. With a frustrated sigh, he slammed the
book closed and tossed it down on the desk. The dance
master was here again. He had no quarrel with the
man, but the girls, especially Chelaine, invariably
turned the lessons into a two-hour period of entertain-
ment, full of amusement and far too much giggling to
afford any time for serious practice.

He rose and left the study. Above the strains of a
minuet, a silvery peal of laughter floated from the
ballroom, eliciting a frown from him as he recognized

Chelaine's voice. What, he thought as he headed down the hall, was so damned humorous in a session of dance practice?

He paused at the entrance to the room. Lucy was at the spinet, her face flushed by more than mere exercise. She strained to keep her attention on the keyboard, but her gaze kept wandering to the dance floor, where Adrian Kinmont was showing Chelaine a step.

As often as she'd practiced, Chelaine still had difficulty maintaining the proper posture, head high, eyes directed at her partner, while she tried to move through the minuet without tangling her feet in her voluminous, belled skirts and petticoats. Already she'd missed a movement and nearly tumbled. Now as she smiled at Master Kinmont and dipped in a curtsy, her heel caught in a hem. She wavered, regained her balance with a blush, but again he'd instinctively reached out to rescue her. The first time she'd laughed and Lucy had joined in, not out of pettiness, but because her spirits were high. This time, though, Chelaine felt awkward, embarrassed.

"Perhaps I should practice with Chelaine."

She startled at his voice, her complexion tinged a deeper rose as she glanced at the doorway and found Stephen lounging there, a hint of disapproval in his eyes. Kinmont released her, retreating to a discreet distance as Stephen sauntered toward them, his gaze fixed on the tutor. "I suggest you take a well-earned rest, Master Kinmont. Instructing two girls at once must be a wearing experience." Lucy sensed a sudden tension and sighed. At a nod from her brother, she directed her gaze at the sheet music, then lightly settled her fingers on the keys. A peek at Chelaine showed her dismay, both at what seemed a reprimand for their instructor and Stephen's assumptive intervention as he caught her hand and took up a pose opposite her.

Kinmont stood back, watching the pair, wondering if he faced a dismissal. Aside from the stipend that helped him support a large family, he'd enjoyed tutoring these two young ladies. Lucy was accomplished, Chelaine only needed practice to manage the intricate steps more easily. From a novice, she'd made great improvement, and all she really needed was more confidence. Now the easy, good-humored atmosphere had vanished, and as tense as the girl looked, there was every chance she might falter again. The earl nodded at his sister and she began to play.

Stephen made a leg, Chelaine responded with a deep curtsy, and despite her earlier mistakes, she was determined not to let him fluster her. Concentrating, she paid more mind to the movement of her feet this time. Stephen *was* a graceful partner, and whether it was his self-confidence or her own commitment to execute the steps successfully, they moved through the slow, stately dance with an ease that astonished her. When the music stopped, Stephen bowed and came up with a smug, pleased smile. She returned it rather stiffly, her gaze directed past him, seeking Kinmont's approval. He nodded and smiled, but the smile faded as Stephen followed her gaze and frowned slightly.

"Master Kinmont, if I could have a word with you," Stephen released Chelaine's hand to gesture toward the hall, "in private?" The man paled and tried to manage a smile, acknowledging the request with a half-bow before he headed across the room, pausing to wait for his employer. Chelaine looked upset; she exchanged a worried glance with Lucy, then caught at Stephen's forearm. His features were expressionless and her hand fell away. Nodding to Lucy and smiling a bit to reassure Chelaine, he apologized for the interruption. "You'll excuse us, ladies?"

Chelaine watched him join Kinmont, wondering if he was going to reprimand him for the lighthearted nature of their sessions. She sighed once they were out of sight, her shoulders slumped, and she wandered over to Lucy, who looked almost as dejected as she.

Strolling down the hall, hands clasped behind his back, Stephen considered how necessary the lessons were. Lucy didn't need them, and while she'd faltered through a dance with Kinmont, Chelaine had acquitted herself superbly with him. "Kinmont?" The dance master started at the address, clearly anxious. He was in his mid-thirties, balding slightly, stocky and bespectacled. "I'm quite pleased by how well my ward has progressed under your tutelage. And I'd have seen no reason to cease her lessons if I hadn't returned home. I've the leisure time to continue her practice—and I'm sure a twice-weekly journey through the snow has been a burden on you."

"M'Lord, you are displeased—"

Stephen shook his head and paused, turning slightly to raise his brows at the protest. "I've just complimented your skill, sir. If I've given you cause to feel uneasy, I apologize. I simply don't see the need to continue the lessons. I have nothing but the highest regard for your abilities—I shall pen a note of recommendation to that effect. Now, as for your reimbursement. You expected to receive payment for lessons through April. I'll be most happy to settle that amount on you, with a bonus of five guineas for all you've done to teach my ward the rudiments of dance etiquette."

The offer was generous, overly generous, but Adrian

still felt he'd incurred the earl's wrath. "I appreciate your benevolence, m'Lord but . . ." He hesitated to voice his feelings.

"Do go on, sir. Whatever troubles you, feel free to speak your mind."

"Well, sire, 'tis just that I feel I've disappointed you. If my conduct displeased you in any way, I should like to know how, so I may correct any errors in my comportment."

"The girls have enjoyed your lessons, Master Kinmont. There's no harm done in making a task more easy by keeping the mood carefree. I assure you, this is not so much a dismissal as a commendation for your efforts, freeing you to take on students in the town. I'm sure there will be many young ladies in need of practice, those who have been invited to my sister's debut. My note should open many avenues of revenue for you."

Kinmont's relief was obvious. He would miss the girls' lessons, but the earl's settlement and his patronage would assure his family a healthy income. "I can't thank you enough for your generosity and kind flattery, m'Lord," he said with a bow of his head. "Should I finish today's lessons—or just bid the young ladies farewell?"

"I suggest you come along to my study. I'll pay you and write out the note, then you may take your parting of the girls." He led Kinmont toward his study, entered, and offered the man a seat. "Lucy and Chelaine will be disappointed, but I'm taking them along to Boston for a shopping spree." He grinned, more to himself, and as he drew out a ledger and a sack of coins, commented, "The idea of spending money appeals to any female. This visit to town should cushion any protests they might broach."

Soon enough, with his pocket nicely plumped by the settlement, Kinmont returned to the ballroom. The earl explained his decision, and while both girls evidenced the expected disappointment, it was clear that the dance master hadn't been chastised and dismissed, as much as let go.

Stephen looked pleased, Master Kinmont beamed and made a point of thanking the girls for the pleasure of tutoring them. He bowed over Lucy's hand. For Chelaine, he had an offering of praise. "For a lady who commenced lessons with no experience in dance, mademoiselle, you have proven to be a most adept student. I've no doubts you will be one of the most graceful ladies to take to the floor at Lady Lucinda's ball."

Chelaine thanked him, still curious over the sudden end to the lessons. Stephen looked more than pleased, he appeared smugly content. "Lucy, why don't you show Master Kinmont to the door?" he suggested, and while his sister saw nothing but courtesy in the directive, Chelaine felt an uneasy stirring. She did *not* want to be alone with Stephen, had managed to keep him at a distance for weeks.

"I'll come along, just to say fare—"

"You've already said your farewell, Chelaine. Lucy can manage quite well."

Chelaine watched with growing apprehension as Lucy led Kinmont off. Despite the size of the ballroom, she felt cornered, just as she had that night in Stephen's suite. Still, what could he do in broad daylight, with servants coming and going? That thought pushed the uneasiness away. She clasped her hands together and faced Stephen. He'd had some purpose in sending Lucy off—she waited patiently to hear it.

"I shouldn't be too disappointed," he commented, approaching her to pause nearby. "You danced well with me. And there'll be more time for such practice in the weeks ahead."

"Why should you care if I'm disappointed? You were generous in allowing me the chance—"

"We're alone, Chelaine. There's no need for false humility. I had a reason in arranging these few minutes with you."

"I guessed you had. Fortunately, we are not in your—"

"Tsk! Someone might overhear," he cautioned. Catching her hands, he parted her interlaced fingers and tucked her right hand in the bend of his elbow, gestured toward the terrace doors, and before she could protest, led her toward them. "We can admire the garden and speak more privately."

"The garden is covered by ice and frost, Stephen. It's an unusual time of year to admire it."

"Ah, but no one questions the master's whims." Stephen caught a glimpse of her brow arched in disagreement. "Well, no one dares but you," he admitted wryly. "Nobility is allowed its eccentricities. If I wish to admire a winter scene, I've the right."

"You may admire whatever you please." He *always* did as he pleased, no matter the inconvenience or protests of another. It was useless to struggle against his will. "What is so important it had to be said in private?" she asked, then with an insincere smile, added, "Oh, *do* forgive me! I should not have been so inquisitive. You'll tell me when it pleases *you* to do so."

Matching her sarcasm, he inclined his head toward

her. "You're forgiven the impropriety. I make allowances for your youth and a manner that often borders on impudence. Now, Lucy will know of this in a short while—"

"Know of what?"

"It's impolite to interrupt. If you can hold your tongue, you may hear me out before she returns." Chelaine's mouth stretched thin in a brief grimace, eliciting a smile that overlooked her desire to retort with some well-aimed barb. "I've decided to take you both to Boston, and as far as Lucy need know, you're along to shop and play havoc with my bank account." He had her attention now, with the allusion to something to be kept from his sister. "I thought we might inquire among the Acadians still held in internment to learn if anyone has word of your sister's whereabouts."

Chelaine gaped, thoroughly taken back by the unexpected and, oddly for him, thoughtful offer. His hand came up to tip her chin gently, closing her mouth as well as raising her head so he could study her wide-stretched eyes.

"You can see why I chose to speak with you first— before you made some stubborn protest that you didn't care to shop." She recovered slowly, obviously searching for some other motive behind his offer. "Your thoughts are as clear as if you'd voiced them, dear. No, I am not out to disarm you or influence your opinion of me. I know that far too well."

"Then why?" It was all she could manage despite a riot of conflicting emotions. Hope, pleasure, distrust, so many she couldn't sort through them.

"You might call it a reward, an acknowledgment of how much effort you've put forth to adjust to our way of life." She still seemed shocked, incredulous. "I'm not entirely without some redeeming virtues. You've seen how I indulge Lucy. She tries to please me and I pamper her. When we aren't engaged in a verbal battle, I enjoy your company. It seemed to me one way to make you happy."

"But—"

"Aren't you allowed happiness, Chelaine? You seem to question any good fortune that comes your way. I wonder . . . were you always so cynical, or have you gained that wary distrust only since we met?" He drew his hand away from her jaw. "Don't answer, I know you've had cause to feel a certain caution of my motives. Surely your treatment since your arrival has shown my own change of heart?"

"And in return for your kindness . . ." Chelaine paused. Stephen actually appeared wounded by a suggestion he meant to influence her opinion by his act. "I'm sorry . . ." The apology drew a raised brow. "I *am,* Stephen, truly! It is a kind, generous offer. Do you truly think there's a—"

"Goodness, what are you doing over there? The room is freezing, and you two are standing in a draft!" Lucy startled them both and left Chelaine wondering if she'd overheard them. Stephen knew she hadn't. Lucy never paused before entering a room, she just bounced in no matter who was present.

"It *is* chilly, but Chelaine loves the view," Stephen jested. "It reminds her of how icy Acadia can be in the winter." He glanced down at her and noted a bare hint of a smile just at the corners of her mouth. "Let's go warm up by the drawing room hearth," he suggested, and as he led her toward the doorway and Lucy, added, "Shall I tell her the surprise or allow you?"

"It was your idea," Chelaine reminded him. Her

smile was genuine now as she glanced aside and upward, with a note of conspiracy only he understood.

"Well, then—if I can pry you away from the boredom of being housebound by the weather," he teased, "I've just been telling Chelaine of my decision to take you both to Boston. You can add to the fortunes of the town's shopkeepers and spend until you're dizzy."

Lucy clasped her hands together and could barely contain a squeal of delight. "Boston! Oh, Chelaine, we'll have such a grand time!" Stephen threw back his head, laughing over her jubilance. She calmed down enough to wink at Chelaine, and as her brother came close, catch his free arm. "Stephen, darling, I could *never* get dizzy spending. You may feel lightheaded, though, when the tradesmen send their bills!"

Chapter Ten

ALTHOUGH SHE'D BECOME USED TO LUXURY, CHELAINE accompanied Lucy on daily shopping sprees and found herself amazed at how freely she spent. In each shop they were greeted with respect, even fawned upon by the shopkeepers. Lucy tried on hats, gloves, shawls . . . anything that took her fancy was boxed and sent along to the town house, the bill of sale forwarded to Samuel, who acted as Stephen's secretary in settling any accounts due.

Chelaine balked at Lucy's insistence that she feel free to purchase anything she wished. It was one thing for Stephen to indulge his sister's whims, another for her to be extravagant with his money. "But darling," Lucy explained, "Stephen earned his own fortune. He sees no use in hoarding it like so many others. There's no advantage to being rich unless it affords you these little pleasures. And if I were to tell him of your hesitance, why, he'd be offended! After all, you're family." Even then, Chelaine expressed reluctance, convinced only when Lucy added, "He takes pride in his appearance.

The Hartes must be fashionable—it's expected of us, you included."

Who could argue with such reason? She wasn't a Harte in name, but as Stephen's ward, she was expected to act the part. If she failed to follow suit, it would seem he was less generous with his poor cousin. And, too, once Chelaine lost her inhibitions, she found the chance to indulge in flattering fashions a purely feminine delight.

Stephen spent his days tending to business matters. As he'd promised, he'd made inquiries about her sister's whereabouts. Chelaine was less concerned over Elise's son, André. They were never close—she'd only mentioned him to Stephen in passing. If he did locate her sister, she'd be fretting over her younger son's fate.

Many of the Acadians interned and guarded at a house near the almshouse, off the Common, had already had their service sold at auction. Stephen had gone alone to question those who remained, refusing to let her accompany him. To her mind, it only made sense that the refugees would be more willing to deal with one of their own kind, but as Stephen had pointed out, Chelaine no longer looked as if she belonged among them. Her fashionable attire would only lead to crude speculation over such fortune in the light of their own impoverished states.

The observation was valid. She had acquired the look of an English lady, and the simple, plain life she'd lived in Acadia now seemed foreign. She was, oddly enough, a displaced identity, no longer Acadian, not quite integrated into the customs and culture of the colonies.

Once Lucy had tired of afternoon teas with her friends and exhausted the round of shops, she determined to return home. Her début was still months away, but a number of craftsmen, drapers, painters, and upholsterers were all busy at work, transforming Hartehill into a suitable setting for the grand ball they'd planned. Chelaine had stayed on, anxious for any word of Elise. Lucy accepted Stephen's excuse that he was trying to locate distant relatives on Chelaine's maternal side of the family, unrelated to him but still of concern to Chelaine.

Stephen visibly relaxed once they were the only occupants of the town house. In front of the servants, in public, he maintained a very proper, formal affection for his young ward, but when they were alone, that façade dropped away. There were nights he read aloud to her from one of the many volumes lining the walls of his study, afternoons spent teaching her a popular card game called whist. He took her to lectures, they lunched at respectable taverns favored by the upper classes. The weather kept them from exercise, but he'd promised that as winter thawed into spring, they would ride the trails about the great Common. At that suggestion, she'd admitted all she knew of riding had been the short-legged, sturdy Acadian ponies, and then bareback, with only a halter to guide the animals. With his usual competence, Stephen had dismissed her worries. By spring, she'd have lessons in riding the English style, sidesaddle, with a fashionable riding habit and a mild-tempered mare of her own choosing.

Her plan to win Stephen's heart and vanish, leaving him to wrestle with the anguish of her disappearance no longer held the appeal it once had. In adapting to his idea of refined womanhood, she had somehow effected a change in him. The arrogant, frosty aristocrat had vanished, replaced by a warm, charming man eager to see her contented. As the days passed into weeks, Chelaine forgot the guile she'd practiced. It was almost as if she'd won and couldn't recall why the desire for revenge had seemed so important. A summons to Corbeau was the furthest thought from her mind.

Stephen had kept his vow, but there were moments, when they stood close, when she felt a strong attraction to him. It was impossible to share the same house and not be aroused by his bold, handsome features, by a dawning awareness that the passion his lovemaking had stirred once was with her still. As honor-bound as he was to deny himself satisfaction in sharing her bed, she knew he chafed under the self-imposed restriction. Her room adjoined his, a common door connecting the bedrooms. Some nights, when she tossed restlessly, struggling with memories of how skillfully his hands and mouth had brought her such pleasure, she noted a light beneath that door, guessed that the same feelings tormented him. Yet the vow stood between them, a wall as solid as any structure, cemented by his given word, by her inability to let him know her desires.

Now March had come, with milder temperatures, the snows melting into rains, with occasional bouts of warm, balmy weather. The other day Stephen had taken her for a fitting of her ballgown for Lucy's debut, and while waiting, surprised her by ordering the riding habit he'd promised. Today, after breakfast, he'd suggested a ride in the carriage, told her to dress warmly enough for a brisk March wind, and refused to tell her anything about their destination. He was evasive, hinting at some surprise that awaited at the end of the ride, only adding to her excitement by the now familiar twinkle in his eyes that usually preceded something delightful.

161

As the carriage passed along the narrow, winding streets, Chelaine plied him with questions. He looked smugly pleased, relaxed and enjoying her attempts to wheedle some hint from him. "Stephen . . . tell me *something*," Chelaine pleaded. "Just a hint, a tiny hint?" He shook his head, responding with an engagingly crooked grin. "Oh, you are so . . . so—"

"Frustrating?" he supplied, and chuckled at her exasperation, then tossed back his head in a rumble of teasing laughter. "Or heartless?"

Chelaine wriggled, settling back against the plush, comfortable seat, a faint pout pushing at her lower lip. She stole a glance sideways through the thick fringe of tawny lashes and nodded. "Both," she replied, "and more. You know I have no patience for surprises."

The cool breeze had dusted Chelaine's cheeks with a healthy rose flush. Her mouth, in profile, had a sweet, child's indentation that, combined with a sensual fullness, tempted him to satisfy her curiosity. "One hint, then, imp," he allowed. "Have you noted what direction we're headed?"

Chelaine glanced about. She was familiar enough with the different sections of Boston now, the South End where they lived, the North End, the Battery. The carriage was heading north on Hanover Street. Ahead lay Fleet Street and Scarlett's wharf, where the brig lay at berth. She faced him with a wide-eyed astonishment. "The wharf . . . surely we are not going sailing?"

"No," Stephen admitted, "we're not, but we are bound for the ship."

"But why? If not to . . ." Fine lines of amusement radiated from the corners of Stephen's eyes, those fascinating pale blue irises that were more startling for the deep, almost black lashes that framed them. He'd offered one hint, and a stubborn set to his chin made it clear he'd say no more.

Stephen saw her struggle against more inquiries. A soft sigh indicated surrender; she would wait. As she gazed ahead, a blend of eagerness and anticipation lighting her face, he studied her. Chelaine had undergone a fascinating transition in three months, giving him cause to wonder what she'd be like in six months, a year, even longer. She'd dazzled him on his return, adjusted to her fate, and even since they'd come to Boston, shown him more intriguing facets to her nature. He'd taken her to visit Olivia Markham's home. The widow's elegant drawing room was a renowned haven for an interesting mix of scholars, artists, musicians, the sophisticated echelon of Boston culture. She had been timid at first, happy just to sit and listen to witty, philosophical debates, but she had absorbed much; her thirst for knowledge and her beauty had made her a favorite, welcome addition to the coterie.

The carriage had turned on Fleet Street, proceeded past the King's Head Tavern, and come to a halt at the wharf. Stephen stood, slipped past Chelaine, and alighted, reaching back to lift her slight figure and swing her down beside him. Here the wind blew stronger off the water, tugging at Chelaine's wealth of shiny curls, and she drew up a lace shawl, tossing one end over the pale azure cape of lightweight wool, before accepting his offered arm. Together they strolled toward the *Lucinda's* berth, and the expectation reflected in her fine, even features brought a smile to his lips.

On board, James Avery was there to greet them. He hadn't seen Chelaine since her arrival, and the difference in her appearance left him open-mouthed with admiration, his manners forgotten as he gaped. Stephen discreetly cleared his throat, and the mate blushed, grabbing off his cap, acknowledging his employer with a curt bow, a deeper one for Chelaine. He stepped back out of the way, as Stephen led Chelaine toward the companionway, but his gaze returned to her, then lighted on the earl with open envy.

Once they were below, Chelaine paused by the stairs. "Stephen, tell me now, at least!" She offered him an enchanting smile, one hand resting on his upper arm, an irresistible appeal that brought an indulgent sigh from him.

"All right," he relented. "Enough suspense. I managed to locate your nephew, André. Several weeks ago I learned he'd been indentured to a farmer in the Connecticut Valley and sent a man to buy off his time. The farmer balked, but he received more than adequate compensation. André is here . . . waiting in the cabin. I've set him—"

Shock rooted Chelaine in place, but only for moments, before an incredulous delight transformed her face. She took one, quicksilver glance toward the cabin, then without thinking, arched and circled Stephen's neck with her arms, her mouth pressed to his in a jubilant, grateful kiss.

She was clearly carried away at the relief of knowing one of her relatives was safe, but even as she seemed to realize embarrassment at her unrestrained reaction, Stephen's arms closed about her. There was a second of hesitation, a stiffness that faded fast as his tender, stirring kiss called up feelings they had both denied for so long.

Chelaine felt the hunger in him, controlled even now, but her own response left her lightheaded, setting her skin burning, awakening that sense of yearning coiled in the pit of her belly. She clung shamelessly, desire pushing all caution and reason aside, André forgotten.

It was Stephen who drew away, in obvious reluctance, to gaze down into her eyes, puzzling just a moment over her desire, helplessly drawn back for one more kiss before he gently caught her wrists and lowered her arms. She looked frightened . . . not of him, but of how quickly an impulsive kiss had blossomed into passion. "Don't blush so, love," he cautioned in a low voice that betrayed his own feelings. "I promise not to make more of this . . . gesture of relief." His fingers lightly brushed the wispy tendrils of hair back from her temples before he stepped back, not sure of his own ability to control the longing to hold her close again. "Compose yourself. André is waiting." He turned and took a step upward, pausing to smile back at her. "I'll be on deck. You deserve privacy for a reunion."

Chelaine watched him climb the stairs, wondering if what she had done in a thoughtless moment had changed their easy, carefree companionship. She couldn't love him, not an English lord who'd bonded her to him with a piece of paper, she couldn't . . . and yet beyond the flare of wild physical yearning, something more than affection, something mysterious bound her to Stephen in a way no legal document could.

At the cabin door, she hesitated. She hadn't seen André for nine months—no, longer, for she hadn't been home much the year before. She would have been far more happy to know Elise awaited her. André was dull, stolid, a simple man who'd run the farm and tended their cattle after his father died. But he was kin, the son of a sister who had raised her. For Elise, she raised a smile, then entered without a knock.

André Brevard wheeled about at the sound of the door latch, expecting to see the tall, suave earl who'd purchased his indenture from the exacting taskmaster, Josiah Gorme. It was the earl's representative, no servant, but a hired man of letters, who'd done the bargaining, paid the farmer, and brought him here. He'd been fed well, allowed to rest, and given a new set of clothing to replace the threadbare rags he'd worn through the harsh winter. He assumed he'd traded one master for another, but why he was being treated so generously puzzled him, and there were greater surprises in store. The earl had come to meet him, offered his hand as if they were equals, then destroyed his papers. Still more, he'd offered him a job working at his country estate, set a generous wage, and left André stupefied at such benevolence from a stranger. He had a right to know why, and if his question had been couched in a belligerent tone, the Englishman had ignored the hostility.

He was free because it would please Chelaine, yet another reason to gape. The last he'd heard, she was tagging after her fool of a brother, playing at rebel when she should have been settled with a husband and children. All the earl asked in return had been his pledge to keep André's relationship to Chelaine between themselves. How she'd managed to wield such power with the man waited on her appearance.

And now she was here, standing in the doorway, so changed he'd never have known her if they'd passed on a street. He ignored her smile, his eyes narrowing contemptuously as he surveyed her rich clothing, his thin mouth twisting in a sneer as he met her eyes. Now he understood. However she'd come to Boston, she'd found a protector in the earl.

Chelaine's smile faded. She'd expected surprise and, if not affection, at least some relief that she hadn't suffered as so many other women had. Taller than Stephen, thin, still gangly, all arms and legs, André glowered at her from a face that looked haggard. His appraisal and the disgust in his eyes struck her like a physical blow. They hadn't even greeted each other, and she wanted nothing more than to turn and walk away.

Instead, she raised her head, staring back, refusing to back down from his glare. She shrugged off her cape, draped it over an arm, and after a deep breath, said, "I never thought to see you alive, André. You haven't changed so. For a man who has been saved from hard labor, you have the air of an ungrateful clod. You might at least ask how I have fared."

"There is no need to ask. You look what you are—the well-kept whore of that English bastard."

There had never been any feeling between them, she had tolerated André for his mother's sake, but such galling arrogance from a scarecrow figure who owed so much to Stephen filled her with rage. She took several steps forward, drew back her arm, and brought her hand up to slap his cheek with all the force she could muster. His head rocked aside from the blow, slowly he straightened, ready to return the smack, until he saw the livid fury that blazed from her eyes. She wasn't frightened, stood her ground, daring him to follow through. It wasn't just the assurance that she could call on her lover. Chelaine had changed more than her appearance. He had disliked her when she lived at home. Much as his mother had loved her sons, she had doted on Chelaine, a wild, unruly brat not even her own.

"You resent me still," Chelaine acknowledged, and her disgust for him far outweighed his spite. "André, you were born old and sour—time has made you more so. I am sorry Stephen found you."

"If I had known it was your traded favors that bought my freedom," he retorted, "I would have stayed in bondage."

She started to tell him he could go back to it and suddenly realized he'd said freedom. Stephen had said nothing of freeing him. It only made her nephew's ingratitude all the more incredible. "He freed you?"

"And says he will pay me well to work for him," André admitted. "It was a chance to regain some honor, but with you sharing his bed, what honor is left to the family?"

She was still stunned by the unnecessary generosity. It would have been enough for Stephen to indenture him, allow him easy work and decent food and clothing . . . but to free him . . . Chelaine turned away, sick of the sight of a man she refused to believe could be her relative. She stalked across the room and paused at the desk, then glanced back, just once. "Think what you want of me, but if you dare say anything disrespectful to the earl, I will see you whipped and driven off his property. Is that clear?" He nodded, some of the righteousness wiped from his features by the threat. Taking several deep breaths, Chelaine fought for control. "Have you considered anyone but yourself? Elise is missing. Stephen will search for her. Or perhaps you are above permitting such kindness. I am not." Her chest rose and fell in a simmering rage. "How she ever bred you . . ." Her lips curled down in disgust; she left off condemning a fool not worth the effort.

Still resentful, but thinking now of his mother, André made an attempt to ease the enmity he'd caused. "I will say nothing to *him*," he promised grudgingly. "But answer me this . . . how did you come to be his—"

Chelaine still faced away from him, leaning slightly on the desk for support. Her head came up, and she straightened with stiff hauteur. "I am not his whore. He has been kind and decent in a way you could never understand. If it makes any sense to you, I am indentured." She owed him no explanations; the fact that she'd said that much raised her anger to a hysterical pitch. "Now get out," she ordered. "I'm sure there are arrangements to see you taken to Hartehill."

André obeyed because she had a commanding presence that seemed to merit obedience. He crossed to the door, opened it, and paused. "Chelaine, I—"

"Get out!" Chelaine shrieked the command, and an immediate shame at her loss of composure left her drained. As she heard him clump out into the hall, her head bent, shoulders slumped, tears spilled over, hot, salty tears of shame, not for herself, but for all the trouble Stephen had gone to for André, for her.

Stephen came in, closed the door, and paused behind Chelaine, but she was shaking, crying so she had no idea he was there. He reached out instinctively to comfort her, then drew his hands back, waited until she straightened and wiped at her tears before he softly said her name. Even then, she took a few moments to compose herself before she turned to offer him a tremulous smile.

He'd heard her shout . . . how much else had he heard? "Stephen, I am sorry . . ." The attempt to apologize renewed her tears. She covered her face and wept.

This time Stephen didn't hesitate. He closed his arms about her, holding her close, stroking her hair until she finally ceased weeping. Even then, he kept her close, the urge to protect her so strong he nearly left her side to demand an explanation from Brevard. He hadn't liked the young man on first sight, but for Chelaine's sake he'd dismissed the lad's sullen air. He'd settle with him later, though. Chelaine finally drew back, still trembling, but not with hurt, he saw as he gazed into her eyes; she was angry.

Despite that very personal pain she had known after they had made love, here in this room, Stephen had been nothing but good and kind. For the first time, she saw herself as she had been on her arrival, sullen, resentful, wary of any generous act. It was as if André were a mirror that reflected her own rude ingratitude. She had no reason to feel anything but hatred and a vague pity for André, but he had shown her a view of herself that left her aching with shame. Suddenly, she realized how the two of them, she and André, had spoiled the day for Stephen. He had set out to please her, to surprise her with a gift that could not be bought and wrapped. She reached out and slipped her arms around his chest, hugging him close. "There was no way of knowing he would act so terribly," she said softly. "For what you did, I owe you more than I can ever repay."

His arms were closed about her; the fact that she was there was payment enough. He'd learn himself whatever it was André had said to upset Chelaine. For now, all he wanted to do was ease her distress. "What can I do to make the day less of a disaster?" he asked.

That he could still think of her almost moved her to tears again. In place of them, she made a great effort at a bright, calm smile. "I am sure we can salvage it in some way. Stephen? Answer one question for me . . . please?"

"Anything. What's troubling you?"

"Why did you bother to free him? It was enough to buy his papers and have him work at Hartehill."

"After laboring for a dirt-scrabble farmer, I thought he could use a fair wage in exchange for work at the estate. I've bought some cattle. You said he knew husbandry."

"There were other men, local men, you might have hired."

"At the time, I wanted to please you, sweet. Now, it seems to have had the opposite effect."

She gazed up at him, puzzling over this complex man who had seemed arrogant and shown himself to be the opposite. "You still hold my indenture," she reminded him. "Why?"

"I knew your feelings. Frankly, I was afraid you'd bolt . . . and, I—it was my only hold on you."

"But I stayed." She bent her head, hiding a smile as she admitted she'd considered it. "And now, are you still unsure of me?"

"God, No!" Stephen smiled and released her, rounding the desk to pull open the top drawer. "If I can free that belligerent oaf . . ." He drew out a familiar parchment and started to tear it, then paused, offering it to her. "You should have the honor, Chelaine. It was never more than an empty threat." She nodded, understanding, taking the paper to tear it into quarters, laying the pieces on the desk. She was free at last, oddly enough, when she no longer wanted to be. "I'll stay,

Stephen," she promised with a gentle smile. "At least until you tire of my presence."

"Small chance of that, mademoiselle. I've grown accustomed to sharing your days." A brief, unspoken flicker of understanding passed between them. His vow had kept him from sharing her nights. And honor still bound him, despite what they both longed for.

Chapter Eleven

DESPITE THE PLEASANT SURPRISE THAT HAD EVOLVED INTO a disaster, Stephen had resolved to make the remainder of the day a memorable one for Chelaine, special enough to make her forget what had transpired. He'd left her briefly in the cabin to freshen her face and rinse away the traces of her tears, gone above deck, and drawn André off to the bow railing, away from the crew.

In a low conversational tone that seemed as if he were merely discussing the younger man's duties at Hartehill, Stephen interrogated him. He made no threats, but there was a latent danger in the hard, merciless gaze that had André shaking, faltering, as he explained what he'd said to infuriate Chelaine. When he came to the moment when he'd called her a whore, he stuttered, unable to pronounce the slur, though he'd said it boldly enough to her. Intimidated by the sheer force of the earl's personality, wondering how the wild, spoiled orphan who had made him miserable since childhood had made such a clear conquest of this sophisticated nobleman, he found his vest lapels caught in two strong, elegant hands, turned a deathly shade of white and confessed. He uttered the word faintly, closed his eyes to shut out a look that had transformed the strong, well-formed face into a devilish mask of pure malice. Any moment, he expected those hands to close about his neck and snap it. When he was suddenly released, he fell back against the railing, dared to sneak a look, and found the earl's features composed, regarding him with a look that seemed to see through him, as if he were nonexistant.

That short interrogation left him more terrified than any threat of the whipping Chelaine had mentioned. Somehow, he knew that any further disrespect to her would bring a vengeance worse than death. This man was not only capable of dealing out punishment, he would do so without any qualms.

"You'll go along to my estate now," Stephen said. He would have liked to throttle André, crack his spindly frame and leave him bedridden for life, long enough to regret his ill-chosen slander, but as little as she cared for him, André was a blood relative of Chelaine's. He was satisfied he'd instilled the fear of something worse than God's wrath in the lad. "One of my men will see you there, with instructions to find you a place to sleep. Each morning you'll rise and tend my herd of cattle, you will keep to yourself, speak only when addressed by the man who oversees my lands. When Chelaine and I are in residence, you will keep a proper distance, forget she and you share the same bloodlines. You are a servant, nothing more." Finally he stepped back, his gaze still pinning André in place. "You do understand my feelings?"

André nodded. "I . . . I w-will beg her p-pardon if—"

"She's suffered enough indignities from you. You owe your life to the lady. The matter is finished." Stephen turned his head, called for one of the older members of his crew, a burly, thick-chested man who could be trusted to escort André to his new home and keep him intimidated. Leaving him quivering at the bow, Stephen met with his crewman, issued orders, and walked away.

By the time he'd joined Chelaine below, his countenance was cheerful, with not a hint of what had taken place. "You look as lovely as ever," he commented, and offered her his arm. "Have you thought of something you'd enjoy? I am entirely at your disposal, m'Lady. Your wish is my command."

Chelaine found the easy, lighthearted teasing a delight. It seemed André had done little damage to their relationship. Stephen was back to his charming, casual relaxed self, still eager to keep her wrapped in a protective cocoon that kept the harsh realities of life at bay. "A brisk stroll along the Battery ropewalks would be nice," she suggested, then in place of a smile, she gazed up at him, searched his eyes for something she sensed, intuitively. "Stephen, you owe me nothing. I am happy just to be with you. You decide what we'll do. Please?"

For all that he guarded his feelings, ever alert to hide them behind a mask, Chelaine had been able to penetrate the exterior, almost as if she could see his heart, soul, his thoughts. He wasn't sure he cared for the power that allowed her. For the first time in years, many years, he felt exposed, naked, vulnerable. Vulnerability was a danger, yet he knew she'd never use it against him. He'd made her happy; as long as she was content, Chelaine was his. No paper bound her now, and while he'd never forsake his vow or force himself on her, each day brought them closer to a feeling of intimacy. She wanted him, as impossible as that might be for her to admit, she did. It remained to be seen if she would reach out.

"A brisk walk would be a splendid way to start anew," he agreed. "Afterward, we'll take lunch at the Marblehead Inn and . . ." Stephen grinned at a sudden idea, one which couldn't possibly have any disconcerting results, "then find some way to amuse ourselves."

The exercise and fresh, salty air invigorated, while a long pause at the end of the ropewalks, overlooking the gray-green waters of the bay, gave them both a measure of tranquillity. A meal of chowder and fresh mussels satisfied the strong appetite raised by the walk, and afterward, this time informing her of their destination, he headed for a livery stable to study and appraise the horses available for sale.

The finest was a rare, very expensive Andalusian mare, gentle but spirited. Chelaine found her own mount, though—or rather, the dappled gray gelding found her. They went roundabout for a while, Stephen insisting on the Andalusian, or at least a mare, while Chelaine stayed by the gray's stall, gently stroking his velvety nose, laughing as he nudged her when her attention strayed. The matter was decided; Chelaine loved the gelding, it seemed to sense her affection and played on it, and Stephen gave in, purchasing the animal and settling an amount for his care and grooming. Chelaine left reluctantly, with Stephen's promise that she could return and visit before warmer weather permitted her to ride the mount she had dubbed Rogue.

Later they returned home, changed, and dined, then set off to see what was of interest at Olivia Markham's salon. Apparently the day's pleasures had banished André from Chelaine's thoughts. Her mood was high, exuberant; she entered the drawing room on Stephen's arm and was immediately swept away by Olivia, to be introduced to several new members of her select assembly. Olivia, a strong-willed, intelligent, and independent woman who never missed an opportunity to flirt with Stephen, returned to engage his attention.

This time, Chelaine felt confident, at ease enough to offer her own opinions. She lacked the broad, formal education of the erudite gentlemen who gathered about, enchanted by her beauty, but with a common sense often lacking in the learned, she charmed them with bluntly honest observations. All the while her rapt attention seemed to be fixed on whatever fresh topic was bandied about, she kept an eye on Stephen. There were few ladies present, most of them older women who fancied themselves poetesses. A younger set was there as companions, brightly garbed and bored, mistresses who'd accompanied their lovers only to keep a tenacious watch over the men who kept them. Stephen drew more than his share of flirtacious glances but stayed with Olivia, his features often animated with appreciative humor at her stylish grace and wit.

Stephen enjoyed Olivia. She always flirted, but they'd known each other for several years, and he'd seen her exhaust a number of lovers, ending the affairs gently when any one of them seemed too involved or possessive. She was wealthy enough to do as she pleased, discreet enough not to shock society, and fiercely chary of losing her independence. There was a time he'd considered a serious flirtation, but he preferred her intelligent companionship more important than a brief fling that might end the occasional visits that enlivened the boredom found in mixing with a more conservative crowd. She was worldly enough to be satisfied with the casual bantering, wise enough not to pursue him when a few, subtle hints brought nothing to fruition. She leaned closer now, her brown eyes twinkling with mischief as she pointed out that his lovely ward seemed to have captured more than a fair share of the attention through the evening. "You really should allow the girl a tutor, Stephen. She's quickwitted, but broadening her education can't do any harm." He agreed with the observation, glancing across the room. Chelaine was poised on the edge of a settee, one man on either side, two standing before her, all of them entranced by whatever she was saying. She had a glass of wine in one hand, a sparkle to those amber-gold eyes, a glow to her fine, ivory complexion. She wasn't out to make him jealous, but nevertheless he experienced a twinge of it.

"She's bound to come under seige by every youngblood and beau monde in Boston after that début for your sister," Olivia added, a smile teasing her mouth as she noted Stephen's bold, patrician features sharpened by an interest that was more than the wary concern of a guardian watching over a young innocent's reputation. She took a quick look at Chelaine, and her eyes returned to Stephen. It was intriguing to think that there might be something more than fondness between the two. Stephen's views on marriage were well-established—the institution was fine for others, absolutely out of the question for himself. What a fantastic, thoroughly shocking effect it would have on the town if the suave, confirmed bachelor wed his beautiful cousin! They were, after all, related in the second degree. The idea caught Olivia's fancy, aroused the romantic in her soul, and titillated her irreverent disregard for all that was staid and conventional in the upper strata of society. If it came to pass, the fairy-tale romance would shake the foundations of Boston with tremors that would make the great earthquake of the past November seem minor in comparison. "I like Chelaine too well to see her lost to a boring life of domesticity, darling." Stephen's gaze returned to her, one brow lifted, measuring her intent. Olivia looked serene, guileless, but there was something conspiratorial in the depths of her large dark eyes. "Perhaps before you approve any match for her, you should take the girl on a tour of Europe . . . you know what I mean, expand her horizons and—"

"Olivia, my dear, you know my fondness for you," Stephen interjected, "my admiration for all of the qualities that make you so special." She acknowledged the flattery with a nod and a smile that deepened a dimple to the left of her mouth. "I shouldn't mind awfully if Chelaine benefited from your sophistication. However . . . in regard to any matchmaking, she'll be free to choose whomever she wishes, provided he's decent enough and sincerely loves her. As for marriage, not all women find it a bore. With the right man . . ." Stephen's voice trailed off. He'd heard a silvery peal of laughter from across the room, recognized Chelaine's voice, and absently frowned as one of her admirers handed her a fresh glass of wine.

"Don't let me keep you, Stephen, darling," Olivia said, and stretched to touch his cheek with a light kiss before urging him toward his ward with a gentle push. "Perhaps it's time for you to see Chelaine safely home, before a bit too much spirits and flattery leave her vulnerable to one of the gentlemen she's entranced."

Chelaine had just taken a sip of her second offering of wine when the men surrounding her parted. She glanced up through the thick fan of her lashes, felt oddly guilty in light of Stephen's wry study, offered up the most artlessly innocent smile before she remembered that he'd spent so long a time in Lady Markham's company.

"You'll excuse us, gentlemen," Stephen said with a smooth, commanding sweep of Chelaine's captive audience. He took the glass from her, handed it to one of the men, and firmly seized her hand, promising they'd be back another evening before he led her toward the hall to bid their hostess farewell.

Chelaine felt a little dazed by the deft way in which Stephen had extracted her from among the gentlemen's company, leaving her barely a second to smile a good night. He wasn't angry, he hadn't assumed his former arrogance, and yet she had been handled, escorted away, and left with the feeling that he had rescued her from embarrassing herself—or him—by imbibing to freely. She *was* intoxicated, but not from the wine. Tonight she had felt at ease, her confidence high and enhanced by the fact that those worldly intellectuals had actually listened to her comments and found them worthy of merit. For a girl who'd arrived a few short months before, in borrowed clothing, with nothing of her own but an English delivered with a heavy French accent, she had made herself a place. That alone was a heady feeling.

Her smile for Lady Markham was a bit strained. She

had taken to the woman immediately, sensing acceptance, in no way threatened by the wit and elegant, gracious personality that set the tone for her gatherings. Still, she'd seen how charmed Stephen had been by her, and more than a little jealousy underlaid her somewhat reserved gratitude as she made a curtsy. "I feel very honored to be included among your guests, m'Lady," she said, and rose, startled when Olivia gave her a warm hug and answered that she was welcome at any time. Perhaps she'd misjudged what seemed a flirtation, reading more into it out of a possessive feeling for Stephen. For him, Olivia offered her hand, received a courtly bow and the light brush of his lips before she included them both in a gracious smile and left to return to her guests.

The carriage ride to the town house was notable for the lack of conversation. Chelaine felt torn, struggling with the day's pleasure and an end to it dampened by what seemed a silent censure on Stephen's part. Finally she breeched the awkward quietude. "Have I done anything to embarrass you?" she asked.

The question surprised Stephen. He'd been lost in thought, dwelling on Olivia's suggestion of a match for Chelaine, her reminder that every eligible bachelor present at the upcoming début ball would be out to pay court to so enchanting a girl. As her guardian, he'd have to suffer through the night. It loomed ahead, a magnification of the envy and jealousy he'd felt this evening. "Embarrass?" he repeated, then shook off his own brooding to assure her she'd only made him proud. "I simply felt the day had been wearing enough. You handled yourself with an admirable poise. Why would you think you embarrassed me?"

"You didn't seem pleased when you came to retrieve

me. It seemed . . . it seemed as if you'd disapproved of the wine. All I had was the one—"

"You're very young, vulnerable . . . I imagine the compliments you received were more effective than wine." He glanced at her, but only an occasional lamppost illuminated the streets, and her expression was lost in shadows. "You acquitted yourself graciously, Chelaine. I'm not embarrassed, nor am I put out. I chanced to look over and thought it was time to return home."

"I'm surprised you remembered me at all. Lady Olivia kept you so entertained—"

"Chelaine . . . you wouldn't be jealous? Olivia and I feel comfortable with each other. There's no more to it than that."

"Oh." She wasn't convinced, but at least Stephen cared enough to make light of the flirtation. "I am sorry. Forgive me for mentioning it."

"Lord, there's nothing to forgive! This was to be your day. If it ends with a sad note, I'll feel as badly as I did this morning."

Chelaine sighed. She'd allowed one sour note to spoil all his efforts. "You were too kind, Stephen. I owe you so much and forget my gratitude too easily."

"Forget you owe me anything," Stephen insisted. "There's as much pleasure gained in giving as receiving, sweet. I'd only consider you ungrateful if you refused to let me indulge you. Allow me that, at least."

"Yes, Stephen." Her voice came out soft and meek. With an effort she amended her tone. "I *did* have a lovely time. And there will be more such days, I know."

Stephen promised there would, and again, for the short distance to the house, they lapsed into silence.

Once at home, he insisted she go up to bed, pressed a light kiss on her brow, and watched her climb the stairs before he went to his study and poured himself a drink. She would sleep soon, but like so many other nights, he faced hours of restlessness, and an increasingly difficult struggle between conscience and desire.

If Stephen knew his own troubled feelings, he'd guessed wrong in thinking sleep would come easily to Chelaine. After her maid helped her out of her gown and turned back the bedcovers, Chelaine dismissed her and sat before a small dressing table, reviewing the day from beginning to end. André was just a troublesome memory, and the afternoon and evening had more than made up for the ruined surprise. As she drew a brush through her hair, her eyes were fixed unseeing on the mirror. Two memories consumed her: the wanton way she had responded to Stephen in the companionway, a crystallization of the vague, unnamed yearnings that had often disturbed her sleep; and the open show of jealousy as she'd seen firsthand how devastatingly handsome, how desirable other women found him.

She could deal with neither. Both were emotional, and if she'd learned one important lesson from Stephen, it was to control her feelings. Finally she set the brush aside, frowned at herself, and rose, stubbornly set on banishing everything but a desire for sleep. She settled in, drew up the covers, and turned down the lamp wick. Despite her determination, sleep eluded Chelaine. She lay there, listening for his footsteps in the hall, watching for the glow beneath the door between their rooms. She couldn't judge the time, but it seemed an hour passed . . . no footsteps, no light. Finally, in sheer exhaustion, her eyes drifted closed, she tossed for a few minutes, tangling in the bedsheets, then a heavy, irresistible, languid feeling settled over her and with it, sleep.

Dreams, reflections of her conscious confusion, came and went, a shifting panorama of scenes. She saw herself in Stephen's arms, felt the wild consuming need for his kisses, the sure, confident hands that could make her feverish as they roamed over her skin. A cruel, haunting voice echoed in the background, naming her a whore until she backed away from Stephen, half believing the taunts. He seemed to dissolve, fading as she watched, whimpering aloud, giving voice to the pain of losing him. The scene abruptly shifted, and she found herself by a stream bank, cringing from a faceless man whose hands roughly mauled her flesh. The voice was louder, more strident, repeating the curse like a litany. Then she was alone, crouched, hands pressed tightly over her ears. Another whimper tore from her throat, a hysterical helplessness shook her with sobs.

Somewhere between sleep and reality, disoriented, Chelaine found herself sitting up in bed, face buried against her knees, the thin fabric of her nightgown dampened with real tears.

The connecting door suddenly opened, startling her, and she bit down hard on her lip to still an outcry. A dark shape loomed in the doorway, seeming to fill it, silhouetted by light.

"Chelaine?" Stephen raised the crystal candelabrum in his hand, saw her wild-eyed, tear-stained face lift. She stared as if he were an apparition, and he repeated her name softly, raising the candelabrum higher, illuminating his features before he approached and set it on the night table. Recognition had dawned in her eyes; as he came back to sit beside her, she stifled a sob and reached out, circling his neck tightly, burying her head against his chest. For minutes he held her, one hand smoothing her tangled waves, his voice low and reassuring, whispering soft, soothing words.

Whatever nightmare had terrified her so left her body vibrating, every muscle quivering. She cried softly now, clinging to him as if whatever had frightened her would return if he released her. Finally she grew more calm, reason returning with several deep, shuddering breaths.

"It was a dream, nothing more than a bad dream, love," he whispered, continuing to stroke her hair. "Tell me if you want. I'd not let any harm come to you, real or imaginary." Stephen drew back far enough to study her features, offered her a smile of assurance. "You're safe." He gently pried her hands from about his neck, eased her back, and reached to draw up the tangled covers.

Chelaine rose up, one hand clutching at his arm. "Please . . . don't go yet," she pleaded, embarrassed but unwilling to see him leave.

Stephen wagged his head, covering her hand with his own, squeezing lightly in reassurance. "I'm just off to fetch a glass of wine for your nerves, to help you rest," he explained, and promised, "I'll only be a minute or two." He left her then, pausing by the hearth to stir the embers with a poker and add a split of cherrywood.

When he returned from his room, he carried a stemmed goblet of port. Chelaine's face was still pale, but the tears had ceased. She'd moved more to the right, allowing him room to sit. While she sipped at the wine, her eyes remained fixed on his, almost as if she were afraid he'd disappear. "I'll not leave until you're at ease." That seemed to relax her, and when she finished the wine, he took the goblet and set it on the table. "Better now?"

Chelaine nodded, inclined her head, and a spill of waves briefly obscured her expression before she looked up, a hesitancy in her eyes. "Stephen?"

"Yes, sweet?"

She reached out, lightly tracing the curve of his cheek with her fingertips. "Don't leave me alone."

Stephen's nerves jangled a warning. He stared, imagining something more in Chelaine's eyes, a reflection of his own needs, when it was only distress that made her reach out to him. He sighed, caught her hand, closing his fingers firmly about her own. "Chelaine . . . don't."

"Don't what?"

"You know what I mean. I came because I heard you cry out, because you needed me. You're calm now. Lie down and try to sleep." He turned and stared at the hearth, frustration evident in his profile. "I'm going back to my reading. If any more dreams trouble you, I'll be—"

"Why do you stay awake so many nights reading your books?"

He faced her again, a slight frown furrowing his brows. "Because I find it increasingly difficult to keep my vow. Chelaine, it hasn't been easy, sleeping in the room next to yours. I find ways to divert my attention." He sighed once more. "I've been thinking . . . it's time you returned to Hartehill. For your sake—and mine."

"I don't want to go."

Her face had a familiar, stubborn set, chin firmed beneath a tiny pout. "If you must hear it more bluntly, I thought I could control my desire for you, but now . . . now I want you more than ever." The admission was a relief. "There, enough reason to send you packing, back to the safety of Hartehill."

Chelaine sat up, sliding her arms around his neck, locking her fingers together at his nape. Their faces were mere inches apart. "What if I feel safer here, with you?" she questioned.

Gently, he tried to disengage her fingers. For so slender a girl, she had a tenacious grip. She looked alert, composed, while he, who prided himself in complete mastery of his emotions, floundered in the face of such determination. There was an immediate danger here of forsaking his given word, forgetting all but an overpowering longing to close that short distance and kiss her. Disconcerted, he pried her hands apart, forced her to lie back, and planted a palm on either side of the pillow. "You've no idea what you're doing to me."

"Tell me, then." Her gaze swept over his face, returning to settle on his eyes, a hint of a smile glinting in her own.

"Chelaine, 'tis a dangerous game you play," he warned, trying to look stern, intimidating. "I've kept my needs under control, but a man's desires can only hold back so long."

Her brows lifted above a wide-eyed, puzzled look. "And men, they are the only ones who struggle with desire?"

Now it seemed as if he were dreaming. She seemed to be admitting her own longing, but Chelaine would never do that. "The wine's gone to your head, girl," he insisted, then tensed as she laid her hand on his chest, just below his throat, raised her fingers to curve them about his neck. "Go back to sleep," he growled. "While I've still enough conscience to—"

"I am not sleepy," Chelaine asserted, her fingers teasing at his skin, flexing and splaying like a contented kitten. "And neither are you. If neither of us can rest, why can you not keep me company?"

Stephen groaned, briefly closing his eyes. This wasn't happening. He'd dreamed everything—her nightmare, his rush to comfort her, and now this . . . all his imagination. Opening his eyes, he found her openly smiling. If anything, she looked more enticing.

"You want to stay, Stephen."

Chelaine's voice was a low, silky purr. Again he faced away before turning on her with an angry exclamation. "Christ, how simple you make it sound! If I stay, you'll have more than company." She registered no alarm at the warning. "Have you forgotten you accused me of spending my lust on you?"

"Passion, Stephen," Chelaine reminded him. "Lust is such a 'crude' term."

For so many months he'd not touched another woman, nor, oddly enough, cared to. Chelaine occupied his waking thoughts; when he slept at last, he dreamed of lying beside her. With a control that nearly strangled him, he bent his head, pressed a light kiss on her brow, and said firmly, *"Go to sleep."*

Now that she'd committed herself, Stephen's reluctance frustrated her. She could feel the tension in the muscle and corded sinews of his neck, the reined desire he refused to loose. Raising up, supporting herself on a forearm, she brought her hand to his temple, running her fingers through the thick, crisp waves before she pressed her lips to his in a tentative, searching kiss.

A shock wave rippled along his spine as Stephen resisted the lure of the velvet-soft lips parted slightly beneath his own. Then, forgetting all, he returned the kiss with the avid hunger of a starving man, his throat vibrating with a low, hoarse moan.

A coil of desire unleashed deep within her as she fell back, responding to the passionate, warm pressure of his mouth. His tongue drove past her lips, stirring a sigh as he teased her, gentle swirling motions of exploration preceding a more urgent stabbing possession of the softness. A burning warmth centered low, at the base of her belly, suddenly burst into a consuming flame, radiating outward, setting her skin afire with a fevered heat. The wine had nothing to do with this wild yearning. It was Stephen, his hands sliding beneath her shoulders, supporting her head as his kisses turned tender, the feel of his chest, hard and muscular, pressing against the soft swell of her breasts.

There was no turning back now. No man could leave a woman whose sweet, pliant body twisted restlessly, arching upward in eager, breathless yearning. Stephen left the honeyed taste of her mouth to nibble at her throat, his tongue flicking at her ivory, silken skin. Half-turned toward him, the thin, opaque gown pooled above her knees, she caught and held a breath as the flat of his hand settled on her smooth, supple leg, slid higher, pushing the material upward. He heard his name in a low, throaty whisper and smiled as a bold, possessive caress elicited a shivered response. No longer as urgent, bent on drawing out the love-play and fully arousing Chelaine, he pulled back to disrobe. Her arms clung, unwilling to let loose of him even for seconds, and unable to resist, he bent for one, stirring kiss.

Stephen was in control now, soothing her with the kiss, his hushed, hoarse voice whispering endearments before he rose and came to his feet, bending a second to blow out the candle wick, straightening to work at the sash of his robe with swift, nimble fingers. Chelaine lay back, staring up at him. His eyes never left hers as he shrugged out of the robe.

He wore nothing beneath it, and as he tossed the garment aside, she marveled at the lean, virile length of his body. The fire cast a reddish glow that illuminated the firm, curving muscles of his upper arms and torso, the shadows and hollows that made his powerful physique seem a model of male perfection. He came back to lie beside her again, drawing her close. The heat of his skin penetrated her gown, firming her nipples, and a shiver of anticipation coursed over her.

"So much for my vow," he said, before his lips brushed hers. Chelaine's hand came up, cradling his head. As sure and self-possessed as ever, a stark contrast to the wild, desperate hunger that shook her to the core, Stephen settled on his side, his hand following the curve of her thigh, slipping beneath the gown to close over the fullness of her breast, a thumb lightly brushing at her nipple as his fingers played at the firm flesh surrounding it.

Chelaine arched against him, stretched to kiss his sculpted, sensual lips, drew back briefly to confess, *"I never took a vow."* This time no modesty interfered. Nothing mattered but the ache of desire, the feverish passion, the release only he could give her. She clung to him, giving into his will, raising her arms as he tugged the nightgown up and over her head, to toss it away. Stephen rolled, one leg between hers, his upper body pinning her back and her eyes closed, surrendering to an exquisite pleasure as his head lowered, a warm breath teasing before his mouth settled over her breast.

Chapter Twelve

STEPHEN LEANED AGAINST THE CASEMENT OF CHELAINE'S bedroom window, one hand parting the drapes. The sky was still a velvety indigo but beginning to lighten with the approach of dawn. In another hour or so, the streets would come alive with tradesmen and vendors, at their tasks before the populace roused, breakfasted, and came forth to haggle and quibble over their merchandise and prices. He'd always liked the vitality of living in the town. Hartehill had a quiet, peaceful tranquillity, yet he imagined he could adjust to the slower pace of country life.

The drape slipped from his hand, he glanced back at the bed. Except for a lighted candlestick flickering on the night table, the room was dark and shadowed. Crossing past the end of the bed, Stephen paused and wrapped his hand about one of the newel posts, his face lighting with contentment as he took these quiet minutes to enjoy the sight of Chelaine sleeping. The stub of candle that remained cast a glow over the bed, catching the strands of burnished gold among the profusion of honey brown curls tumbling about Chelaine's head and shoulders. Curled on her side, one hand beneath her cheek, she looked angelic and young. Long lashes cast spiky shadows, hiding the amber eyes that had always fascinated him. The sweet, childlike curve of her mouth belied the passions of a woman just emerging from girlhood, the wild creature whose desires matched his own. That he loved her so no longer aroused his wonder; he didn't marvel over his decision to make her his wife, only at the length of time he'd taken before realizing his life would mean nothing without her.

A velvet box sat beside the candlestick, within it the ring he'd ordered from the jewelsmith. Chelaine would be startled by his proposal, but he had no doubt she'd accept. Now he drew off his robe and laid it across the end of the bed, slipped back into the side of the bed that still bore the impression of his weight, and drew up the sheet. On his side, facing her, he reached out to brush a wispy tendril back from her forehead. The silken texture of her hair never ceased to amaze him. Everything about her was soft and feminine, her skin smooth and velvet, a creamy ivory shade glowing with health.

She stirred restlessly a moment and settled back with a faint sigh. With a feather-light touch he traced the curve of her shoulder, swept his hand behind the graceful column of her throat, and unable to resist the urge, leaned forward to press a kiss against the warm, scented hollow at the base of her throat.

Somewhere between awareness and dreams, Chelaine stirred at the tender brush of lips against her skin. Her dreams were of Stephen; when at last her eyelids lazily drifted open, it seemed the warmth radiating from him, the light, teasing kisses were part of the dream. A shiver tingled her skin as she realized they were real. Blinking away the last vestiges of sleep, she raised her hand and followed the taut, corded muscles of his arm until her fingers tangled in the dark, thick waves at his nape. "Stephen . . ." His breath teased her ear now, stirring a giggle. "How can you wake so amorous when—"

"Easy enough, my love," he answered, nibbling at her earlobe, drawing on the petallike skin with his teeth. "You stir my senses no matter the hour." He pulled back enough to smile at her. "Your fault . . . no woman has a right to look enchanting day and night."

His mouth came down on hers then and all thought vanished, reason replaced by a need that was alarmingly easy to rouse. When he finally drew away, she clung, her fingers grasping his hair. His lips curved in pleasure at her response, he kissed her once more, then covered her hand and reluctantly pulled away. Setting his hands between her shoulders he rolled onto his back, raising her slightly, settling her atop him. His intent hadn't been to make love, but with the supple feel of naked flesh next to his own, his body responded of its own accord. Chelaine shook her head, the mane of curls teasing his chest before she lowered her mouth and kissed him, then made an attempt to roll free. His hands closed firmly along her ribs, keeping her with him.

"What hour is it?" she questioned. If night was still upon them, there was time to dally, to enjoy the love-play. Each night he spent beside her, only to return reluctantly to his own room at dawn. It was stealthy, yet they couldn't chance arousing the servants to gossiping. His fingers curved around the swell of her breast, a slow, leisurely exploration, and while she tried to ignore her response, her tone was breathless when she repeated the inquiry.

"We've at least an hour before sunrise," Stephen replied, and stared in fascination as a gentle brushing of his thumb teased a dark rose blush from her swelling nipple. He knew her protests before she voiced them. With a sigh of resignation, he eased her slight weight aside, then flashed a roguish grin. "You know you didn't want me to stop."

"What I want and what must be are at odds," Chelaine answered. "If Mary found us just once—"

"I could lock the door."

Chelaine pursed her mouth, fixing him with a chiding look. "She'd hear us."

"A pox on your maid! This *is* my home."

Stephen looked like a boy denied a favorite plaything. She knew he chafed at sneaking back and forth, but there was no way around it. "And I'm your ward, sir," she reminded him. "Or it must seem so to others."

"Aye," Stephen acknowledged, "'tis the reason I stay so close . . ." he leaned toward her, touching the corner of her mouth in an affectionate kiss, "to guard you well." With that, he left off his pursuit; pleasant as it was, the stir of intimacy had strayed him from the reason he'd awakened her. "You dislike this nightly trysting as much as I . . . it's time to put an end to it, love."

What was he suggesting—that they live openly and let all of Boston know she was his mistress? He'd taken such care to protect her reputation. Such a suggestion didn't seem credible. "Have we a choice? I—"

Stephen caught the tip of her chin, curling his fingers about it to raise her face. Her expression was troubled, but that would vanish with his proposal. "We do have a choice, sweetheart. If we were wed, there'll be no need for us to part at dawn." He smiled, musing, "Think how wonderful 'twould be to lie abed, to make love in the morning, before breakfast."

Shock stretched Chelaine's eyes wide, every fiber, every muscle and nerve went tense before she lay back, her face turned away from him. "How can you jest at my expense?" she asked incredulously.

"I've never been more serious. Chelaine? Look at me." Slowly she obeyed, disbelief and something else, pain, reflected in an accusing look. "Do I appear to be joking? Would I hurt you so thoughtlessly?" His knuckles grazed the slant of a cheekbone, and he was drawn to kiss her, his eyes set on her mouth, but she turned her face aside and he settled back. "You can't be as shocked as you appear. I know you set out to win my heart . . . is it so difficult to believe you've succeeded?"

"I . . . I never thought it would come to this," Chelaine said dazedly. She *had* set out to win him, but with spite and vengeance for the hurt he'd dealt her. Now that purpose seemed cold and calculated, now she loved him. Why *did* the idea of marriage leave her stunned? The reason was simple and clear—at least to Chelaine. She had played a role, practiced it so well it had become a part of her; but she knew herself, even if Stephen had lost sight of the old Chelaine. He was English, an aristocrat. And she, despite the silks and satins she wore, despite the affected manners of a lady, she was a common farm girl, a French commoner. Both countries were on the brink of declaring war. As much as she loved Stephen, she didn't belong in his world. "Why is it so important, Stephen? Why now? We have been happy."

He stared at her, confused, shaken by the very fact that she hadn't instantly accepted his offer. "I told you why. I'm tired of slipping in and out of your bed. With the party a week off, I thought, if we announced our betrothal that night, we could be wed by the end of May." She'd admitted to happiness—why would she balk at sharing the honor and protection of marriage? He scowled, more to himself than at her. "Chelaine, *talk* to me. I can't guess at your thoughts."

Stephen had guarded his freedom for so long. His plea now was as impassioned as frustrated. He wanted her. Desire was the strongest bond between them. He was possessive enough to want her bound to him in a way that was far more permanent than the term of indenture. What of that certain day in their future when desire no longer overruled reason? He was so logical, he prided himself on mind over emotion. Sooner or later, he'd see the mistake in marrying a girl who'd come to him as a bondservant. "Stephen, I *did* want you to fall in love," she confessed. Her motive, so justified then, seemed cunning and sly now. "I thought only of hurting you, as you had—"

"—done," Stephen finished. He drew away, the warmth gone from his eyes, replaced by a chilling condemnation. He knew she'd set out to win him—there was no crime in that. What hurt was her admission that she'd never intended for it to come to marriage. He *knew* he'd made her happy, since they'd come together again that night of comfort, he'd put aside all else to spend time with her. Edward knew the business well enough to handle it himself now; the past six weeks had given him ample opportunity to learn every facet of the merchant trade. How much of her contentment had been real, how much feigned? Had she used him only for—what?—as some kind of stud, to satisfy the physical urges he'd awakened in her? Passion, desire . . . had they nothing more than that? He was too furious to think clearly, too hurt to consider anything but his own pain. "You're to be congratulated, Chelaine," he snapped, and swung around, planting his feet on the cold floor, combing his hair out of his eyes with his fingers.

"Stephen, wait . . . *please!* I never meant . . ." It was hardly true. She had meant to strike back at him, but she loved him. Losing him now would leave her empty, devoid of feeling. She touched his shoulder, thinking that the contact would reach through his anger. He only caught at her fingers, held them tightly as he stared over his shoulder with a scathing look that made her flinch, then shoved her hand away.

Stretching, Stephen caught at his robe, stood and drew it on, tying the sash with short, jerky movements. Chelaine said his name softly, in a voice trembling with emotion. He was already at the door, his hand grasping the handle.

"Please . . . I had reason to hurt you once, but that's forgotten—"

"Not by me." Stephen glanced back, his features as hard as stone. "You've had your revenge, now sleep with it. You may find it a chilling bedpartner, though." With that barb he entered his room, firmly shutting the door.

Chelaine stared at the door. More than its solid oak separated them. She had done this, and more than for her own suffering, tears came welling to her eyes for his pain. She lay back, condemning herself for an idiotic, impulsive desire for vengeance that had cost her so much. Corbeau . . . she had adored him with a child's devotion, never knowing more than the stories of his daring. This love was real, too important to lose. Even if Stephen hurled insults at her, she had to explain how she'd changed, why she'd abandoned any thought of vengeance.

With resignation, she rose, wiping at her tears. Stephen would only see them as a means of manipulating him. Outside, the sun was rising, a stream of light poured through a slight parting in the draperies. Chelaine turned to pinch the candle wick and suddenly saw a small, black velvet box next to the holder. She picked it up, opened the hinged lid, and her mouth rounded in shock. A large, faceted sapphire, oval in shape, surrounded by diamonds, sat against the velvet. She took the ring out, tried it on her left hand. The fit was perfect. Stephen hadn't proposed on a whim, he'd given the idea of marriage enough thought to have this made for her. More guilty than before, she slipped the ring off and returned it to the box.

Crossing to a chair, she retrieved her robe and donned it. The box was closed within her right hand; with her left she reached for the door handle, then hesitated. It took every ounce of willpower she possessed to turn the handle.

Stephen lay on his bed, his arms beneath his head, eyes closed. At the sound of the door opening, his lids lifted slightly. Chelaine stood there, her complexion pale, her expression unsure, timid. She'd come this far, he had the impression she wanted to try and reconcile. He sat up, swung his feet down, and watched her come toward him. Several feet away, she stopped. Her left hand was closed, holding something. As she parted her fingers, he saw the ring box. He'd forgotten it and now . . . now she was returning it. A brief ray of hope at her appearance faded. His head bowed, then he overcame his feelings, looked up, and held out his hand. "You didn't have to bother. It's yours if you like."

"You gave a great deal of thought to your offer, Stephen. If you still feel . . ." She could see regret in his eyes. If the feelings that prompted him to purchase it for her were gone, she couldn't keep the ring. She stretched, placing the box in his hand. "Stephen, I owe you—"

"Nothing. It was typical of me to assume too much. I began our relationship arrogantly," his fingers closed tightly about the box before he set it on the bed. "I'll not end it so. I deserved what I got."

"You say this, yet hate me too much to listen."

"Hate you?" His brows met in puzzled surprise. "No, I never could. There's just no more to be said. You were right." He glanced at the ring box, the corners of his mouth curved down in self-mockery. "I let my emotions rule my head." His expression turned thoughtful. "Odd, how we've changed. You and I have acquired some of each other's traits. At least there's that good to come of what we had. You've conquered your wild emotions and I . . . for the first time in years, I've stopped seeing everything so bloody indifferently. Bitter lessons, but needed."

Chelaine cried again. Not weeping or sobbing. The tears rolled down her cheeks so silently Stephen never knew until he looked up. Then the sight of her so forlorn was more than he could bear. *"Please*

. . . *don't*, don't cry, Chelaine. I feel badly enough as is." He came to his feet, wanting to comfort her, realizing he had no right. "At least I can set my conscience at ease. You're free to go at will but . . ."

A glimmer of hope ceased the flow of tears. "Yes?"

"Well, Lucy loves you like a sister. Don't rush into any decisions. The party is coming. After that . . . Chelaine, you're welcome at Hartehill as long as you wish."

"It is *your* home, Stephen."

"Yours as well. I've only one favor to ask. I brought you here. I'd not see you go anywhere without adequate provision for your comfort. Wherever you choose to go, you'll need money, contacts. Promise me you'll consult me before you decide anything."

He *had* realized his error, not only in carrying her off as his captive, but in allowing desire and passion to cloud his thoughts. "You have done enough. I want nothing—"

"I'll have my way, Chelaine." She looked up, eyes expressionless. "One last time."

She had meant to say she wanted nothing but his love, the happiness they'd shared back again. She nodded. "Yes, then. I'll do as you wish. I'm not sure what I'll do. But that doesn't matter at the moment." She backed away, started to turn and took a deep breath. "Stephen . . . can you forgive me?"

She didn't see his incredulous look. "You fought back the only way you could. In your place, Chelaine, I'd have done the same."

Her head came up, she stood stiffly proud for a few moments, then inclined her head. "No, you would have been more open, more honest." Her eyes were

200

squeezed tightly shut, her hands closed into fists before her, but she fought for control and won. She did owe him that—no maudlin scenes. "I *am* sorry. It was just not meant to be." Then, with as much dignity as she could manage, she walked back to her room and closed the door.

Chapter Thirteen

FOR THE PAST WEEK, HARTEHILL HAD BEEN A BEEHIVE OF activity. The house had been refurbished, painted, papered, and the new draperies that hung in the ballroom matched the silver brocade material of the reupholstered divans, sofas, and chairs ranged about the perimeters of the deep, rectangular room. Maids had polished, dusted, waxed, extra staff had been hired to help serve, to act as grooms . . . all for one gala event that would last perhaps seven hours.

Chelaine had kept busy, overseeing many of the small tasks that sent a nervous Lucy into a fluttering fit of anxiety. She'd made sure the maidservants all had spotless uniforms, rehearsed the duties of each, and on this last day, personally chosen baskets and baskets of flowers from the gardens, arranged them in tall floor vases, and seen to their placement in the ballroom. Smaller bouquets adorned the refreshment table and buffet, and several crystal vases sat on the foyer and hall tables.

Now there was nothing left to do but await the arrival

of the guests, among them the most élite, distinguished citizens of the Bay Colony and its urban hub, Boston. Lucy was with her maid, still dressing for the important evening that would formally introduce her as a young lady of marriageable age. Chelaine had dressed early, stopped in to give Lucy a reassuring hug, and left to wander toward the stairs, pausing there to settle her own feelings.

She and Stephen had returned together, the morning following his proposal and its painful aftermath. They were estranged, no more than polite strangers, each determined to keep their differences hidden for Lucy's sake. Several times through the week she had tried to breech the cool distance that lay between them but courage failed each time she caught a glimpse of those icy blue eyes of his.

She had played a role for months, tonight would be another, and if she ached with misery, her mirror told her she had managed to hide her feelings behind a pleasant countenance. Most of the ladies would wear their hair in upswept, curled coiffures. Chelaine had chosen to brush hers loose and catch it back with combs at the sides, letting the rest cascade in a spill of shiny curls and ringlets that ended just below her shoulder blades. She wasn't flouting fashion so much as unconsciously styling it as Stephen liked. Her gown was the height of fashion, a clinging, snugly fitted bodice and skirt of periwinkle blue velvet, with a layered, ruffled petticoat of translucent ivory silk to set off the simple lines of the split skirt. Ruffs of matching silk trimmed the three-quarters-length sleeves, and a fine edge of creamy lace flattered a rather daringly low-cut neckline. At the bottom of a gold-link chain, the diamond-edged sapphire hung, just above the shadowed V between her breasts. Stephen had sent it back to the jeweler, ordered it made into a pendant, and given it to her that morning. As beautiful as she'd found it at first sight, she found its pale blue sparkle chillingly reminiscent of Stephen's eyes, of the condemnation in his expression that awful morning.

With a sigh, she swept down the stairs, gracefully managing what had seemed awkward months before, a slow, ladylike descent, head high, one hand extended and draped on the banister, the other grasping her skirts to manage their volume. She would acquit herself well this evening, calling on all the poise and composure she had struggled so to learn. The début had made her uneasy from the first, but she had counted on the support of Lucy, Edward and, of course, Stephen. Now it seemed Lucy would be caught up in the excitement, the center of attention. She couldn't begrudge her that; Lucy had looked forward to her début for over a year. And as for Stephen, though they had to stand beside one another for the reception line, she doubted she'd see him after that duty was done. Edward remained, her only hope of a friendly, familiar face among the many strangers.

Halfway down the stairs Chelaine sighed and sank down on one of the wide steps, mindful not to wrinkle her skirts. She propped her elbows on her knees, her chin on her hands, and considered the ordeal that loomed ahead. No one was about to note the unladylike pose. The servants were occupied with last-minute tasks. It was selfish to dwell on her own misery when Lucy faced the most exhilarating night of her young life. Despite their closeness in age, Chelaine felt far older. Too much pain, too much knowledge of a world filled with strife and suffering separated them.

Chelaine sighed once more, then tried a smile. For Lucy, she must shake off this melancholy spirit or ruin the night's air of gaiety.

Suddenly her eyes focused on a figure at the bottom of the staircase. Stephen lounged against the wall, arms crossed, strikingly attractive in a coat of indigo velvet. A starched cuff showed fashionably beyond the wide, turned cuffs of the coat sleeves, matching a snowy cambric shirt and stock. A silver gray vest complemented the deep blue coat. His only allowance for ornamentation was a silver braid scrolled on the turned cuffs and silver buttons that fastened his fitted breeches just below the knee. Unlike many of the gentlemen guests, he'd chosen to wear his hair unpowdered. He'd mentioned often enough that he disliked wigs and thought powder a pretentious affectation of the élite.

How long had he been there? She paled slightly, before a stubborn refusal to let him intimidate her allowed her to return his steady, enigmatic gaze. For a second, so briefly it seemed illusory, she saw a reflection of her own feelings in his eyes. Sadness, longing, loneliness. She blinked and the impression vanished, surely a figment of her imagination. Catching hold of the banister, she rose and inhaled deeply before beginning her descent.

Stephen straightened, smoothing the creases from his coat and breeches before he gazed up again. When she was some three steps above him, Chelaine paused, a challenging tilt to her head as her chin came up. "You've no idea how enchanting you look," he observed in a lazy drawl. "No idea whatsoever."

Those disturbingly light eyes swept over her figure before he offered her a smile that tugged at her heart. Chelaine returned the smile, once more in control of her emotions. He was pleased, but there was little solace in his announced approval. She had imagined that soft, tender glance. All he cared for was a proper appearance for his guests. Like the jewel that hung about her throat, she was an ornament, a means of displaying his wealth and generosity. If that was all he wanted of her, Chelaine would grant his desire.

"The gown is not too daring?" she inquired. Her voice was light, even toned, the question less important than a show of amiability. Stephen offered her his hand, and she came down to the hall level.

"You've no need to feel timid," he assured her. "Why should a girl . . . woman . . . with your figure hide her charms? The ladies may feel threatened, but you'll have the rapt attentions of every man present." Still holding her hand, he asked her to turn about.

Chelaine complied, revolving, keenly aware of his scrutiny. She was no longer bound to obey any commandment, but for all he'd done, for the months of contentment, she owed him this. As she faced him once more, his eyes slid over her, lingering at her narrow waist, pausing at the curves of her décolletage, rising to meet her eyes with unabashed admiration. She lowered her lashes, a burning warmth suffusing her cheeks. Stephen stepped closer, and she held a breath. The air between them seemed charged. She was so aware of him, aching for the lost intimacy, her pulses raced, a drumbeat she recognized as an echo of her heart thrummed in her ears.

Crooking two fingers, Stephen gently raised her chin. Even then she shied, unable to meet his eyes. For a week, he'd wrestled with his feelings. Acting like a sullen, resentful schoolboy denied his wishes, he'd tossed off careless words he couldn't call back. It was a wonder she could bear his touch, much less stand for his inspection. "You'll conquer every heart, my dear."

There was only one heart she longed to conquer, and that was lost to her. Stephen seemed to consider her as available for suitors as his sister. "I don't want any man's heart," she retorted, put out by his cavalier attitude. "The only reason I will be sociable is for Lucy's sake." Her mouth thinned in an irritated line as she glanced away, her fingers absently toying with the heavy jewel that felt so cool against her flesh.

"D'you feel comfortable with that?" The large sapphire and its surrounding diamonds seemed too gaudy for Chelaine. "I'd take no offense if you chose not to wear it."

"I have nothing else suitable," Chelaine answered. The color went with her gown, and while it *was* dazzling, she truly didn't feel at ease wearing it.

Catching hold of her elbow, Stephen gestured down the hall with a nod. "Come along, then. I may have something you'll like." He led her past the landing and ushered Chelaine into his study. She stood before the desk, openly curious, watching as he retrieved a small wooden box from the bottom drawer, recovered a key from beneath the desk top, and unlocked the box. There were a number of items within, but he came up with a soft, kid leather pouch and smiled.

Rounding the desk, Stephen paused beside her, loosened the drawstrings, and emptied the contents into his open palm. He gazed at it a moment, then glanced at Chelaine, more interested in her reaction. Her eyes widened, her lips parted slightly and then curved with an appreciative smile. The jewelry was a heart-shaped locket of textured gold, an inch across its breadth, almost two inches from the curves of the heart to its tip. He handed it to Chelaine and studied her as she examined the piece.

Chelaine peered more closely, marveling at the fine, detailed pattern of leaves that edged the heart. At its center was a stemmed rosebud in relief, so beautifully crafted it almost looked real. Above the stem there was an engraved letter M, below it an S. Chelaine glanced up, puzzling over the initials that fit her name and Stephen's.

At her curious expression, Stephen took another look. He hadn't seen the piece for years. Suddenly he realized her confusion and explained, "M . . . for Marielle. And the S, that's for Stephen."

"Who is Marielle?" The question sounded vaguely accusing, and Chelaine blushed slightly at the hint of jealousy in her tone.

"My mother. He had this fashioned for her. And I was named for him. Marielle Rose and Stephen." Stephen's face was shadowed by some unpleasant memory, but it was fleeting. "He loved her very deeply."

The locket, set on a filigree chain of golden links, said as much. Its symbolism was subtle but clear now to Chelaine. Marielle, a rose, beneath it, Stephen, all bound on a heart . . . enchantingly romantic and touching. She imagined them together, then realized suddenly that she'd seen them in the family portrait. Stephen's mother had been wearing this very locket, but Chelaine hadn't noted it then.

"It suits you more than the sapphire," Stephen observed. "You'd honor me by wearing it."

Chelaine nodded, pleased by the offer. Stephen's hands circled her throat, reaching beneath her hair to work at the necklace catch. Too aware of how her pulses quickened at his physical proximity, she stood very still and kept her gaze on the locket. Once he had the necklace unclasped, he carelessly tossed the valuable jewel on the desk and took the heart from her, this time circling behind to fasten its chain.

Stephen brushed the wealth of thick curls over Chelaine's shoulder, drew the two ends of the chain together, and deftly secured the clasp, then carefully rearranged her hair, smoothing the silky waves until they rippled down her back as before. He peeked around to find her holding the heart, fascinated by it, and smiled at her delight.

As beautiful as the sapphire had been, Chelaine loved this piece. Suddenly she realized Stephen's hands had closed lightly at her shoulders. Out of sheer instinct, she longed to turn and be held by him once more. This could be the moment to say all those words that wouldn't come earlier. Gathering her courage, she inhaled deeply and faced him, faltering briefly before she glanced upward. "Stephen, I—" She stopped, words failing, transfixed by his languid, heavy-lidded gaze. A dizzying weakness assaulted her . . . as much as she wanted his kiss, she had to speak now or lose the chance. His head inclined, eyes fixed on her mouth. She trembled, beset by a lightheaded feeling that raised a shiver across her skin.

They both wanted the kiss, both seemed swept by an emotion stronger than desire. Chelaine's eyes closed, then her lashes fluttered in bewilderment as she realized that his hands were all that held her up.

Concern banished the intimate moment as Stephen eased Chelaine down on the edge of the desk. Her complexion had gone pale. "Chelaine? What is it? You look ill . . . Good Lord, is that the effect I have on you?"

She felt better already, whatever it was had passed quickly. "It isn't you, Stephen," she insisted. "You've kissed me before and I've never felt faint."

"Your stays," he guessed with a frown, unable to think of any other explanation. The color was already returning to her cheeks. "I'll loosen them. You'll never last the night if you can't breathe." His hands slid along the sides of her bodice; she wasn't wearing a corset. "I should have known. You've no need for any bindings to narrow *your* waist."

"I'm fine, Stephen." His concern made her smile. She almost felt a return of tenderness. "Truly, I am."

"It's nerves, then." His fingers tipped her chin high. "You have no reason to feel uneasy about this evening."

"I'm not, not any longer."

"Chelaine, you're a puzzle. I've never met a girl so lacking vanity. You care nothing for jewels, titles and rank don't impress you. Does anything?"

She touched the locket and smiled. "This." The answer puzzled him more. "It has a value lacking in the other necklace." She came to her feet, wavering a little before she straightened. His hands were there again, steadying her. Now, before she lost the chance, she had to speak her mind. His thoughts had returned to their interrupted kiss. She set her hand against his chest, raised her eyes in a beseeching plea. "No, Stephen . . . oh, please—"

Stephen drew back. She wanted his kiss but this protest . . . he frowned, unable to understand her, frustrated by his desires, unsure now of hers. Banishing the troublesome thoughts, he slid a hand about her neck, his arm circled her waist, pulling her close. His mouth found hers, and after a pause, her lips parted. She seemed to melt against him, despite her protests, responding, arching close.

The hall door suddenly swung open. "Stephen, have you seen—" Lucy paused, startled by the sight of Chelaine in her brother's arms. It was an awkward moment. They parted, Stephen disgruntled, Chelaine nervously turning away, a deep blush coloring her skin. Lucy wasn't sure whether to retreat or explain herself. "Forgive me . . . I should have knocked."

"You'd no way of knowing I wasn't alone," Stephen said smoothly, habit bringing his usual self-possession to his aid. "Neither Chelaine nor I cared for the sapphire necklace. I gave her my mother's locket."

"How wonderful!" It appeared the intimate moment was lost, so Lucy came forward to admire the initialed heart. From the first, she'd felt something indefinable between Stephen and Chelaine. He'd saved her from deportation and an uncertain fate—naturally she was grateful, he protective. They were, after all, only second cousins. It was natural for two such attractive people to be drawn to each other.

They were both strong-willed, but it delighted Lucy no end to learn that her brother had finally succumbed —and to a girl she loved as a sister. Stephen would never make advances, never kiss her unless he intended to wed Chelaine. She could scarcely conceal her happiness. Standing before Chelaine, she studied the locket and nodded approvingly. "It does suit you," she agreed. Out of sheer exuberance, she hugged her, taking the opportunity to whisper a quick, "And the initials are *so* appropriate!"

Stephen heard the whisper but not the words. He busied himself dropping the necklace in the box, locking it, and returning it to the drawer. Despite a calm mien, he was irritated. Chelaine had protested his kiss, then returned it with an undeniable hunger. And to complicate matters, Lucy was probably already imagining a wedding date, while he wasn't even sure Chelaine would want him for her husband. It wasn't the best mood in which to begin an important evening.

"Stephen, you'll have your hands full tonight," Lucy teased, and in answer to his questioning look, explained, "Watching over both of us, darling! At least *I* know which gentlemen you approve of. They're all strangers to her. Perhaps you'd best stay by her side and fend off the more brazen rakes."

"Chelaine can handle herself quite well. I'm not concerned," Stephen replied, and though she faced away from him, Chelaine stiffened at the callous-sounding assessment. She'd had a chance to set matters right and lost it. He was cool, reserved, and distant once more. Desire . . . it had brought them together before and love blossomed. If it was all they had in common, they might begin with it again. He would learn to trust her. If he didn't, she had no choice but to leave. But before she chose that resort, she would try to win him back.

"Well, I must be off," Lucy said. Neither of them looked at ease. How much damage had she done by blundering in so unexpectedly? "I only came looking for Chelaine." She headed for the door, hoping things would smooth over once they were alone.

"Lucy?" Stephen called to her as she started to open the door, and she glanced back expectantly. "Don't make more of this than it is. I know your love of romance. Chelaine was merely carried away by the gift, nothing more."

Chelaine's head turned sharply toward Stephen; she seemed startled, but only for a second. With a quick recovery, she nodded agreement. "Stephen's right. I forgot myself in the excitement. Stephen's been as kind as always and in my gratitude, I embarrassed us both."

Lucy didn't believe either disclaimer, but now wasn't the time to pursue the matter. "I see," she said thoughtfully, then smiled at Chelaine. "Well, don't be embarrassed, dear."

With that she left them, quietly closing the door after herself. Chelaine sighed and touched her hands to her cheeks. They felt hot, a flush of fading desire, confusion, and wounded pride.

"I've upset you," Stephen observed. "It's best if I keep my distance." She heard him but in no way acknowledged the statements, eliciting a disconcerted sigh. "For Lucy's sake," he added, and still Chelaine refused to look his way. He stalked to the door, paused, and glanced back. Her head came up, her eyes calm and composed. "You're no longer lightheaded?"

"I am as steady as you."

"Then I'll leave you to compose yourself."

"I *am* composed."

"Odd, you're blushing like a rose. Try to relax, Chelaine. We've a long evening ahead."

"You needn't concern yourself with me. As you said, I can handle myself well. And *I* have no desire to ruin Lucy's début either."

She was touchy, on edge, giving Stephen reason to wonder what was simmering beneath her apparent cool poise. He seemed to make her miserable at every turn. Perhaps if he brought her such grief, she would be better off without him.

Chelaine started when the door shut. She'd been so close to reaching him . . . now matters seemed worse. What chance had she when he meant to stay his distance? She glanced down. The locket felt warm against her skin. Closing her fingers about it, she shut her eyes and mused aloud, "Marielle . . . was *your* Stephen so impossible a man?" He couldn't have been. The locket was evidence of a love that would never have tried its recipient's emotions.

Chapter Fourteen

"I SWEAR, ALEX, IF I DIDN'T TRUST YOU SO, I'D TAKE umbrage at how you've monopolized Chelaine's time."

Chelaine's eyes widened in alarm before she caught the teasing twinkle in Stephen's own. She'd had a glimpse of him approaching, his features set with a reserved, almost stern expression. Now a faint smile tipped the corners of his mouth.

Not long after the dancing had begun, Alex Peters had appeared at her side, smoothly extracting her from a circle of admirers with an air of authority none of the young men dared question. She'd recognized his name earlier, when Stephen had introduced them, recalling how Stephen had spent several afternoons with him while they'd been in Boston.

"But the young lady has voiced no objections, my friend," Alex tossed back with a grin that deepened the cleft in his cheek to an engaging dimple. He sported a thick, neatly trimmed mustache of a rusty brown shade lighter than his thick, wavy auburn hair. That was only one of the differences that set him apart—above—the other gentlemen, who followed fashion's dictates with clean-shaven faces and powdered hair or wigs. His dark brown coat was plainly cut, his shirt simple and unadorned by ruffles, his fawn-colored breeches neat and pressed—all suitable for the formal affair, but a marked contrast to the fancy dress coats and vests of rich, embroidered materials worn by every other man. A few inches shorter than Stephen, but with a solid, almost stocky build, perhaps a few years older, Alex made her feel comfortable. He belonged here no more than she, but both shared a common bond through Stephen. Now he bowed his head and with a mock seriousness, inquired, "Have I been a nuisance, Chelaine?"

"Au contraire!" she rejoined, out to return Stephen's teasing in kind. "Stephen has been so busy attending to his guests, I am surprised he noticed us at all."

"I noticed. Dancing doesn't require one's absolute attention." They were standing near the refreshment table, and while Alex had just finished a snifter of brandy, Chelaine held a half-full glass of Madeira in one hand. Stephen took it from her, turned, and with a wink and a smug grin, gave the glass over to Alex. "You won't object if I steal the lady away from you?" he questioned.

"This is your right, *m'Lord,*" Alex replied, subtly poking fun at his friend's noble title. His mouth quirked aside, and the dimple surfaced. "But I would like to have her back."

"I'll consider your request . . . and let you know," Stephen drawled, reaching for Chelaine's hand to place it atop his extended arm. "After a spell with me, she may feel disinclined to return."

"I would not take too long to consider it, Stephen.

There is a lady bearing down on you with a most determined expression." Alex gestured past them with a tip of his brows.

Stephen glanced over his shoulder and suddenly stiffened. Chelaine felt his arm muscles tense beneath the velvet coat sleeve, gazed up, and saw a ripple of shock cross his face before he recovered with a look of curious intensity. With an intuitive sense of anxiety, she followed the direction of his fixed stare, saw Edward approaching and with him, slightly ahead of him, the lady Alex mentioned.

The woman was stunning in a way that caused a stir of speculation and whispered asides. Her bearing had a regal hauteur that intimated she was accustomed to turning heads, that it was beneath her to acknowledge the attention she aroused. She was very fair, her plump arms, complexion, and an ample display of swelling décolletage enhanced by the stark, low-cut black gown of velvet. There was no ornamentation on the gown; it needed none with a sparkling, lacework necklace of diamonds spread out about her throat. A large diamond teardrop pendant hung from the bottom of the necklace, catching the light as she walked, drawing attention to the deep V between her breasts.

She sallied forth with such assurance Chelaine felt intimidated as the woman drew closer. Her mouth was full and crimson, her prominent cheekbones touched by a flush of color too deep to be natural. Feathery ringlets framed a face that would have been a perfect oval but for the width of her cheekbones, lending it a triangular shape, an exotic face that commanded attention. Her hair was drawn back, a silvery blond cap of curls secured at her crown above a fall of thick, shiny coils.

Her effect would have set any woman on edge, but Chelaine particularly. The lady's large eyes hadn't left Stephen's face for a second, and in their fixed gaze lay a provocative air of sensuality. Everything about her spoke of a seductive purpose. Finally she slowed her sweeping stride, easing to a halt several feet from them, her faint smile deepening as she extended a smooth, white hand laden with several large, ornate gold rings. "Hello, Stephen," she purred in a silky voice, the simple phrase pregnant with more meaning than any such greeting Chelaine had ever heard.

There was a hesitation before Stephen reached out, caught the very tips of her fingers, and made a leg, acknowledging her with a slight bow. "Vanessa, what a . . . pleasant surprise." Edward had just caught up and looked slightly breathless. His smile faded at an annoyed glance from his cousin, he shrugged a shoulder, and Stephen's gaze returned to the lady he'd brought. "There's no need to ask how you came to be here," Stephen went on smoothly, adding, "but I can't help but wonder what purpose brought you so far from home."

Chelaine felt like a spectator, just part of the background. Indeed, from the way Stephen and this Vanessa gazed at each other, it almost seemed they were alone in the room. She withdrew her hand from Stephen's arm, found the action irritated him, but at this point she no longer cared. Moving toward Edward, she extended both hands, and as he caught them and drew her close, she touched his cheek in a light, affectionate kiss, no different than any other time they met. As she pulled back, she canted her head slightly at the lady and questioned him with an arched brow.

"Forgive me . . . my manners seem to have deserted

me." He held Chelaine's hand forward and cleared his throat to draw Vanessa's attention. Even then, after he pronounced her name, she seemed loath to drag her gaze from Stephen. "Vanessa, this is Stephen's ward, Michelaine Sully." A pair of cool, mossy green eyes did a quick, perfunctory assessment of her; she nodded regally with a vague smile that didn't extend beyond the curve of her full red lips. Edward's smile was nervous. "Chelaine, may I present Lady Vanessa Maysbrooke, Baroness Tipton."

"Dowager Baroness," Lady Vanessa corrected, and extended her hand. Chelaine reached out barely touching fingers, then dipped in a required curtsy that nearly choked her. "Edward mentioned a ward. Somehow I expected more maturity. You look so . . . sweet."

With that, she turned back to grant Stephen a dazzling smile. "How like you to welcome a homeless waif, darling." Vanessa's lashes lowered, her eyes slid toward Chelaine a moment, and her features softened with what appeared to be a sincere warmth. "Stephen, she's a delightful child. You always did have a tender regard for anyone young and helpless. The years haven't changed you."

"Nor you."

Her lashes fluttered, then rose, her face tilted up with a curious expression. "May I take that as a compliment?"

"Knowing me as you do, you may take it as an observation." Stephen glanced at Chelaine. Her features were composed, but he knew she felt nothing but enmity for Vanessa's honey-coated barbs. Only another woman—or someone who knew Vanessa well—could hear the venom behind the condescending appraisal. He allowed himself a frown and turned back to question the woman he had once professed to love. "Dowager, you said? My condolences on Cecil's passing."

Vanessa lifted one shoulder and let it fall in an elegant shrug. "The poor dear lingered, bedridden for over a year. Actually, it was a blessing . . . to end his suffering. It took me some time to settle his affairs, and when I learned I'd inherited property here, I couldn't pass the opportunity to look you up." She stepped closer, so sure of her charm she failed to notice Stephen tense stiffly again. "Edward and I met, and when I learned of Lucy's début . . . well, I had to come and see how she'd turned out. Lucy always was such a pretty thing. Is she about?"

Stephen gestured toward the dance floor. The crowd parted briefly to show Lucy at the edge of the floor, basking in the glow of a number of admiring swains.

"My word! What a beauty she's turned out. I'd never have known her."

"You met her once, when she was six. I sincerely doubt she'd recall the meeting."

"Ah—has it been that long?" Vanessa recovered adeptly from the gushing flattery of a girl she obviously knew by name alone. The music began again, the lilting strains of a minuet, played upon a spinet, accompanied by a violin and the rippling chords of a harp. "Oh, *do* let's dance, Stephen. You can't refuse me that after so many years."

"Chelaine and I were about to—"

"Oh, she won't mind giving you up to a . . . friend of such long acquaintence." Vanessa glanced at Chelaine. "You have the rest of the evening to regain Stephen's attentions, dear. I'm sure Edward would be delighted to be your partner."

"I'd be honored," he piped up, reaching for

Chelaine's hand again. "I never mentioned how . . . incredibly lovely you look, enchanting."

Briefly, all eyes were focused on Chelaine. Vanessa was sure she'd won her way. Edward guessed as much and waited expectantly. Stephen was the only one who searched her face, hoping for some sign that she'd stand up to Vanessa and insist on her prior claim. Her lashes were lowered, shuttering her expression. "Chelaine? I asked *you* to dance." Stephen reminded her.

As much as she despised the woman, as pleasant as it would have been to see her disappointment if she accepted Stephen, Chelaine longed to know more about this sudden, very obvious rival. Edward was the only source for that information. He'd known the lady in England, well enough to escort her here tonight. She dredged up a smile as sweet as she could manage and graciously demurred. "There'll be other dances, Stephen. It would be rude to refuse the lady's request."

Vanessa pounced on the opportunity. "There, you see, darling,"—at the repeat of that endearment, Chelaine's jaw clenched—"the girl doesn't care about one dance. And we have so much to discuss. I've news of people you haven't seen for ages." She moved aside, and rather than place her hand properly on Stephen's arm, she insinuated it between his crooked arm and body, sinuously wrapping her hand about him.

"Edward, when you've done dancing with Chelaine, please return her to my friend there," he pointed toward Alex. "She'll be safe in his care." At that moment, Alex glanced up, and a look passed between him and Stephen, a barely perceptible nod of understanding. "Chelaine . . . I'll expect to find you with Alex."

"Yes, Stephen." The answer sounded appropriate,

couched with respect, the obedience of a girl replying to her guardian. Only Stephen and Chelaine knew the emotions simmering beneath that docile appearance. And at the moment, there was nothing Stephen could do but go off and leave her. She'd made the choice.

Chelaine watched them take to the dance floor. They looked so suited to each other—Vanessa's fair, blond elegance complementing Stephen's dark wavy hair, his sun-burnished, patrician features, the lean grace with which he carried his height and broad shoulders. An ache filled Chelaine, growing worse by the minute, a mix of jealousy and longing.

She had questioned Lucy once about Stephen's commitment to remaining a bachelor. She was vague about the details but recalled a girl he'd loved in his youth, when the family still lived in England. Something had come between them, and Lucy surmised it had soured her brother on marriage. Chelaine finally dragged her gaze from the two, found Edward studying her with a curious look. "How much of a 'friend' was Lady Vanessa?" she asked, trying to keep her voice light and even.

"I thought we were going to share this dance—"

"I am in no mood to dance," she snapped, and appalled by her lack of control, apologized. "I'm sorry, Edward. We can dance later. Tell me what you know of their relationship."

"Surely you're not jealous?" he puzzled. "I know you're grateful to Stephen but . . . I never imagined the two of you together. Forgive my curiosity, Chelaine. I've become very fond of you, enough to hope, well I'd hoped there was a chance you'd allow me to court you."

She was fond of him as well, but a romance had never

entered her mind. How could it when she was so in love with Stephen? Beside him, Edward was a pale, rather dull and proper gentleman. "We can speak of that another time. Please answer me. You knew them both in England, all three of you are close in age."

Edward sighed heavily, then stepped closer to discuss the subject more privately. "All right. Vanessa is . . . was more than a friend. You're sure you want me to go on?" She nodded, and his forehead creased in concentration. "Stephen was nineteen, she was . . . seventeen. We all ran in the same crowd, our homes were close enough to allow for socializing. On the surface, they seemed to be a pair who enjoyed each other's company."

"On the surface?"

"In those days—well, even now, a gentleman paid suit with a good many friends or older couples present. To go off alone . . . just the hint of a tryst was enough to ruin a girl's reputation and marriage prospects. He and Vanessa always paired off at parties; they'd ride the countryside, accompanied by a chaperone." The subject was approaching an intimate confidence; Edward hesitated but Chelaine pressed for details.

"I was the only one who knew. They'd been meeting secretly for months. Stephen's intentions were honorable, he was just . . . carried away. Her father must have got wind of it. Suddenly Vanessa went off to London to visit an aunt. Stephen sulked and brooded for the six weeks she was away."

"And? When she returned?" Chelaine prompted. She pictured Stephen, young, lean, but lacking the experiences that had added character and strength to his features. Vulnerable, as enamored of romance as he was of Vanessa.

"She came home wearing a wedding band, Cecil Maysbrooke's bride. Stephen went wild, even I couldn't make sense with him."

Why wouldn't he have been wild and wounded? Stephen believed she loved him. Chelaine's anger stirred at the thought of how disillusioned he must have been. "How *could* she choose another man over Stephen? He meant to marry her, you said—"

"The choice wasn't hers. As I understood it, her father forced the match. Cecil was a baron, he had money. He was twice her age, but such arrangements were common enough."

"And now she's free," Chelaine said, voicing her thoughts more than addressing Edward. "Does she truly believe she can just stroll back into his life and . . ." Recalling Vanessa's self-assurance, there was no need to finish. Stephen's welcome hadn't exactly been cordial. Did he still love her? Perhaps not even he knew the answer . . . yet. It had only been a week since his proposal. And though that spark remained between them, desire, whatever it was, how could it compete with the intense love he'd felt for Vanessa? She'd returned when he was vulnerable again. Chelaine could do nothing but wait, in uncertainty and misery.

"I haven't the right to ask this, but has Stephen given you the impression that you and he, that you might—"

Chelaine shook her head, determined to conceal her feelings. "No, of course not. He's been so kind and . . . I don't want to see him hurt. Vanessa may be beautiful, but I find her cold and arrogant."

"I don't wonder. She's always been a man's woman." The phrase puzzled Chelaine, and he went on to explain, "She couldn't care less what the ladies think.

Even back then, she had a way of making a man feel he was the only one who mattered. It doesn't seem she's changed." He frowned. "You heard how she spoke down to you. I should have said something."

Stephen should have set her straight. He'd heard Vanessa's patronizing words. Either he didn't care . . . or she influenced him so, he'd noted nothing rude about her comments. Chelaine wanted desperately to leave the room, get away somewhere and think, a chance to bolster a composure that threatened to crack.

"Unless I am mistaken, this next dance was mine."

Lost in thought, Chelaine startled. She hadn't heard Alex approach. He was interceding again, though why he should object to Edward confused her.

"Chelaine has no desire to—"

Alex stepped closer, his hazel green eyes darkening with a scowl. "The lady can speak her own mind."

Before the two faced off in an argument over her, Chelaine interrupted. "I haven't had anything to eat, Edward. Would you be kind enough to bring me a plate from the buffet?"

He hesitated. Despite the fact the man was a friend of Stephen's, his manners and arrogance begged a proper setback. Still . . . he glanced at Chelaine, questioning her with a look.

She nodded, assuring him she would be fine. With a sweet smile, she said, "Please? I *am* hungry."

"Then it would be my pleasure." He returned her smile, but as he brushed past Peters, dealt him a scornful look that left no doubt as to his opinion of his worth.

Still preoccupied by the threat Vanessa posed,

Chelaine shook her head at the posturing between the two. Typically male, like two roosters challenging for supremacy. "It wasn't necessary to be so abrupt," she chided. "After all, he *is* Stephen's cousin."

"Does it matter? Cousin or not, the man upset you," Alex insisted. "Stephen charged me with your protection. You were to return to me after the dance ended." He reached out, tipping her chin until their eyes met. "You did not dance, you talked. And it distressed you." He glanced at Edward, moving along the buffet table, glowering before he faced her again. Chelaine's eyes were wide, the long sweep of her upper lashes framing a puzzled gaze. "I came to rescue you from that—"

"*—loup?*" Chelaine purposely employed the French term for a wolf, and while Alex blanched a little, covering his surprise with a brow ruffled in bewilderment, his reaction confirmed a startling revelation. That sense of kinship she'd felt earlier, the notable differences between Alex and the other gentlemen . . . all seemed logical in the light of what she now knew. She was facing Corbeau, in a ballroom with a number of government officials present who would love the chance to collect the bounty on his head.

Stephen's friend . . . as she recovered from the shock, a growing anger pushed away all else. It seemed the night would be one surprise after another. Firmly tucking her hand in the crook of his arm, she inclined her head toward him. "We must talk, privately." A protest of innocence was out of the question. She knew the truth and meant to have an explanation. Alluding once more to her talk of wolves, she lowered her voice to a hushed whisper. "There are too many shepherds present . . . one in particular who would be astounded to learn—"

"Enough. Where do you suggest we speak?"

"The study." Chelaine had an odd sense of detachment, of control. "And smile, Alex. We mustn't attract attention." He took a quick, cursory survey and managed a pleasant expression. No one seemed to be paying them particular mind. "A slow stroll into the hall shouldn't draw much notice." Alex nodded agreement and led her across the room. Couples moved aside to let them pass, but no one seemed to think anything was out of the ordinary.

Only one person watched their progress. From the buffet, Edward had kept an eye on them, at first because he disliked the man, then with more interest as he saw Peters stiffen in shock at something Chelaine said. He'd recovered so quickly, Edward doubted anyone but he had noticed. Chelaine exuded an aura of command; she spoke, Alex Peters listened. He'd glanced about uneasily, then nodded, assenting to some request of Chelaine's before they moved off.

The scene was intriguing enough to lure Edward from the table. He followed at a cautious distance, able to keep them in sight by Peter's height. They paused by the wide doorway leading to the hall, and as they turned to the right and disappeared momentarily, he hurried to see where they were bound. He stopped where they had, peering around to check the hall. One couple strolled toward the ballroom, a servant passed bearing a tray of bread and rolls for the buffet, and the hall emptied a while.

Chelaine's irritation was visible now. She seized hold of the door handle of the study, jerked it and pushed

back the door, to disappear within. Stephen's friend—
Edward had reason to doubt the man's loyalty—
paused, surveyed the hall with a stealthy air, then
followed Chelaine and closed the door.

After a few minutes, Edward ventured forth, smiling
at a matron who passed, before he halted next to the
study door and assumed a casual stance, covering his
intention to eavesdrop by picking at the food on the
plate he'd carried along.

For a number of minutes, Chelaine was too indignant
to speak. She paced the glazed-brick area in front of the
fireplace, pausing once or twice to confront Alex, so
irate all she could do was sputter the first words of an
accusation before she resumed the stiff, angry stride.
"How can you . . . why . . ." Finally she gave up,
flinging her hands wide, even more frustrated by her
inability to understand her conflicting emotions. In
contrast, Alex looked cool, imperturbable, and resigned as he leaned against the door, one ankle crossed
over the other, arms folded, waiting.

"Why are you so furious?" he asked after she'd
crossed her own arms and faced him, with a slippered
foot tapping out the anger that held her stiff and glinted
in her eyes. "I understand your shock but—"

"I am incensed by your claim to be Stephen's
friend," she snapped, then prudently lowered her
voice. "When you came to me that night, you betrayed
his trust."

"A man can be loyal to more than one friend,
Chelaine. I came to offer you the chance to leave, to
fulfill my obligation to Henri." Alex glanced down at
the carpet that stretched between the door and hearth,
his mouth thinning as he considered answers to other

questions that would surely follow. With a sigh, he looked up and met her eyes. "What gave me away?"

"Your English is flawless, but it is not your native tongue. I thought nothing of it until you spoke several phrases that echoed what you said that night in my room." He inclined his head, as if saluting her astute observations, a sheepish smile drawing her attention to his thick, full mustache. "And that—" she gestured with a hand, "your mustache. Everything came together with shocking clarity."

Alex brushed at the wiry bristles adorning his lip. He had amended all else to permit himself to move among the colonials without arousing suspicion, but this one feature he refused to give up. "So, now you know the identity of Corbeau. You are one of a select few who possess this knowledge." He gazed at her intently. "You would never betray me."

"You are so sure?"

"For a girl who has been infatuated by the elusive Corbeau so long, suddenly you make me out the villain." Chelaine's cheeks, already stained scarlet with anger, blushed a deeper color. "No, for many reasons I am confident of your cooperation. Answer me this— what have I done that offends you so?"

Chelaine's mouth pursed. What had he done? By firing on Stephen's ship, he'd begun a quest that would eventually see them face off. "You must have recognized the brig. Why fire—"

"I had no choice. We emerged from a secluded cove and the brig was upon us. She had greater firepower. I had no desire to engage, for my sake as well as his. Yes, I recognized the *Lucinda*. My shot was a well-aimed diversion, permitting me to sail away in the confusion before Stephen recognized my schooner. Had I been his enemy, a broadside would have crippled the brig."

That was true enough. Her anger was receding, replaced by reason and clear thought. She had idolized Corbeau and now he faced her, a congenial man, not strikingly handsome but attractive. The reality was not as dashing as the romantic image she'd always carried with her. "You are French . . . Acadian?" He nodded, and she went on to ask, "How is it you speak English without an accent?"

"Much practice, enough to fool the British," he admitted. "I speak several languages, all useful in various ports of call. In my trade, it is necessary to blend into the background, without attracting notice." He cocked a brow and grinned; the dimple appeared again. "I have not kept the dogs at bay by advertising my accomplishments. So—now that you know, what will you do? Your indignation for Stephen's sake says much. I care for him as well."

"But you know he's determined to see you . . . to see Corbeau hang. Have you never considered what would happen if you met at sea?"

"That will never come to pass."

Chelaine was torn between loyalty to Corbeau and her love for Stephen. It seemed inevitable, sooner or later their paths would cross. "How can you be so sure? Stephen knows you rendezvous at Baie Cristal. I learned of it soon after he came home, would have sent word but you said you wouldn't sail again until spring."

"Perhaps the one trip, then no more. I have no reason to smuggle supplies any longer. Acadia is lost to the British. Corbeau will fade away, alive only in the minds of our people—and they are scattered far, carried away like seeds on the wind, to settle wherever destiny drops them. When they die, Corbeau will not even be a memory."

"Then if you're through, tell Stephen the truth. Your reason for firing on him makes sense. He won't pursue a friend."

"What purpose would this serve? What gain? He will forget his pursuit when there are no longer reported sightings of Corbeau. He already loses interest, he has not spoken of it for months. You have made him happy. A contented man forgets all else."

Chelaine turned away, faced the hearth, and grasped the mantel. Alex couldn't have spoken with Stephen in the past week or he would know of the estrangement between them. And with that determined, haughty woman present, the chances of a reconciliation were slim. She would not embarrass herself or Stephen by staying if he and Vanessa . . . she bowed her head, wincing at the thought of them together. "What Stephen and I had is over," she admitted in a soft voice.

Alex pushed away from the door and crossed to Chelaine. "Is this what you want—or he?" Reaching out, he caught her arm, and with a gentle tug, brought her about to face him. She seemed composed, not happy but resigned. "Chelaine, he—"

"I will not speak further of the matter," she insisted, and her head came up, chin firming stubbornly. "If I wish, will you still take me away?"

"You know I will, but why would you leave—"

"I have my reasons. And I'm not yet sure . . . I just wanted to know I could count on you."

"You must consider this well before you take such a step. Be sure of your feelings, Chelaine. If I come for you, there will be no turning back." Alex searched her face, found it impossible to discern what lay behind a purposely enigmatic gaze, and sighed. "When you send your ring, I will meet you here." Her eyes widened at the suggested rendezvous site before he went on. "You know the orchard beyond the gardens? There is a trail that winds through it to the river landing. I will come that way, at dusk on the day I receive the ring. You remember where to send it?" She nodded, but he asked her to repeat the address.

"Brattle Street, number twenty-four."

"Good. You have my promise, Chelaine."

In the hall, Edward moved away from the door, his bland expression covering astonishment as he assessed the importance of what he'd heard. A servant passed, he stopped the man to hand over the plate, then wandered back toward the ballroom. Stephen and Vanessa had finished dancing, but she still clung to him. They stood near one of the sofas, each had a stemmed wineglass in hand, and while Vanessa flirted outrageously, Stephen had a bored, withdrawn look.

Vanessa had been a bit of good fortune. For weeks, Edward had seen evidence of the growing attachment between Stephen and Chelaine. He liked her well enough, but until she'd appeared, Stephen was committed to his freedom. Edward was in line to inherit the title, along with a good portion of the fortune his cousin had built, admittedly, through diligence and intelligent investments. Now Chelaine was a very real threat to Edward's future. If Stephen married her and sired an heir . . . to forestall that chance, Edward had brought Vanessa. She hadn't a prayer of winning Stephen, but by Chelaine's reaction, her presence could cause a rift, had already through his own version of the tragic love affair ended by Vanessa's "forced" marriage.

Now he had a much more potent weapon. He was as stunned as Chelaine to learn that Alex Peters was the smuggler Stephen sought. Not only that, but it seemed there was a very real chance Chelaine might go off with him. It would serve no purpose to reveal the truth to Stephen . . . yet. He had no proof; it would be their word against his. It was certainly an extra card to play, something in reserve, an added advantage. Stationed at the doorway, with equal views of the hall and the ballroom, Edward toyed with the secret, turning it over, testing the ways in which he could best use it. A flicker of movement caught his attention. Stephen had finished his wine, taken Vanessa's glass and set both aside, and nodded toward the terrace doors, not far from where they stood. She looked chagrined; obviously she'd made some gaff, perhaps a catty allusion to Chelaine. Stephen's stride was long, indicating irritation as he drew her toward the garden.

Suddenly Chelaine appeared at Edward's side. When he'd left off eavesdropping, her voice had been composed. Now she looked furious again, fairly vibrating with what appeared to be righteous ire. He couldn't imagine what set her off, nor could he question her. "Where on earth did you disappear to?" he asked. "I fixed a plate, and suddenly you'd vanished."

"I . . . I left Alex and went upstairs to freshen up," she answered, and Edward seemed to accept the lame excuse. Before he could remind her she'd claimed to be famished, she caught hold of his forearm, glanced about, and gave up a search for Stephen, to turn on his cousin with an engaging smile. "Have you seen Stephen?" His face fell slightly. "Oh, Edward—I've been rude to you again. I promise to make it up, but I *must* talk to Stephen."

"Well, I did see him over by the terrace doors. Why don't we walk over and see if he's still about?" There was a slim chance of catching Stephen in a compromising position, especially if Vanessa tried to take advantage of the moonlit garden setting to make a play for him.

Forcing herself to calm, Chelaine tried to forget what had sent her stalking from the study, propelled by a desire to put as much distance as possible between herself and Alex. He hadn't pressed for an explanation of why she might want to leave but seemed to accept her admission that she and Stephen were finished. Suddenly he'd set his hands against the mantel, one on either side of her shoulders, with a distinctly amorous demeanor. Reminding her that they were very much alike, that she'd always dreamed of him, Alex bent forward, kissing her before she realized his intent. Shock numbed a reaction, but as his arms closed to embrace her, she pushed at him, and when he stepped back, puzzled, swung her palm and slapped him. Her hand was still warm from the blow.

Where was his loyalty to her brother, not to mention Stephen? How could he abruptly turn into a brazen rogue? He'd laughed at that description. "But it is part of my reputation! You want to leave, we will go away; perhaps settle on Martinique, swim in the Caribbean, laze on a white beach and—" She couldn't believe her ears and must have stared at him incredulously, for he'd laughed again and explained "One lesson I learned, in this very short life—go after what you want. You are beautiful, you no longer care for Stephen, what is there to stop us?" She reminded him he was married. But he wasn't, that was a lie. He was widowed, free . . . just as she was. With that, Chelaine had swept past him and left the study, without a backward glance.

"You seem tense, dear."

The comment drew her from her reverie; she managed a smile that denied the observation. "No, I'm still a little concerned about Vanessa," she admitted. "By now, she may have Stephen—"

They had come up to the terrace doors, opened to admit the cool evening air to the stuffy atmosphere of the ballroom. At the far edge of the bricked terrace, where the garden paths began, Stephen stood with Vanessa. He faced away but there was no mistaking his tall, lean physique. The woman's plump white arms, glittering with heavy, jeweled bracelets, were about his neck; her fingers possessively twined about his nape, she arched against him in a stretch that brought her mouth to his.

Chelaine whirled about, her complexion white, eyes stricken before she shut them. Edward closed an arm about her shoulders in support. Even before he whispered a caution to calm herself, Chelaine knew he'd seen them as well. She felt lightheaded once more; without Edward to hold her, she had a feeling she might have fainted. He circled her, his body between her and the guests, allowing her the needed time to take several deep breaths and recover . . . enough so that she felt steady on her feet and was able to follow him to a divan, settle on it, and rest. He stayed beside her until the color returned to her face, then excused himself briefly to fetch a wineglass and offer it to soothe the shock to her nerves.

"You must get hold of yourself," he insisted, seated beside her, holding her free hand, chafing it with his. "I'm sure she was the one who made the advance."

"Stephen didn't seem to be protesting." Chelaine's voice was dull, a numbing sensation covering emotions that might have erupted, unchecked, in a scene she could never explain. Oddly enough, it was what she had learned from Stephen that came to her aid. Control, mastery, the ability to mask one's feelings with a serene expression. As shaken as she was, she drew on some vague inner strength, and with the wine to take the edge from her raw, exposed nerves, she appeared to be poised again, if still a little pale. Edward said nothing more, merely held her hand, his concern so touching she came out of her own, selfish introspection to offer him a dazzling smile. "I've ignored you far too much, Edward. You've endured my distracted air, come to my aid when I so badly needed support. How can I make it up to you?"

Brightening visibly, he returned her smile and made light of his help. "You owe me nothing," he insisted. "But I suggest that, aside from the pleasure your company would afford me, you might avail yourself of the opportunity to show Stephen you're unconcerned by his behavior. There's no need to reveal what we saw. But if he's given you so little consideration . . . stay with me. We'll dance, you'll forget that scene. Be gay, Chelaine. It suits you more than despair."

"I am not despairing." His brow arched in doubt. "Truly. I recover from shocks very easily." There'd been so many in a brief time, it was true, she'd become immune to them, though this last had nearly been her undoing. "We'll dance, then. I can't think of anyone I'd rather be with." She meant it sincerely. Stephen was lost to her, she wouldn't allow Alex near her, Edward was the natural choice. She didn't want to encourage him, but he seemed pleased just to have her attention. Finishing the wine, she set the glass on a nearby table and squeezed his hand. "This next dance, and all the others, are yours if you desire."

He rose, his firm grasp bringing her to her feet. With a delight that was genuine for many reasons, he bowed, set her hand on his, and gestured to the dance floor. "Mademoiselle, I will hold you to that offer. You are mine . . . for the evening."

The hour was late, the guests, including the younger set who'd lingered past the departure of their elders, were gone. Stephen exhaled a deep sigh of relief as he bid the last couple farewell. He'd managed to set Vanessa back on her heels, left her fuming in the garden after a kiss that had proved he felt nothing but distaste for her. He'd only taken her to the garden to reprimand her for her cruel remarks about Chelaine. She was still as shallow and single-minded as she'd been at seventeen.

When he returned to the ballroom, Chelaine was dancing with Edward. Every time he tried to get near, she moved off, ignoring him. All he could think of it was that she had set out to enjoy the evening, to show him that she had her fair share of admiration. On the fringes of the floor, watching the dancers, he heard a number of comments about her, all flattering, complimentary. She was stunning, a dazzling beauty, so sweet, utterly charming, so poised for her age. All astute observations. He was justly proud of her even while he wrestled with jealousy over the rapt attention she allotted his cousin.

He'd caught Alex off to the side to inquire why Chelaine seemed so absorbed with Edward. He was a decent-looking fellow, but there were more handsome bachelors eager for a brief spell in her company. Only after Edward left, to escort Vanessa home, did she divide her time between several of the older, more seasoned beau monde. By then he'd given up any hope of catching her for a dance together.

Now, as he left the foyer, he loosened his stock, rubbing at an irritated spot chafed red by the starched collar. Lucy had already gone to her room, exhilarated, bouyed by the evening's success, but exhausted. He was himself, and as he'd kissed her good night, he'd mused aloud that he was thankful she was the only sister he had to launch among society, even jesting that he was too old to go through such a lengthy, elaborate affair. Eyes sparkling, she reminded him that he might face another such ordeal within a year. When she decided to wed, the celebration following the ceremony would exceed this evening's splendor. His mouth twitched in an attempted smile before she giggled and assured him he would bear up. Before she turned to bound energetically up the stairs, she teased him further. "Before then, darling, you may have your own wedding to deal with. Chelaine will be at your side to soothe your nerves by the time mine comes about."

Not likely, he'd thought at the time. If Vanessa hadn't showed, they might have reconciled. He wasn't sure where Chelaine was at the present, but he meant to corner her and have it out. Even if she was already in her room, he'd demand to have a reason for her avoidance of him.

The servants were moving around the ballroom, clearing tables, straightening the room before it received a thorough cleaning the next day. He headed there, on the chance Chelaine was still downstairs. He'd reached the study and was passing it when she suddenly emerged from the ballroom. She didn't see him at first, then when she glanced up, she paused, met his eyes, and up came that chin in a familiar stubborn tilt.

"I'm glad you haven't retired," she said coolly. "May we talk . . . in your study? I won't keep you long."

"Of course, I'm at your disposal. In fact, I was searching for you for the same reason." He gestured to the study door, backed up a few steps, and as she came up, swung it open, allowing her to enter before him. She headed straight for his desk, and even before he'd closed the door, she had raised her hands, working at the catch of the locket. "Exactly what are you doing?" he inquired. "That piece belongs in your jewelry box, with—"

Chelaine ignored him, silently cursing the awkward catch, fumbling at it before she finally managed to unfasten it. Stephen came up behind her, she could feel the bewilderment and anger radiating from him. With a deep breath she turned, held up the locket and offered it back.

Stephen stared at the heart and the lacy golden chain that pooled beside it, then his brows drew together, nearly forming one dark line. "That was a gift," he said before his eyes shifted to meet hers.

"You have done enough . . . for me," she replied, just catching herself before she'd said "to me." "I don't want to give anyone the impression there's anything between us. Thank you for allowing me to wear it."

He was scowling now, his features stormy, giving the impression his voice would boom with thunder, but as he snatched the locket from her hand, he spoke evenly, in a chill, taut tone. "After this evening, there may already be speculation."

Chelaine shrugged. "A few people remarked on it. I told them how kind you were to lend so valued an heirloom . . . that I accepted it to please you."

"What an accomplished liar you've become—"

"I had the best of models to learn from."

Ignoring the remark, he went on, "You know *you* were pleased to wear it." He tossed it on the desk, and Chelaine started at the clink it made as it landed. "Why were you trying so hard to avoid me? Each time I came close, you moved off with Edward."

"I didn't notice," she lied, with an innocent look designed to irk him. "You were so occupied throughout the evening—"

"You set out to make me jealous. I don't deserve such treatment from you."

"No, you don't," Chelaine commented thoughtfully. "If I offended you, I offer my apologies. After all this time, I've forgotten my debt to you." As composed as she appeared, Chelaine gazed at him and saw the image of Stephen holding Vanessa, kissing her. It took all her resolve not to throw it up to him. He *dared* chastise *her* about how she'd treated him . . . she looked down before she lost control.

"You owe me nothing." Stephen turned aside, wondering how they'd come to this when he'd meant to settle their differences and ask her, once more, to be his wife. "I'm returning to Boston tomorrow afternoon. Will you be coming along?"

His face was turned in profile, stubbornly set, rigid with an anger he had no right to feel. She was the one who'd been dismissed, left while he traipsed off with the "love" of his life. "I have no reason to go with you. And you can no longer command me to do as you wish. I am free."

"That you are!" he snapped, and wheeled about, crossing to the door in several long strides, jerking it open and disappearing without another word or look. The door rattled on its hinges, vibrating a minute after he slammed it.

Chelaine swallowed hard. It felt as though a knot constricted her throat. She couldn't even cry. There was nothing left, not even tears.

Chapter Fifteen

CHELAINE SAT ON ONE OF THE WROUGHT-IRON BENCH seats in the garden, a flower basket of cut irises and jonquils next to her. The late spring morning was clear and sunny, a soft breeze ruffled her hair, tugging at the cotton lace that trimmed her light calico frock. She was lost in her thoughts, oblivious to her surroundings, the expression that lent her features a sad cast came of a melancholy air of resignation.

Lucy was away. She'd accepted an invitation to visit a friend in Portsmouth the night of the party. For the six days that followed, she had vacillated, unable to decide whether to send her regrets or go for what would be a two-week stay. Her concern centered on Chelaine; she had taken the notion to heart that Stephen intended to marry her, and when Stephen had left the next day, bluntly asked him why he hadn't bothered to say good-bye to Chelaine. Just as bluntly, he'd told her it was none of her business, then softened the reprimand by assuring her she'd let the scene in the study take her fancy. *She* might desire such a match, but neither he nor Chelaine did. Chelaine had overheard; once he was off, she hastened to confirm what Stephen said. Still, Lucy was troubled by the subdued, withdrawn mood that seemed to indicate at least Chelaine had hoped for some commitment.

Even at the last minute, with her bags already in the carriage, she'd hesitated. She couldn't leave Chelaine alone in an empty house—she would cancel the visit. Edward had come calling; she appealed to him to convince Chelaine to accompany her. Chelaine adamantly refused, and Edward had supported her. He would visit often, she wouldn't lack for companionship.

Now, five days past, Edward stood at the back door to the terrace, studying Chelaine. He'd hushed the maidservant who'd shown him to the terrace, sent her away. As enchanting as she was, he'd never quite considered Chelaine in the light of desire. In the beginning, of course, Stephen's overprotective, watchful air had seemed to transmit a hands-off attitude. And even while their relationship in public was quite proper, he'd seen an occasional look, a blush, subtle hints of a growing attachment that went beyond affection between a ward and her guardian.

His feelings had changed; he'd begun to imagine how passionate a creature she might be. Peters had mentioned a man called Henri. It was possible Chelaine wasn't as innocent as she appeared. If she'd been involved with the pocket of rebels who'd harried the authorities in Acadia, those sort of men would not have left such a beauty chaste and untouched.

"Chelaine?" He called her name softly before crossing toward her. She didn't startle, but as she turned her head, she blinked away a dazed look, then a faint smile briefly brightened her face, and she started up to greet him. "No . . . stay as you are," he said. "You've no idea what a charming picture you made, silhouetted against the flowers of the garden!" He paused, caught her hand, and touched his lips to her fingers. "I admit I watched you a while before I spoke out. No artist could ever hope to catch your exquisite likeness on a canvas."

"Edward, you're making me blush!" Chelaine chided softly. By the look in his eyes, the compliments were sincere, but she didn't at all feel exquisite. A glance in the mirror this morning showed the faint purple shadows beneath her eyes, evidence of nearly two weeks of restless, troubled sleep. Her complexion was pale, she found it hard to have any appetite. "I don't look charming, I look wan and—"

"—unhappy. I know your feelings, dear." He gestured to the basket, and she caught the handle, setting it on the ground so he could sit beside her. "At least you've found ways to occupy yourself."

One feathered amber brow arched at the evidence of her task. "Cutting flowers for arrangements no one will see," she said wryly. "I've done it daily. There isn't much else to while away the hours."

"I should have come sooner, but I was waiting for this," he reached within a coat pocket and drew out a small satin pouch, "to be finished. It took longer than I expected." Loosening the drawstrings, he emptied the contents onto his palm, returned the pouch to his pocket, and held out her ring. Holding it between two fingers, he showed her the layer of brighter gold that reinforced the bottom of the band. "That should assure you such a valued piece won't be lost."

Chelaine's expression was a blend of pleasure and gratitude. Edward had asked her about the ring on his previous visit, noting she was never without it. When she explained it had been her mother's, she'd taken it off at his request and let him see it. He'd remarked on the chance the thin, worn gold might break and insisted he'd have a goldsmith repair it. "How can I thank you?" she asked, as he slipped it back on the ring finger of her right hand. "You must let me reimburse—"

Edward looked offended. "Please, it was my pleasure. I only wish I'd come with a band for your wedding finger." She glanced away, nervous at the comment, then met his eyes with a beseeching look. "Forgive me, I know your feelings."

"I should ask *your* forgiveness," she insisted. "I never meant to—"

"Chelaine, there's no need to explain. You love Stephen. And just because he . . ." he paused, shifting uneasily.

"Because he is seeing Vanessa," she finished, reaching out to place her hand over his. "You don't have to spare my feelings. I've had time to consider their relationship, to accept it. Have you seen him?" On his first visit, she'd had to pry word of Stephen from Edward. After an awkward hesitation, he'd admitted he seldom found Stephen home. Now he looked even more unsettled. "He's well?"

Edward cleared his throat, gazing past her before he sighed and met her curious stare. "I, uh . . . I went to see him first thing this morning and, well, he had just arrived home." Chelaine paled but retained her composure. "It wasn't my place to question him, but I did mention I was coming out to see you." Her eyes widened slightly; with a nod, she encouraged him to go on. "Stephen did ask how you were faring."

"And? I hope you told him I was well and enjoying my time alone."

"I did. I knew you wouldn't want him to know how distressed you've been. We didn't speak long, he seemed tired and eager to be rid of me. Oh, he inquired if you'd asked after him. I said you had."

"That was true." Chelaine sighed and glanced about the garden, out of habit, twisting her ring about her finger. She thought about their last minutes together, how he'd asked if she were coming back to town with him, and wondered how much of a difference her refusal had made. He hadn't wasted any time resuming his affair with Vanessa. The idea of a marriage between them was not only possible, it was probable. For a moment she hated Stephen, despised Vanessa. The woman deserved her enmity; Stephen . . . no, she didn't hate him. She hadn't been able to see past her jealousy that night, all that mattered was showing him how little his attentions to Vanessa had concerned her. He'd reached out, she'd rejected him and allowed that awful woman the freedom to seduce him back into her arms.

"Have you considered my suggestion?" Chelaine had been staring off, trancelike. At his question she came out of her reverie and stared at him with her large, tawny gold eyes misted and liquid with emotion. Earlier in the week, she'd spoken of a desire to leave Hartehill but wondered how she could when there was no place to go. She was far from home, her circle of acquaintances, of friends, was limited to those she had met through Stephen. At the time, he'd been surprised she hadn't just taken Peters up on his promise. She might even now be considering such action, and he moved quickly to forestall the chance.

"My offer of a stay at my estate in Richmond still stands." He caught her hands in his and smiled at his own expense. "Estate hardly describes the place. It's nowhere as grand as Hartehill, but comfortable, with servants enough to attend to your needs. Abby's spinster sister always lived with us; she still keeps house and acts hostess for me."

Chelaine knew he'd been widowed a year before. He wasn't much of a womanizer, and she wondered if it wasn't grief over his loss that kept him from courting another wife. "You must have loved her very much."

Taken aback by the statement, Edward puzzled and then realized she referred to Abigail. "Very much," he admitted, another lie. His wife had been as plain and thin as a piece of wood, the better looking of the two sisters. He'd only married her for her large dowry, and when he'd gone through that to pay his gambling debts, made no effort to conceal his disdain for her. From one drunken night when he'd come to her bed, too besotted to search for one of the slave girls, she'd become pregnant. All he'd felt was a relief that he was free again when she'd died in childbirth. "But I've put that grief behind me now. Before, I meant you to go there as a chance to have a place where you could forget Stephen and consider what you wanted for the future."

"But now?" Chelaine tried not to look crestfallen. If he'd changed his mind, she would find some other place to settle. Now, more than ever, she had to leave. She couldn't turn to Alex, not after the way he'd disillusioned her with his suggestions. Edward's offer had seemed like an answered prayer.

"Oh, Lord, I've not changed my mind, Chelaine! It's just . . . I'm not sure Stephen knows his own mind right at the moment."

"But he's been with her—"

"He may have spent time with her but—"

"When he's only come home in the morning, even I can guess where he's been."

Edward's mouth thinned, he sighed an acknowledgment. "Yes, but that doesn't mean he loves her. I was thinking . . . if you leave for Richmond and I let him know—don't you see, if he came after you it would prove how much he cared."

"And if he doesn't, it will settle the matter." Chelaine considered the chances that he would come. They were slim, but a ray of hope brightened her spirits. "You'll tell him . . . then I'm to travel alone? What if your sister-in-law doesn't understand?"

"I'll send a note ahead. She owes her continued presence in my home to my regard for Abby. She'll say nothing. How soon can you be packed?"

Chelaine's cheeks shaded with a faint rose blush. "I'd already decided to accept your kindness." She canted her head, lips curved in a smile. "Everything is packed."

Edward beamed. "Then I'll take you to the coach station and see you off immediately," his smile dimmed a bit, "before Vanessa sinks her claws in any deeper. Come," he stood and helped her rise. "You go to your room, change into something suited to travel. I'll avail myself of the study, pen a note to Sara—Abby's sister—introducing you and giving instructions to make you welcome. And I'll make a list of the inns and roadhouses on the route that are suitable for an overnight stay." He was excited, Chelaine was caught up by his enthusiasm, and as they strolled arm in arm toward the house, he observed, "I know this will come out for the best, dear." It would, at least for him.

Chapter Sixteen

HANDS CLASPED BEHIND HIS BACK, HIS COMPLEXION mottled and florid, Edward paced the floor of Stephen's Boston study, his agitation a stark contrast with his cousin's pensive composure. When Samuel had announced him a quarter-hour before, he'd found Stephen at his desk counting out coins from a small metal box, an open ledger book before him, settling accounts before his voyage to Nova Scotia.

Chelaine was out of the way. He'd seen her onto the coach that morning. He'd hired a young boy to deliver the copied ring to the Brattle Street address later in the day, then spent several hours rehearsing the tale he'd just repeated to Stephen. Nothing ever ruffled Stephen, but there should have been more of a reaction. He only sat at the desk, gazing at a few coins in his palm, absently shuffling them until the repetitive jingling wore on Edward's nerves. Finally he paused before the desk, leaned forward to splay his fingertips on the polished surface, and impatiently questioned Stephen's lack of reaction. "I can understand your shock," he admitted, "but, God's blood, man, how can you just sit there, lost in your thoughts? I swear to you what I've said is the truth. Why would I concoct such a fantastic story?"

"I've wondered the same myself, Edward." Stephen looked up, a puzzled frown etching creases between his brows. "After all, I could check it easily enough . . . not that I see any reason to. It's just . . ." he shook his head, the fine, clean lines of his mouth thinning, "this idea that Alex could be Corbeau—"

"I know, I know," Edward snapped, "I could scarcely believe it myself. I'm not old enough for my hearing to fail me, though. I tell you, I stood close enough to the door to overhear—"

"Eavesdrop," Stephen corrected, fixing him with a penetrating gaze. "That suits what you did, listening purposely on a private conversation."

"Well, you were off with Vanessa. I saw Chelaine's face go pale, I saw her whisper to Peters. He looked about and nodded grudgingly, then followed her with an odd stealth. Wouldn't such a scene have raised *your* interest?"

"I do suppose it might have. What did you imagine they were about—some brief tryst in the midst of a large gathering of party guests?"

Edward frowned. He'd expected this to be easier. "Of course not! But it's deuced odd to go off in private like that. She looked shocked, angry, and he . . . he seemed surprised, but apparently whatever she'd said was important enough to make him obey without a protest. Listening in may seem unsporting to you, but if I hadn't, you'd have come back from another useless voyage chasing Corbeau to find he'd been and gone, taking Chelaine with him."

"Alex *can't* be Corbeau. My God, I've known him for years, he's my friend! You've seen him—he's neither cunning nor the sort of man slippery enough to make fools of the provincial authorities . . . which Corbeau had done so well for years."

"True. But I know what I heard. He admitted he was Corbeau. He'd come to her before, the first time you were away. Only then, in the dark of her bedroom at Hartehill. Somehow she recognized him and demanded an explanation. She was as shocked to learn he was a friend as I was to hear how he'd deceived you."

"Why didn't you come to me immediately?"

"That was my first reaction. But even now you doubt the truth. I can't say I blame you." Edward sighed and straightened, folding his arms. "If I'd told you then, they'd have both denied it. Just as they would now. That's why I came here as soon as I left Chelaine. He said he'd come for her if he received her ring."

"And you saw her send it off?"

Edward shook his head, wheeled about, and crossed to the fireplace to lean a hand against the mantel. "No, not exactly," he confessed. "She'd just dispatched a hired man—"

"Who would that be?"

Edward shrugged. "That French fellow who's overseeing the cattle you bought. I'm not sure of his name." He grimaced again impatiently. "Does it matter so? I paid no mind to it until after I was with her a while. Chelaine ordered tea, served it herself, and her hand shook, spilling a bit as she poured. Her mood was anxious, preoccupied. I could barely draw any conversation from her."

"Did she ask after me?"

"Yes. I told her you'd been busy, readying the ship for sea. She asked if you were off after Corbeau again. I assumed you were. After that, she appeared distracted, nervous. That's what drew my attention to the missing ring. You know she's never without it. Well, she kept twisting at her finger, as if the ring were still there."

For the first time some emotion surfaced. Stephen scowled at the coins in his palm, set them in a pile on the desk, a dark, brooding intensity in his eyes giving them the look of icy blue chips of glass as he looked up at Edward. "I've seen her do that often enough. A habit she resorts to when she's upset." He set his hands at the desk edge and pushed the chair back, rising to come about the desk. "I can't believe she'd leave me . . . with Alex, yet. Still, as you said, the only way to prove—or disprove—your claim is to be there this evening and see if they meet."

Relief flooded through Edward. "It's the *only* way, Stephen," he emphasized. "But I'd not let you go there alone. After all, I'm the one who brought you the information. My loyalty is to you, and I mean to stand by it. Alex may have posed as a friend, he may even feel some fondness for you, but he's dangerous. He'll be armed. If it came to a matter of his life or yours . . ." Edward flared his nostrils in disgust, then his expression softened in sympathy as he came forward to clamp a hand on Stephen's shoulder. "I know how painful this must be, a betrayal of trust, a shock to your senses. Believe me, if I could have spared you—"

"Your actions speak for themselves, cousin," Stephen replied in a taut, coldly furious tone. "I'd find it odd if you hadn't offered to join me. You should be there, if only to meet Corbeau before I settle the matter to my satisfaction."

"I'm as eager as you to see him trapped. The bastard should know why he's to meet his end."

"No one should be eager to see blood spilled, Edward," Stephen rejoined, shrugging off the comforting hand to cross to the door, grasp the handle, and glance back before he turned it. "Still, there are times that justify such action." He opened the door and stepped back, clearly indicating his desire to be alone without voicing a dismissal. "I'll expect you here by six, no later. We'll ride to Hartehill together."

"I shan't be late," Edward promised, and as he came across, paused to compliment Stephen's composure. "In your place, I'd have been raging, cousin. 'Tis good you've a cool head on your shoulders, the better to handle this affair and come out the victor."

"Once I understood how my trust had been misplaced, I'd a rein on my temper. One must keep one's perspective, Edward. Anger without control gains nothing." His mouth quirked in a mirthless smile. "I've no doubts I'll come out of this meeting and see justice done. After all, forewarned is forearmed."

Edward shook his head in wonder. "You're a rare man, Stephen. You've no idea how much I aspire to be like you." With that he nodded and made his exit, allowing himself a faint, smug smile only after the door had shut and he was free to indulge in a feeling of self-satisfaction.

Once he was alone, Stephen returned to his desk, gathered up the money, and returned it to a felt pouch, then set it and the ledger in the strongbox. Next he rang for Samuel, asked him to have his mount saddled and brought around. "I'm off for the brig," he explained. "If anyone comes by, I'll be there until half past five." Samuel had a worried set to his worn, creased face but held back commenting on the earl's stern, stubborn expression. He knew him well enough to keep his opinion to himself. Whatever Edward had said to disturb Lord Stephen, the master would take care of.

Chapter Seventeen

STEPHEN SAT AT THE DESK IN HIS CABIN, HIS FEET PROPPED up, chair tipped back, eyes closed. On the desk top, near his right hand, sat a half-full glass of brandy, his second since he'd come aboard. Edward's visit had been a shock. Stupid of him not to realize. All the signs had been there, but he'd been too absorbed, too much in love to think clearly.

A knock sounded at the door, stirring a scowl even before his eyes opened. He'd left strict orders not to be disturbed. "What is it?" he snapped. "Avery, you'd best have a damned good—"

The door opened, just enough for Samuel to poke his head in. When Stephen's dark scowl faded, the old man slipped in, closing the door firmly behind himself. "I knew your orders, m'Lord, but—"

"What was so urgent it couldn't have waited?"

Samuel glanced back over his shoulder, took a deep breath and sighed.

"'Tis your cousin, sire."

"What does *he* want now?" Stephen's mouth thinned, his eyes narrowed as he swung his feet to the deck. The planks shuddered as the front legs of the chair slammed down. "Whatever the hell he wants, it can wait on the evening."

He'd served Lord Stephen for many years, seen him in every mood, but the master'd never taken out his temper on him. "Beggin' your pardon, m'Lord, 'tisn't Edward but Mistress Chelaine. A constable brought her to the house."

The chair scraped against wood as Stephen abruptly came to his feet, his expression concerned as he rounded the desk. "Constable?" he puzzled. "What's happened? She's not hurt—"

"No, sire. She was . . . uh . . . she set forth on a public coach and at a stop, the authorities made a check for papers and, well, she didn't have none." The earl's surprise mirrored his own when they'd brought Chelaine to the town house. "I vouched for her, but the officer, he wouldn't take my word, had to hear it from you, he did."

Clearly Samuel was put out at such an affront to his credibility.

"Where is the man?"

A thumb gestured to the hall. "Waitin' out there, m'Lord. With herself. She's none too pleased, neither."

Some of the shock had worn off, now Stephen considered this odd turn of events, one hand absently rubbing his jaw. "I'd imagine not," he agreed. He turned and paced across the room, thinking, a slight smile playing at his mouth before he did a turnabout and nodded at Samuel. "See them both in, if you would."

"Aye, m'Lord." Samuel expected rage, at the least irritation, but Stephen's features had relaxed. He stood there with arms folded, a curiously contemplative look clouding his eyes, one might even say, bemused. Samuel shook his head. The older he got, the less he understood. Turning back, he opened the door and swung it wide. The grizzled, authoritative constable stood there, hat in hand, one thick, ruffed eyebrow raising as he stared past Samuel, did a quick survey of the luxurious cabin, and then drew his hat forth, using it to gesture Chelaine before himself.

Chelaine sailed forward, ignoring the man, her head held high, as righteous as any lady might be in similar circumstances. She paused in midstep as she saw Stephen, flushed, and her chin tipped even higher, including him in a scathing look of condemnation.

The constable followed, his lined, craggy face bearing a disgruntled look. Even though the gentleman before him was in shirt sleeves and vest, his patrician bearing intimidated. With a bow, the officer introduced himself. "Lord Braden? The name's Rush, Constable Rush. I am sorry to bother you, but this young woman claims to be—"

Stephen straightened, fixing the man with a cool, appraising look. "The young lady happens to be my ward, sir. She was on her way to visit a cousin . . . with my permission." Stephen glanced aside a moment. Chelaine's indignation was fading into wonder at the outright fabrication. "I find her detainment inexcusable, a humiliation for her as well as myself." He raised his head, glowering at the public servant, who seemed to wither visibly under the chill regard.

"But 'twas my duty, m'Lord. There's rules to follow, I've orders . . ." He was no longer confident of his judgment and wished he'd let the young lady pass without a fuss. "She bein' French and all, what with us close to a war with them—" He was already mired in trouble and paused before a careless phrase made matters worse. Twisting his hat in his hands, shifting his stance, he gave a great sigh and offered one last excuse. "If the lady'd had proper identification—"

"I presume you'll take *my* word she's no French spy?" Stephen questioned caustically. "Michelaine is offended enough by this treatment. I should like the name of your superior, in order to lodge a—"

"'Twas my duty, sir," Rush insisted, a sheen of sweat frosting his broad, lined forehead. "P'rhaps I was overvigilant." He faced Chelaine with a suddenly respectful mien, bowing deeply as he apologized. "M'Lady, my sincere pardons to you. I should have known—"

Chelaine bristled. The man had treated her like some sort of criminal, all because she lacked some document to prove her identity. "You are *not* forgiven," she said with a hauteur that was intimidating even without the icy glare that accompanied it. "I was humiliated, dragged off as if . . . as—"

"My dear, the officer has admitted his error. No doubt it was a degrading situation, but you're safe with me now," Stephen interjected. "Rush, I'll let this pass, but next time, have a mind for someone who *looks* suspicious. Even if she'd forgotten her papers, the lady is what she appears, a person of quality and refinement." Out of the corner of his eye, he could see that his reprimand had mollified Chelaine's irate mood somewhat. He nodded a dismissal at the man. "You may take your leave."

"Aye, m'Lord." His blustering confidence banished by a misjudgment that might have been brought to his captain's notice, Rush made a bow to the earl and attempted one for the offended lady, then beat a hasty retreat, past the smug old servant, out the door, away as fast as his feet could carry him.

"He might have taken my word," Samuel muttered, glaring after the man.

"I quite agree," Stephen said, and smiled at Samuel's offended air. "Thank you for seeing Chelaine safely here. I'd like you to stay aboard a while. And remind Avery I want no other disturbances. For any reason."

Once they were alone, Chelaine lost her righteous demeanor. She had escaped the belligerant official only to be left with Stephen to face. Even though her gaze was fixed on the deck, she could feel him studying her. Cornered, forced to come up with a reason for having left him without a word of explanation, she caught at her bottom lip and clasped her hands together, refusing to glance up.

"If you'd bothered to consult me, I might have saved you this humiliating experience," Stephen commented, and strolled forward to pause directly before Chelaine. "No one travels through the colonies without proper identification. But then, you couldn't have known that."

That was true. Edward had said nothing of such papers. She had departed in such a rush, he must have forgotten to ask if she possessed them. Her lashes fluttered, lifting just enough to peek at Stephen's expression. He wasn't angry, nor even upset at discovering she had decided to leave. Still, as relaxed as he appeared, there was something, a hint of tension beneath his usual composure. He towered over her as if awaiting some excuse. Refusing to be intimidated, she took another deep breath and stood taller, glancing up with a confidence she didn't feel.

"If I had known, I would be far from here by now."

"May I ask where you were bound?"

"You may ask whatever you please."

The implication was clear enough. He could ask anything; she was under no obligation to satisfy his curiosity. "You'd have left, without the courtesy of a farewell?" He clicked his tongue in dismay. "After what we have been to each other, you owe me some explanation." Chelaine's eyes narrowed, refuting the claim. "I thought we had an agreement? You were to let me know of any such decision, so that I could—"

"Provide for me?" Chelaine interrupted. "You have done enough. My only desire was to leave. I took nothing but what you gave me."

"I'm not accusing you of stealing away like a thief." Now she was staring past him, ignoring him with the same regal hauteur she had employed with the constable. The other had deserved it. Stephen's patience frayed a bit. "Considering your stealth, I find your attitude rude and inconsiderate. You will explain yourself, Chelaine." Her eyes came back to his, widening a bit, questioning his imperious tone. "*Now!*" he snapped, and she startled, then took a step back.

"I am not yours to command any longer," she asserted, but Chelaine's voice lacked the confidence to carry off the claim. "I am free to do as I wish. Why should you care where I—"

"I *do* care. Despite our differences, I'd hoped you would take the time to reconsider your feelings for me.

Or are there none left?" He wanted to reach out and grasp her shoulders, shake off the icy reserve that held her aloof and distant, but knowing her as he did, she would only become more obstinate at such an act. "If you don't answer me, I'll—"

Her eyes flashed with a sudden rage at the hint of a threat. "You will do what?" she demanded. "There is nothing you can do to hurt me. I saw no need to bother you with my intentions. What we had is over. I wanted to leave your life the way I entered it—abruptly, strangers with nothing in common."

Stephen's breath came out in an incredulous huff, he half-turned, rolled his eyes heavenward, and shook his head. Glancing back, angry now, "Nothing in common? What is it you feel, then—hate? Or just indifference?"

"My feelings are no concern of yours. You had no thought for them after that . . . that black-draped bitch came back into your life!" Chelaine started past Stephen, her resentment manifest now in the narrowed cast of her eyes, the tension of a stride that meant to put distance between them. A hand closed on her upper arm, bringing her up short. She glared at the strong, dark fingers that firmly held her and then looked up, challenging him to set her free.

"You had no reason to be jealous of Vanessa. Who filled your head with such nonsense?"

"No one needed to say anything. I know what she once was to you." His fingers loosened slightly, but as she tried to jerk her arm free, Stephen held firm. "You may think I am naïve, but I am not blind, Stephen. I saw her in your arms. That was enough—"

Stephen pulled her about, his other hand grasping

her shoulder. "I had no idea you witnessed that. Yes, we were in the garden, but I took her there to set her back on her heels for the way she spoke to you."

"You did not seem to be arguing. I suppose you kissed her to take the edge from the reprimand?"

His hands tightened for a second, then he released her, a stunned expression widening his eyes. "Christ! You saw *that?* My God, no wonder you avoided me . . ." His hands came back to rest lightly on her shoulders. "Chelaine, if I'd known, I could have explained it then."

She stepped back, shrugging off his touch. "Who was I to demand any explanation?" she questioned. "Not your wife, nor even a mistress any longer, jealous of a rival. You loved her once and lost her. She was back and free to marry. Both of you were free."

"And you've been brooding over that for two weeks," he said, voicing a thought aloud. And Edward had undoubtedly dropped hints of a renewed love affair, perhaps even suggested she leave rather than suffer alone, abandoned. "Lucy's been away. I imagine Edward came to visit, to entertain you with the latest gossip?"

"Several times." Chelaine thought she heard a touch of jealousy in Stephen's inquiry. "At least *he* cared enough to wonder how I was."

Stephen reached out and caught Chelaine's right hand. Her fingers stiffened with resistance, then went limp. She still wore the ring. Raising her hand, he turned it and pressed a light kiss on the smooth soft flesh of her palm. Her fingers tensed, began to curl in, but not before he saw that the worn underside of the band had been reinforced with a layer of new gold. He released her then, glancing up to find her studying him with an open curiosity. "You've had your ring repaired," he commented. "I know how dear it is . . . I should have seen to it myself."

Surely there were more important matters than her ring. Chelaine moved past him, crossing the room, putting distance between herself and Stephen. He knew his power to influence her with a mere touch. Pausing by the desk, she noted the brandy glass. She could use something, wine perhaps, to soothe her nerves, but she needed all her wits about her. "Edward was considerate enough to take it to a goldsmith. Now I have no need to worry I might lose it."

"Edward is a most uncommon man. I owe him more than you can imagine," Stephen replied.

The mention brought to mind Edward's visits. Chelaine tried to recall whether he had told her Stephen was seeing Vanessa. No, all he'd said was that Stephen was away from home often, he could seldom be found at the town house. She had assumed the worst. He had professed his own love for her, though she had firmly rebuffed any idea of a marriage. Perhaps he'd thought, once she was settled in Virginia, he might convince her to change her mind. Now Stephen had denied any affection for Vanessa . . . how much could she believe him?

"Chelaine?" Stephen stayed where he was, watching her, wanting to bridge a distance that had nothing to do with the fifteen or so feet separating them. Her head came up, she seemed willing to listen. "What I had with Vanessa was over a long, long time ago."

"She was the reason you never married."

"She was."

At that admission, Chelaine turned, her heart pounding, though her features remained expressionless. She leaned against the desk, her fingers tightly gripping the edges the only evidence of emotion. "Must I hear how great a love you shared?" she asked.

"All you'll hear from me is the truth," Stephen swore, and flinched at the dubious glance she cast his way. "I was young, not much older than you, and Vanessa . . ." he paused and grimaced, still counting himself a fool, even after so many years. "Vanessa made me think I was the most handsome, charming, desirable man she knew." The memory brought a smirk, a self-mocking chuckle. "Can you imagine, at nineteen I was so worldly, so debonair . . . so gullible. In my conceit, I believed she was devastated by my wit, entranced by the poems I wrote extolling—"

"Poems?" Chelaine questioned incredulously. The Stephen she knew was charming, yes, and handsome enough to make any girl swoon, but she could never have thought him romantic enough to write the sort of verse he had read to her from his volumes of love poetry. "You actually—"

There was enough light streaming through the windows to see Stephen flush, his sun-burnished complexion darken in embarrassment.

"I did. That alone should tell you what a fool I was." He went on, telling her what followed, his expectations, his disappointments, sparing Chelaine the more sordid details of the old affair, confessing how dumbfounded he was to learn Vanessa had chosen to marry a man twice her age, all for the lure of his title. "She couldn't understand my reaction. For her, nothing had changed. We could still meet, only more discreetly."

Chelaine had never heard Stephen so open and vulnerable. It was so unlike the man who guarded his feelings, who kept the world guessing at his thoughts, whose suave command of every situation made him seem cold, unyielding, obdurate. Vanessa had hurt him so, he distrusted all women, used them, even gave them a pleasure to equal his own, but never again let any female wield that kind of power over his heart. "How could she come here, thinking you had forgiven her?"

A great, weary sigh rushed from Stephen's chest. His eyes had been fixed on the carpet, seeing nothing, as he called up the old, bitter memories. Now he glanced up and over at Chelaine. "You have to understand how Vanessa's mind works. Her entire life, she got what she wanted by using herself as a lure. It made her a baroness, something she craved more than love. Through mutual friends, she knew I was still a bachelor." He made an effort at a smile, again seeming amused at his own expense. "A more lofty title beckoned. If in her youth, she sold herself for a barony, think how determined she was to see herself a countess."

The woman was repulsive, her vanity so great she had swept in, sure she could win Stephen back. "So . . . you told her how you felt." Stephen nodded. In his eyes there was a look that beseeched her to understand. She did, now, but she couldn't help but question why they had kissed. "You are eloquent when you wish. Your words did not convince her?"

"Apparently not. I told her it was you I desired, that if you consented, you'd be my wife." At Chelaine's startled expression, he nodded. "True. You'd refused me once. I don't give up *that* easily. She scoffed at the idea, challenged me to prove I felt nothing for her."

"And you had to kiss her? Why not turn your back and walk away?"

"I should have, especially knowing what I do now. I truly thought I'd settled my feelings long ago. I spent a year in London, gambling, whoring, working her out of my system. And even when I left for America, I still held onto my resentment. Then, years passed. I never thought of her. But she wanted proof, and some small remnant of vengeance remained. So we kissed. You saw that, but not the rage that followed when she realized I felt nothing." Again he sighed, then slowly came toward her. He paused, and only a short distance, less than a foot, separated them. "I had no idea you'd come looking for me. I still thought you were with Alex."

Chelaine blinked, confused by the statement. How could he know she was with Alex? She was the one who'd insisted on drawing Alex to the study. If he'd seen them . . .

Seeing her bewilderment, Stephen reached out and lightly ran his fingers along her cheek. He wanted to take her in his arms, but there was more to confess. If they were ever to have a chance, he had to be completely honest. He was no coward, but what he faced now made him inwardly cringe. He drew his hand away and stepped back. She had listened with compassion, understood much about him now, but she had to know everything.

"It was no accident that you recognized Alex, Chelaine."

Fine lines creased her brows as she tried to make sense of what she heard. Vanessa was forgotten, but this . . ."You *knew* he was Corbeau?"

He had so much to explain, had practiced a deception so long, Stephen wasn't sure where to begin. His mouth suddenly went dry, he reached around her and

265

retrieved the brandy, downed it in several swallows, and set the glass down before he backed up again. "You thought he was . . . I meant you to." Her eyes grew wide, he swallowed hard, trying to organize his thoughts. In frustration, he ran his hand through his hair, combing it back with his fingers, giving him a moment's pause.

"After you and I . . . after I proposed, and you seemed to reject me, I couldn't find a way to make you see how much I loved you. I tried, the words wouldn't come. I should have told you before I stalked out of the bedroom. You wouldn't have believed me, though, even if I'd put my damnable pride aside."

"You are making no sense, Stephen." Chelaine wasn't sure she wanted to hear what Stephen struggled to confess. She had an inkling of suspicion, but the idea that was beginning to form in her mind was too farfetched.

"I realize that," he admitted. Raising his hands, palms open, he gestured for a brief indulgence. "Alex came to your room one night at Hartehill. Mid-January, the seventeenth—"

"It was the eighteenth. You were still away. He came because Henri sent him to find me, and I—"

"You chose to stay. I wanted to know whether you'd take the chance to flee."

An icy chill formed in the pit of her belly, spreading throughout her, raising goosebumps on her skin. "And you learned that I was staying because I awaited your return, because I had set my mind on winning your heart. You knew all along I wanted revenge, that I'd summon Alex once I had it."

Guilt was written plainly on his face, etched in creases that lined the sides of his mouth, in a tracery of fine wrinkles that radiated from the outer corners of his eyes. Nothing Chelaine could have said would have made him feel worse than the condemnation in her eyes.

"Just as you knew my 'rejection' came of fear that all we shared was passion, that after it waned, you'd see we were wrong for each other," she went on, relentlessly pursuing the discussion even though pain darkened those incredibly blue irises. "You were confident, arrogant as Lord Braden, you were daring and fearless as Corbeau, but at a moment when you could have saved me so much grief, when a few words would have changed my fears to happiness, Stephen, you were afraid."

"I said it was my pride."

"What pride?" Chelaine spit the words out as if they were a curse. Was he the only one with any pride? Had he considered hers when he began this charade?

"Damn it, Chelaine, I know what I've done!" Stephen heard his voice, a wounded bellow that ached for mercy even when he knew he had no right to ask it. "Yes, *pride*. I was through playing Corbeau. Playing . . . that suits your image of me, right? Always a gamesman, a man who loves a challenge and cannot bear to lose. Corbeau . . . the very name leaves a sour taste in my mouth! I was Corbeau, I fancied the adventure, I delighted in the risks . . . more than any noble cause, I ran the gauntlet because I enjoyed it. You idealized him, a selfish bastard who sailed for the glory." He rubbed his knuckles across his forehead, his breath coming fast and hard as he denounced what he had been. He squeezed his eyes shut as if they hurt, then opened them and stared at her.

"I thought you had adjusted to living here. I can't

change who I am . . . even if I wanted to. You had to love *me,* not some romanticized idiot who had to flout the British just for the thrill of it."

A part of her was furious, another part watched him struggle and longed to reach out in compassion, to ease his torment. The fury was stronger, not an uncontrolled rage but a cold, merciless anger that would not allow mercy, allowed for nothing until everything had come out. "So, you couldn't tell me. You set Alex to do your bidding. He must be very loyal to you, to follow whatever deed you set him."

"It's a loyalty born of blood, Chelaine." Stephen felt drained, and there was so much yet to reveal. "Alex is my cousin. Older, maybe wiser, but he always followed my lead. We worked the smuggling together. When I was at a rendezvous, dropping supplies, he'd lead the navy a chase. We covered each other, like the time—"

"He fired on your ship, giving you reason to sail on to Halifax, proclaim your indignance, with a broken bowsprit to prove Corbeau had attacked you."

"It didn't happen quite that way. I'd met at Baie Cristal with Henri. He was worried, his impetuous, headstrong little sister had gone off, disobeyed him. She was overdue to return, likely captured." Stephen stared at Chelaine. For the first time the anger in her faltered. "I promised him I'd find you—you heard the rest from Alex that night. Alex had the brig, we met. *I* fired the shot that broke the bowsprit, changed commands, and sailed for Halifax."

"To see if I was among the interned." Now she saw the reason for his decision to indenture her. He'd expected to go searching through the colonies, to keep his promise to Henri, and finding her there . . . it explained much, but why continue to act the arrogant aristocrat once they'd sailed? So many other memories rose, altered now by his confession.

"And Alex, you wanted him to disillusion me. He made Corbeau seem no better than any other man, with the same desires, but without your honor." Stephen colored again, shifting his stance, ashamed. "Your idea worked, Stephen. I left him, knowing I could never go away with such a man. I sought you, I was willing to forget pride, and even if you rebuffed my attempt, you were worth pursuing."

"Until you saw me with Vanessa."

"Yes. I could have faced anything to make you love me, but at least I had enough pride left to turn away. What little remained saw me through the night."

"Lord, I can imagine how you felt," Stephen said in a low voice so laden by remorse it came out raspy.

Chelaine's head inclined; as she shook it, her hair veiled her expression. "No, Stephen, you cannot."

Now it was out. She knew the truth. As much as he loved her, he could do nothing but wait. It was within Chelaine's power to forgive him or make him suffer, deservedly so, for all he'd done. She was so still, so quiet. He refused to think what his life would be like if she left him. "Chelaine? What can I say? I've been arrogant, overbearing, stubborn—"

"To say the least. Those admissions are so humble, I can scarcely believe they came from you." Chelaine raised her head, brushing her long waves over her shoulders. Her face was expressionless, no indication of judgment or indictment.

"Humility has never been a virtue of mine."

"It can be learned, Stephen. I speak from experience." Chelaine glanced past him, gazing at the berth. Her face clouded with a pensive, withdrawn look, the long sweep of her lashes hiding her feelings. Lost in the past, drawn back to an earlier time, she saw herself lying there on that stormy night, the pleasure still with her, a sense of contentment, a vulnerable girl who had abandoned modesty. Surprised by her own passionate arousal, by an attraction to a man reason dictated she should despise. Then, the questions, pressed even though a growing alarm jangled her nerves, showing clearly on her face. Finally, the loss of intimacy, stripped away and replaced by shame and fury.

Watching Chelaine, following the direction of her fixed gaze, Stephen wondered what memory suddenly shadowed her lovely face with a fleeting pain. He said her name softly, then again before she heard. She blinked, her eyes returning to his, clear and calm. "What were—"

Chelaine's hand, fingers tightly balled in a fist, hurtled upward, her knuckles connecting with his right cheek, just above the jawbone, slamming with a force that split his lip and rocked his head back and to one side. All he knew was a sudden explosion of pain, a sense of nerves throbbing, the feeling of heat that preceded swelling. Eyes closed, head still turned away, he instinctively raised his hand, wincing as his fingertips explored the bruised bone. Gingerly he worked his jaw back and forth, brought his hand away, blinking at the sight of a smear of bright crimson blood on his fingers. A trickle pulsed from his bottom lip, where his teeth had sliced the corner.

With the back of his hand, he blotted at the blood, then slowly, eyes narrowed, faced her. She'd struck without a hint of warning. A second, greater shock awaited. There was no fear in her eyes. In fact, her hand was still balled, arm tensed, waiting for any move

270

CHELAINE

that might prompt another blow. Judiciously, he took several steps backward. Once, it seemed like an eon past, she had slapped him and remorse had followed. Not this time. There was only satisfaction and that disconcerting air of challenge.

Finally, feeling fortunate that he could form words, he quirked a brow, straightened his posture and eyed her. "What in God's name was *that* for? Just in general . . . or for some specific wrong?" He blotted at the trickle of blood again and flinched. His lip felt twice its normal size. "I thought you loved me."

"I do."

Her voice was calm, she slowly relaxed her fist, inhaled deeply and exhaled with a sigh. She looked . . . mollified, as if the blow had exorcised all the rage and resentment that had been building for so long.

"One hell of a way to show it," he observed. "I'd have preferred a kiss, not that I deserved one." He could feel a pulse pounding at the edge of his jaw, a frown only renewed the throbbing. "You didn't answer. Why *did* you slug me?"

"You *knew* I was a virgin, that I told the truth about the man who attacked me." He nodded, a guilty flush blending with the reddening bruise beginning to discolor his jaw. "And you knew Corbeau was never my lover."

"I can explain that."

Her hands rested at her waist, elbows flared. "Do so."

"Your brother—my friend—entrusted me with the task of finding and rescuing you. I never thought I'd locate you so soon. Once I had you aboard, you were safe—from the army, from the chance you'd be sold in

271

bondage to some farmer who'd work you day *and* night. Your brother told me you were beautiful. I just didn't count on how beautiful."

"This is why you hurt me? To save me from one man's desires and—"

"—give into my own. I know. Not very heroic or gallant. Exactly my thoughts when the brandy began to wear off. The drink, the storm . . . whatever, I forgot you were Henri's baby sister. All I knew was that you enchanted me. I wanted you and, it seemed, you wanted me as well."

With an indignant toss of her head, Chelaine dismissed the excuses. "So, you blame the brandy, the weather, me. I suppose nothing would have happened if we had not matched drinks? I did nothing to encourage you."

"Your very presence, as innocent as you were, was an enticement. One, if you recall, I resisted for many days. Do you have any idea how fetching you looked in that clinging nightgown? Or moving about in Lucy's ill-fitting gown, your charms all too evident? D'you think I didn't feel what my crew did when they ogled you?" Stephen looked righteous, comically so. "I didn't touch you 'til the liquor loosed my desires. And I'm not the one who had to prove myself with a drinking match." The blood had ceased flowing, but his lip pulsed each time he formed a word. "I should have stopped that nonsense after the first drink." He made a half-bow. "My fault. I stand condemned."

"Why didn't you stop it?"

"Wasn't one blow enough?" Stephen straightened, leaving himself open for another punch. "Go ahead. Get it over with. I guess I deserve it."

Chelaine raised her hand slowly, uncurled her

cramped fingers and now, vaguely chagrined that she had hurt him, no matter the justification, felt her resentment ebbing. She pressed two fingertips lightly to the corner of his mouth, wincing along with him. It struck her suddenly that this tall, broad-shouldered man who could easily knock her flat with a swipe of his hand was stoically prepared to let her hit him again. She sighed. "Does it hurt terribly?"

Stephen's eyes shifted to her, as he puzzled over the concern that softened the query. "Yes, awfully," he admitted, then caught at her wrist to stay her from a soothing touch that would only worsen the throbbing. "I'd never have believed you could throw a punch that solid."

Chelaine smiled. "There's a good deal you don't know of me. I grew up with three boys close in age. When you are outnumbered, you learn."

"I hope your other surprises are less painful. Anything you'd care to tell me?"

Chelaine shook her head. "Only that I love you."

"That's far less painful." Stephen smiled, despite the cost in pain, reached out and slipped an arm about her waist, pulling her close. "You're sure you're done beating on me?" A teasing tone softened a stern look. "I don't know of another woman who'd have dared what you just did," he mused.

Chelaine stared up at him, her lashes up and framing a smugly satisfied look. "But I knew you would not hurt me in return."

"You did, did you? Why were you so sure?"

"Because you do not hit women. And because you knew you deserved it. And, too," she added, leaning even closer to smile into his eyes, "you love me too much to hurt me any more."

"True, all true. I also have a healthy respect for your audacity, spirit, and a surprisingly sound left-handed punch. The last alone should keep me in line."

"I do not want you intimidated, Stephen. I'll take you as you are, part Corbeau, part Lord Braden."

"I've a request of you, Chelaine."

"Yes, Stephen."

His brow lifted. The raging virago had turned demure and obedient. Unable to resist, he lowered his head and pressed his mouth to hers, ignoring the jolt of pain as their lips met, the ache canceled by the sweet, yielding kiss. He drew back inches, enough to gaze into her eyes.

"Chelaine, be my wife. Forget what we've been through. I'll make it up to you. I swear, I will cherish you and let no harm come to you for all our lives."

Chelaine's fair brows drew together in a puzzled look. "Stephen, you had no need to ask. You could not rid yourself of me if you tried."

Her claim seemed to echo Henri's warning. Then Stephen had laughed, taking the claim in jest. Now he realized Henri had known her very well. "Why would I ever wish to?" he asked. One hand cradled the back of her head as he rubbed his cheek against the silky waves at her crown. "Whatever you want, whatever I have to give, anything, everything, is yours. I'm as tenacious as you, my love. Nothing will ever come between us."

Even as he said so, Stephen suddenly remembered Edward. His cousin had tried to keep them apart. Failing that, he was set on a course of action that would bring about the end he had conceived of for Stephen. After this evening, nothing would stay him from making Chelaine his wife. The future Countess Braden knew nothing of the plot, though, and it would remain so. He wanted his mind clear of worry over her safety when he met Edward. He didn't quite trust her with the knowledge. She'd come to listen to reason, a far way from the undisciplined, willful girl she'd been in Acadia, but she would never sit still while he went off to finish this business. He'd think of some excuse to keep her here, but for a while yet, they had time . . . and the privacy to make up for lost time.

Chapter Eighteen

THE DOORS OF THE ARMOIRE LAY OPEN. STEPHEN STOOD before the left, adjusting his crisp, linen stock, straightening his sleeves, studying his reflection in the mirrored panel before he reached for his coat and slipped into it. He gave a shrug of his broad shoulders, settling the tailored lines of the coat until he was satisfied. Peering closer, he examined the purple-red bruise to the right of his mouth. The flesh was still puffed and tender, the corner of his lip swollen.

"How *will* you explain that?"

Focusing past his own image, Stephen studied Chelaine. "I've come up worse in a fair match with a male opponent," he observed drily, "but 'tis the first wound suffered at the hands of a lady. I'll just claim I decked some fellow who admired you too boldly." He chuckled and gave a shake of his head. "Christ, if word ever got out . . ." Chelaine plumped the pillow beneath her head, and the movement drew his attention back to her. She lay on her side, the sheets rumpled behind her and at the foot of the berth. Her tawny curls spilled over her shoulders, as silky as the translucent chemise that covered her curving figure to midthigh. There, lacey garters secured the opaque silk stockings that sheathed her long, lithe legs. She wasn't consciously posing, but he sensed she knew intuitively that the artless dishabille enchanted him. Transfixed by the sight, the bruise forgotten, Stephen felt a surprising tug of desire.

They'd spent the last hour in each others arms, and he was ready to strip again and join her. If not for Edward . . . Stephen silently cursed and shut the armoire doors, walked past the desk and retrieved his hat, continued on to drop down on one knee at the berth edge, facing her.

Chelaine reached out, her fingers lightly smoothing the thick, wiry waves back at his temples. "If you stay," she said softly, "I'll tell you a secret." Her fingertips were at his cheek now, tracing the prominent ridge, sweeping down in a touch both soothing and alluring. His head bent, Stephen gazed upward with a rueful look she acknowledged with a lowering of long, feathery lashes that cast spiky shadows on cheeks suffused with a rose tint.

"I thought we'd agreed . . . no more secrets," he reminded her. "What is this that can't wait on my return?"

"Oh, it can," she admitted, then leaned forward to kiss his brow. "I just cannot understand why this talk with Edward cannot wait for another day."

"We decided on the meeting earlier, love. Since then, I've found more reason to confront Edward. He'll answer for his intrigue, I want it settled."

Chelaine's mouth pursed in a slight pout before she sighed and gave in. "He seemed sincere when he professed to love me. Even when I told him there was no chance, he offered his friendship."

"With all deference to your considerable charms, sweetheart, my cousin had nothing in mind but separating us. Have you forgotten who brought Vanessa to the ball? Or who implied she and I had become lovers?" Chelaine's lips twitched in irritation. She hadn't been so much gullible as Edward had been cunning.

"I practiced deception long enough to recognize a façade," Stephen said. "Edward never impressed me with the intelligence to carry off such maneuvering. My mistake, underestimating him." His eyes warmed suddenly as he dismissed Edward and smiled at Chelaine. "I'm off now. You've the look of a sleepy kitten. Take a rest—I'll be back before you miss me."

"I miss you already." Her fingers toyed with his, before she glanced up with an openly seductive look. "There is nothing I can do to make you stay?"

Stephen caught at her fingers, raised them to his lips. "My dear young lady, your sensual appetite will age me before my time. I told you once, when your emotions became more disciplined, you'd make a fool out of the most jaded man."

"I may seem insatiable," she acknowledged, "but only for you. And though you have been a libertine, you are not jaded. I have saved you from that appellation."

"And I'm grateful for being rescued." His lips brushed her hand in a lingering kiss, then he rose, smoothing the creases from the tight, fawn-colored breeches that covered his lean, muscular thighs. "Now be a good girl. Close your eyes and rest. There's little else to do . . . until I return." She smiled at that promise. "I'll be back no later than nine. On my honor." Inwardly he cringed. It was a lie. If he returned by ten or eleven, he'd be lucky. For now, all that mattered was his assurance she'd remain aboard, safe, out of harm's way.

For a while after Stephen left, Chelaine lay back, eyes closed, reflecting on what had turned out to be the strangest, most disconcerting day of her life. Despite his heritage and wealth, the title she scorned, she had fallen in love with Stephen. Even before Alex had tarnished Corbeau's image with his amorous, unprincipled advances, she'd abandoned her girlish infatuation. Few women could hope to see their most romantic dreams realized, but suddenly she had all she'd ever hoped for, all she'd come to cherish, neatly melded in one man.

She should have known. Stephen's rank and privilege were a perfect foil to cover his activities. He was at home on the seas, he had wealth and ships at his command, but more than this, the power and force of his personality suited the daring, devil-may-care smuggler whose exploits had cheered the Acadians and frustrated their enemies.

Now she knew why Stephen had spent nights away from home. He was preparing the brig for a voyage to Acadia, taking his aunt to her old home, the property he had purchased in November. Alex was away in New York, taking on a load of furniture aboard the schooner, pieces that had been duplicated to match the furnishings of the home where he and Stephen had been born. Stephen had touched only lightly on his early youth in Acadia. There would be time ahead to ask him all she wanted to know.

The thought of Edward's sly manipulations still

rankled. Stephen was more perceptive than she, though, and he'd been taken in as well. No matter— after Stephen confronted him tonight, she would never have to see the conniving man again.

Stretching langorously, the tension and buried desires of three weeks apart vanquished by Stephen's tender lovemaking, Chelaine sat up, swung her legs over the edge of the berth, and slid her feet to the deck. She rose and headed for the corner beside the tall armoire to cleanse herself at the washbasin. The water was chill, but it refreshed her, banishing any thought of sleep. A bath would have been a pleasant indulgence, but she hesitated to call for Samuel. There was no shame in letting him see the rumpled bedclothes, only a desire to avoid the surly old manservant.

Alert now and bored, she wandered about the room. It looked the same as it had six months before, only she had changed. She frowned at the memory of the sullen girl who'd come aboard, a child-woman who had no command of moods that were capricious, often volatile. Life with Stephen had altered that; when she considered the conversation he'd had with her brother, she could almost hear Henri bemoaning how wild and spoiled she was.

She wasn't his wife yet, but Chelaine felt no guilt at poking about searching for something of interest. She opened the armoire, found it the same, the drawers full of neatly folded shirts. Glancing up, she gazed at her reflection, noted the glow that warmed her complexion. Her hair was as unruly as ever, but Stephen seemed to love the mane of wild curls. She dragged her fingers through it, smoothing the tangles, at least for some semblance of a coiffure. Gazing past her reflection, she spied the sea chest, still in place behind the small, circular table between the two wing chairs. *That* might hold something interesting.

Circling the chair, she went down on her knees, lifted the metal latch, and struggled to raise the heavy, curved lid. Inside there were stacks of papers, tied with ribbon, a few rolled parchments that appeared to be maps, several books. Layer by layer, she sifted through. About to choose one of the books and settle in to practice her reading, she suddenly saw her buckskin shirt and leggings, neatly folded, and beside them her soft, doeskin boots. Her mouth rounded in surprise and delight. Stephen had told her he'd tossed them overboard. They reminded her of home, and just for a lark, she reached in, drew them out, and quickly shed the chemise and stockings, to don her old attire.

The shirt stretched taut across her breasts, more tightly than she remembered. The breeches were snug as well. She laced them loosely and pulled on the knee-high boots. They still fit . . . at least her feet hadn't plumped with the rest of her. She stifled a giggle, imagining Stephen's shock if he returned to find her dressed so. As she came to a standing position, something else in the bottom of the chest caught her eye. A knife lay there, sheathed in a finely tooled leather scabbard. Had it been there on the journey from Halifax? If so, she was glad she hadn't known. In her anger and hurt, she might well have taken the weapon and used it on Stephen. The thought horrified her.

Fascinated, she drew the blade from the sheath. It was shiny and double-edged, the hilt layered with ivory, a ruffled surface that provided for a good grip. Obviously made for a man's larger hand, heavier than the simple knife she'd carried, it was a finely crafted, wickedly sharp weapon. She discovered how sharp when she nicked a thumb with a bare touch of one side of the blade. She hadn't used a knife for so long, had had no need to, and the last time only stirred memories better left forgotten. Still, Chelaine wondered if she could use one as accurately as she had in Acadia.

It was too much temptation to resist. She glanced about the room. Stephen wouldn't be pleased to find dents in any of the furnishings and the deck was as smooth and gleaming as the desk and chairs. There were two support timbers, columns with arched reinforcements attached to the above deck. The wood was stained dark but rough. She examined one, smiled at finding a whorl, a knot that remained of the tree from which the timbers had been hewn.

She backed toward the door, allowing herself some ten feet, with room behind her to allow for her raised arm. The whorl was about her shoulder height. As strange as the unfamiliar knife was, once she took up a stance, balanced on the balls of her feet, her confidence returned. She brought her hand up, aimed and snapped her wrist. The blade tip lodged in the timber some nine inches below her target. Chelaine frowned, then shook off disappointment. At least she'd hit the column. She retrieved the knife, adjusted her aim, and this time struck the bottom edge of the knot. Once more, a triumphant grin, as the blade struck dead center.

It was enough. She was satisfied, whatever the skill was worth, she was as good as ever. Returning to the table to slide the sheath over the blade, a sharp rap at the door startled her. Stephen . . . back so soon? She called his name. In answer, Samuel's dry, froggy voice asked permission to enter. Forgetting her attire, she replied, grimacing at having to face him.

Samuel opened the door, paused, and gaped. His expression altered to disapproval as he glanced down, then up, taking in the unsuitable clothing she had worn when she'd come aboard in Acadia. He knew his master intended to marry Chelaine, knew she'd been told about Corbeau, but to find her like this, with a knife in hand yet . . . He shook his head and tsked several times.

Chelaine bridled at the censure. Despite her attire, she drew herself erect and fixed him with a haughty stare. "You had some purpose in mind, other than clucking your tongue over my appearance?"

"Aye, that I did, mistress," Samuel replied, impressed by the authority in her voice. "'Twas shock what made me forget it." He came forward, holding out an envelope. "This just come. Captain Peter's boy, David, brung it. Figured you'd give it to His Lordship." Chelaine reached out and took it, barely glancing at the name scrawled on the front.

The old man nodded, studying her with interest, a rather smug look twinkling in his bright blue eyes. "Is there something you wished to say?" she asked.

"Yes. If you're goin' to be the wife of an earl, them clothes'll never do. Thought you'd given up dressin' like a boy."

"How I dress is no concern of yours!" Chelaine snapped. "I merely tried these on . . ." Why was she explaining herself to him? "Unless I call for you, you may keep your distance. And keep your opinions as well."

Now she sounded like she should. In her finery, the

girl would bowl the gentry over with her beauty and poise. "Beggin' your pardon, m'Lady," her eyes widened at the respectful title, "I been with Himself for a long time. I just wanted to say I knewed you was a matched pair from the first."

Now Chelaine stared, startled by the confession. "How is it you knew this before any other?"

"Well, you got the same tempers, you're both stubborn and started off wild."

"The earl might not approve of that judgment."

"It's the Acadian blood," Samuel observed sagely. "Lord Stephen, when he come to live in England, he was as spirited and . . . willful as you. Did fine, though, made himself a place."

"Then you no longer see me as unworthy?"

His eyes grew wide with wonder. "M'Lady, you was always worthy. It just took some temperin' to bring it out." Chelaine offered a faint smile, thanked him, and received a bow. "However, were I you, I'd change back to you dress 'fore the earl gets back."

"I had planned to."

Samuel gave another nod of approval and left her. Once the door had closed, Chelaine examined the envelope. She considered setting it aside, but it might be important . . . and she had a right to look. Carefully, she tore the end open. A small round object dropped, and she bent to retrieve it, forgetting the envelope as she blinked in surprise. The object was a ring, not just any ring, but exactly like the one she wore on her right hand. Bewildered, she turned, found herself near the chair and sat, unable to make sense of it.

Alex's son had brought the envelope. She stared at it

now and peeked within. There was a note she'd missed in wonder over the ring. She withdrew it and opened the folded paper. Alex's name was scrawled at the bottom, Stephen's at the top. Apparently he'd returned earlier than expected. She struggled to make out the handwriting. Alex had written to say he'd received the ring an hour ago. He was meeting her as planned, but he wanted to let Stephen know her decision.

Meeting? Chelaine glanced at the ring again. It was a duplicate of hers, a copy even with the same worn look. How could . . . suddenly she thought of Edward. He'd shown himself to be a liar, a greedy man who'd plotted to assure himself Stephen would never marry, to protect his position as the heir to a title and fortune. He'd copied her ring . . . to trap Alex? That would gain him little. If he'd sent the ring to Alex, he knew what reaction it would bring. She thought back to the night of the party, her conversation in the study. When she'd emerged, Edward was in the hall. He must have overheard them. Why lure Alex to the orchard when he was meeting with Stephen?

Suddenly it all made sense. Edward wanted more than their separation. He had set a trap for Stephen and Alex. They were to meet, face off, the earl who'd been hunting Corbeau, finally coming upon him. Stephen knew. She remembered his comment on her ring, her answer that Edward had seen to its repair. Stephen was prepared. He had gone out to settle with his cousin, not just confront him with his treachery.

But Alex was back, he was bound for the rendezvous. In the dark, if he came on them, Stephen might be startled . . . lose his advantage for a precious few minutes. She came to her feet, knowing what she had to do. Stop Alex, catch him before he came up the path from the river. If she lost Stephen now, when they'd just discovered the happiness that lay ahead . . . Chelaine closed her eyes a second, wavering on her feet, then, in a loud, anguished cry, she called for Samuel.

Chapter Nineteen

FOR HOURS AFTER HE'D LEFT STEPHEN'S STUDY, EDWARD went over his plans detail by detail, searching for some flaw, some error that might have aroused his cousin's suspicions. Chelaine was safely on her way. Peters would respond to her summons as he'd promised. No doubt Stephen still wrestled with the startling idea that his friend could be the elusive French outlaw he'd sought, but when Alex emerged from the orchard, it would prove beyond a doubt how cunning and deceitful he'd been.

Everything seemed to favor Edward, leading him to believe that some divine providence had preordained Stephen's fate. It wasn't a matter of dislike or even hatred. Stephen was affable, generous to a fault, a man above reproach. He didn't deserve to die, but Edward's needs came first. When he'd given some consideration to what he'd learned, it followed as a matter of course that such a drastic measure would afford him the privilege of a title and the fortune that came with it while he was still young enough to enjoy the inheritance. He pushed aside the guilt that assailed him. Other men had done the same—to closer relatives—and for less gain.

They had met at the appointed time; if Stephen's countenance was dark and brooding, he'd had most of the afternoon to consider Alex's treachery. At his first sight of Stephen, Edward exclaimed over the bruise that shaded his jaw, at the slight swelling of his lower lip. The explanation had given him a heart-stopping moment. A friend of Stephen's had stopped him on the street, confessing he'd seen Chelaine board the southbound coach for Providence, that Edward had kissed her before handing her within.

"I told him he was mistaken," Stephen explained. "Whitby insisted he recognized you both clearly. Even when I said it was impossible, he refused to change his tale." Then Stephen had fixed Edward with a penetrating stare, waiting for his reaction. He'd scoffed, of course, his pulses racing as he'd managed an incredulous laugh, then asked how they'd come to blows. "My mood was testy. Ordinarily, I'd have passed it off as misplaced concern," Stephen answered, sinking into his desk chair to open the polished, rectangular box that held a brace of pistols. "But Whitby intimated I had reason to question your intentions, that you seemed apprehensive, even nervous. I struck without thinking. He returned the blow and we parted before it turned into a public spectacle."

Clearly Stephen believed him over his friend's claims, but the chance sighting had shaken Edward's confidence, dampening his armpits with a nervous sweat fortunately hidden by his coat. The subject was dropped, much to his relief, and once Stephen had loaded and primed the weapons, they had set off for Hartehill.

Skirting the house, they'd crossed a field and tethered their mounts far enough from the orchard so that no restless whinnying would carry there and disturb the quiet. Neither had pursued a conversation on the road, only now, as the sun began to set, did Edward venture a comment in a hushed tone. "We've a while yet. Chelaine won't leave the house until it's close to dark."

Stephen leaned against the thick trunk of an oak, his features expressionless. His answer was a sigh, a flicker of a glance at Edward. "Corbeau will show before then. He'll want to assure himself the area is safe." They had taken a position in a secluded stand of oaks on a rise some fifteen yards from the first of the rows of apple trees. The orchard was in full bloom, the thick green foliage spotted with white blossoms that gave off a sweet odor. The day had been warm; now a cool breeze came off the river, laden with moisture that was beginning to form wisps of ground fog.

Behind and to their right, a grassy meadow stretched up a hill. Beyond it lay the gardens and the house. Lights gleamed faintly from the first floor windows, no other signs of activity. Despite Lucy's absence, the servants still went about their evening routine.

Edward had striven hard to control a nervous energy. Like Stephen, he'd taken a stance by one of the younger oaks, folded his arms, his senses keened sharply for any unusual sounds. The sky was fading from a faint orange-gold to lavender as twilight settled in. He licked his dry lips, wishing he'd brought a flask, any sort of drink, to wet his throat and chase away the tension. Shifting his feet for the third time in five minutes, he finally straightened and wiped his damp palms on the skirt of his coat, then paced a few steps forward, staring toward the orchard, only to turn about and pace back.

"Anxious, cousin? Or just shy of meeting the man face to face?"

Edward responded to the queries with a raised brow that denied any qualms. "Not I, Stephen. He's no reason to expect anyone but the girl who summoned him." His hand covered the pistol tucked within his waistband, patted the weapon before he smirked at the idea of anxiety. "Two against one, with the element of surprise . . . I see no need for worry."

Stephen nodded at Edward's pistol. "If there's a shot fired, 'twill be from one of my pistols. I could have come alone, Edward—"

"I'm just along to back you up," he hastened to assure Stephen. "You've been after Corbeau for months. Are you sure you can shoot him now you know he's been a friend?" There was a chill edge to Stephen's voice that further frayed his nerves. Stephen never learned anything without mastering it, and he was a skilled marksman. If he chose to question Alex at gunpoint rather than finish him with a shot, it would make a simple matter into something more difficult. Before Alex answered anything, before he tried to play on Stephen's sympathies, Edward would have to aim carefully and silence Stephen, then retrieve one of his pistols and finish off Corbeau. The shadows were deepening, he strained to make out Stephen's expression and repeated his question.

Still lounging casually, Stephen raised a shoulder and

let it drop. "Who can ever really know another's thoughts?" he mused, "even one who's been as close as Alex? No relationship is ever all it seems to be." He had one of his guns out now and raised it, taking imaginary aim at a branch before he turned the muzzle toward Edward and smiled. "Take us, for example. You and I played together as boys, we did our share of skirt-chasing. The other members of the family made no effort to disguise their opinion of me. I was somewhat of an outcast, unworthy of the Harte name or whatever faded grandeur it still bore. You were the only one who accepted me. We had our share of good times."

"We did, that," Edward agreed. He'd missed the allusion to their relationship, heard only praise and fellowship in Stephen's remembrances. "A pity we drifted apart over the years. Still, now that I'm in the trade with you, we can take up like the old days." The muzzle remained fixed on him, aimed at his mid-section and he grimaced. "Do point that away, eh? We don't want any accidents."

"No," Stephen agreed, "no accidents, only a matter of bringing a Judas out in the open." He lowered the weapon and stiffened suddenly, staring past Edward, his concentration so intense Edward glanced over a shoulder, straining to see what had alerted Stephen. The orchard was shadowed now, a rising breeze stirring the mist, rustling the branches.

"You heard something?" he whispered, unable to see anything out of the ordinary. The rows of mature trees were terraced, each slightly lower, following the sloping ground that led to the marshy river bank and a private landing that jutted out into the River Charles.

Alex would come that way, in a dory. For long minutes, he listened, but heard nothing, only the stirrings of small animals, a repetitive cadence of chirruping crickets.

Stephen no longer stood so stiffly. As Edward faced him, he shrugged his shoulders. "'Twas nothing. The dark is his ally, Corbeau comes and goes, silent as a haunt, a man who's survived by his keen senses."

"You know his ways well. I wonder that you never caught him."

In the gathering darkness, a flash of white showed Stephen's grin. "When you hunt, you learn the habits of your prey. I do know how he thinks, you might say, how he feels."

"That's an advantage," Edward observed, then puzzled, "Peters never struck me as the crafty sort."

"To suit his purposes, he'd have to appear the opposite of the expected. He'd have been caught long ago if he swaggered about with the air of a man vain in his victories."

"You sound as if you admire the beggar," Edward said. "He made a mockery of your trust, he's coming here to carry off Chelaine."

"That remains to be seen. And one can't help admire an adversary with the wits to elude his hunters so long." Stephen stepped back, one shoulder to the oak, at ease again. "I'd have thought you'd prefer to see Chelaine vanish without a trace," he mused aloud.

"Stephen!" Edward's voice sounded wounded. "Why would I warn you, then? The girl's not good enough for you. You took her in, gave her everything, including your affections . . . only to be repaid by going off with her lover." Stephen's head came up at

292

that term, and Edward eased his vehemence. "You'd be better off without her. Your decision—but I'd toss her out."

"Chelaine won't be going anywhere. After this . . . business . . . is concluded, she'll be my wife."

"What of your pride, man?" Edward managed an indignance that seemed righteous for his cousin's sake. "After this, how can you ever trust her?"

"I trust Chelaine completely," Stephen replied smoothly. He loosened the catch on his pistol and gently, almost like a caress, rubbed a thumb over the smooth, fine-textured wood. "Odd . . . how still it is." At his comment, Edward raised his head, listening. The crickets had ceased their music, the breeze had calmed, a few leaves rustled, but his breathing was louder than any other sound.

Suddenly sweat beaded Edward's forehead, slicking his hands. He could smell his own nerves and fear over the sweet scented blossoms. "Maybe we should separate," he suggested. "More chance of catching him off guard."

Stephen's mouth quirked. "Not a wise decision, cousin. You're edgy already. In the dark . . . who knows, you might mistake me for him."

"True. Still, I'd not shoot unless I saw him clear. If I'd wanted to, I could have come on my own, Stephen, with no risk to you."

"Aye. But you wanted me to have the pleasure?"

"He wronged you. And you'd never have believed my word over Chelaine's. I swear, Stephen, passion has muddled your thinking. What gain have I in her loss to you? Lovely as she is, I'd not have forgiven her."

"But we're different. I've never really given a damn for my title, while you . . . ." Stephen's voice was a low, velvet-toned persuasion, inviting confidence. "Think how grand you'd feel, to hear yourself addressed, 'Lord Braden,' or 'Lord Edward, earl of Braden. His Lordship.' You can't deny you've never reflected on it. The truth . . . between us."

"It may have passed my mind, but I've never coveted the honor. This isn't England, where rank had more prominence. You're young, healthy . . . Lord, why dwell on so morbid a subject?"

"Well, I expect to live long," Stephen admitted. "But one can never set aside the chance of being struck down, a sudden illness, an accident. And if that happened, you'd stand to gain more than a title you find empty of purpose. Just think how far my money would go in clearing you of those bothersome debts. That sort of relief might tempt the most principled of minds."

"To what effect? Stephen, you make it seem as if I'd designs on what's yours. I'd have little pleasure in wealth gained so sadly."

Stephen suddenly hushed him. Somewhere in the distance a branch crackled, then an owl hooted. Stephen remained still, puzzling over the soft rustle that preceded the cracking branch. Finally he shook his head. "Just anticipation." His fingers firmed in a sure grip about the pistol butt. "Strange . . . the owl calling just then. Ancients always thought them a harbinger of death. And we were just speaking of it."

Edward frowned. Stephen's mood was all that was strange. "Something's delayed him," he groused. "She'll be along before Alex."

"No, Edward."

How could he sound so sure? "What if she happens along just as we spot him? He'll be armed—Chelaine might catch a shot."

"You're concerned for her safety now?"

"Only for your sake . . . because you care for her."

Stephen sighed. "Neither of them is coming."

"What!" Edward's voice rose in shock. "If you knew that, then why are we out here?" He was tense and confused, puzzled, unable to think clearly. "You didn't go and confront him?"

"No need to. Alex has been in New York the past few days."

Edward's insides churned with acid, he felt a sour taste of fear mix with a rise of bitter gall. Stephen had known of this when they spoke, said nothing. He cursed his stupidity in not checking Alex's house. A bad error, very bad. His hand slid slowly toward the butt of his weapon, slippery fingers trying for a hold. "But she sent the ring," he insisted, the desperation in his voice as evident as it was to Stephen. Three feet separated them, but once more, the muzzle was aimed, higher this time, at his heart, held in a steady hand. His mouth filled with saliva, his throat constricted, choking him as he tried to swallow. "Chelaine—"

"—is safe," Stephen said calmly. Earlier in the day he'd been furious, but that had abated, replaced by an icy detachment. "She has no idea we're here."

"But she went . . ." His mind a morass of confusion, Edward struggled to salvage something of sense. All he saw was the muzzle of a pistol whose hammer was cocked. "She left you."

"You made several mistakes, Edward. Alex was one. The other . . ." He went on, explaining what had brought Chelaine back to Boston. "She knows you tried to keep us apart, but I spared her the rest."

"Whatever she said, it was all a lie. She doesn't like me. You can't believe I arranged—"

"A trap? Of course you did."

"For Corbeau . . . Alex."

Stephen laughed, but the sound was chill and mocking. "You laid your plans with a stealth that surprised me," he admitted. "If it had worked, you would have had everything, even some acclaim for having killed the scoundrel who shot your cousin."

His limbs shook, his knees threatened to buckle, but Edward still sought a way out. "I can't believe you'd think this of me. I—"

"For a while, in your mind, you owned it all. At least you should know where you failed. No man should meet his end without understanding why. When did your mind turn from meddling to murder?"

"I never meant . . ." Stephen knew it all, he'd figured out everything. "Alex *is* the man you want. Doesn't that mean anything?"

"Alex isn't Corbeau."

Edward shook his head. "I heard him admit it."

"You heard part of a conversation. At the time, Chelaine believed it, too. But she knows the truth now. You wanted to face Corbeau?" Stephen inclined his head. "You can't see me as clearly now, but then my features are familiar enough."

"You? But why . . ."

"My mother was Acadian, I was born there. Reason enough?"

"So now, what? You wouldn't shoot me, your own cousin."

"That tie never stopped you from contemplating the same for me," Stephen reminded him. "Your reason was greed, mine . . . self-preservation. I have too much to live for, Edward."

"It doesn't have to end this way . . . I'll go

away . . . you'll marry her and breed your heirs." His voice was a whine now, more like a woman pleading and begging. "I don't want to die!"

"Neither did I."

Edward edged back. He had no chance to draw his gun before he was shot. His shoulders bumped the tree, stopping him for a moment. Stephen followed with the pistol, moving effortlessly, just a shift of his foot. The moon had risen, its light glinted on the polished steel barrel. Edward slowly pried his pistol free of his waistband, held it between his thumb and index finger, away from his body. Stephen wouldn't fire on an unarmed man. With a quick toss, he threw it into the clearing between the oak stand and the orchard.

Stephen didn't even blink as it sailed past. His eyes remained on Edward, amazed that a man who could callously plot murder for gain would turn into a blubbering coward, mewling for mercy. Suddenly that same, low rustle caught his ear. It sounded like a step, heavier than an animal's tread. He kept Edward in his aim, alert to any movement, while he considered the possibility that Alex had returned, found the ring, and come.

With a sidling motion, Edward inched toward the clearing. The pistol followed him, raising slightly, stopping him at least five feet from his abandoned pistol. "You won't kill me now," Edward said, with some semblance of confidence. "A man without a weapon?"

With slow, even strides, Stephen approached. "This isn't a duel, cousin," he smirked, "no matter of honor to be satisfied. I've killed for less cause than you've given me. You chose the course, I'm only finishing it."

"I . . . I may have tried, but you're alive. Turn me

over to a magistrate, I'll face trial for attempted murder. At least I'd have a chance."

"I'm your judge, you've proven your guilt, I'll act as executioner." Edward shook his head, dazed and disbelieving. "One shot to the heart. Consider it merciful. You've never seen a man hang? The rope chokes off your breath, you strangle slowly, legs flailing. If you're lucky, your neck snaps."

The man who'd meant him to die slumped to his knees, shoulders quivering as he sobbed. Stephen stared at him in disgust. "Get up," he ordered. "Christ, man, you can't even die with dignity! Get on your feet."

Edward fell to one side, his breath heaving, glancing at the gun he'd tossed in the dirt. Stephen guessed at his desire to reach for it and warned him not to try, ordered him to his feet once more. His fingers stretched, dragging at the dirt before he closed them in a fist, struggled up until he was kneeling. As he straightened, he flung his arm out, his fingers opening to hurtle dirt and pebbles upward, toward Stephen's face.

The desperate move gained him a few moment's valuable time. Stephen faltered, fell back a step, one hand brushing at his eyes, long enough for Edward to stretch, scrabble for a hold on the pistol. He caught it and dragged backward, on his knees but erect. Abject terror faded in a mad flare of triumph. He had a chance.

Stephen whirled, feet balanced, body slightly crouched, his gun extended in a steady, two-handed grip. Before Edward could draw the hammer, there was a flash of powder, a cracking explosion, and a ball from Stephen's weapon struck just below his collarbone. The force rocked him back, tearing a gutteral scream from his throat. He slumped forward then, shock waves rippling through his body, touching every nerve. Still he held the pistol, one rational thought clear in the fog of pain. Stephen had to reload and prime his gun. That brief hope brought him up, the pistol wavered in his hand, he gasped as he dragged his left arm over to steady his quivering muscles as he cocked the hammer. Somehow he managed it, blinked away a crimson haze, and aimed.

Moving with a catlike agility, Stephen twisted aside, balancing on one foot, kicking out hard with the other. His boot heel slammed Edward's shoulder, then he dropped and rolled. An agonized shriek echoed, the pistol discharged with a flash and report, the ball whizzing off in a wild shot. Stephen came up on one knee, watched Edward jerk, his upper body suspended stiffly before he sprawled forward, face down in the dirt.

Out of habit, Stephen rose cautiously, assumed a spread-eagled stance, and peered at Edward. A gutteral rasp issued from his throat, a rattle as he tried to inhale, a gurgle that faded to silence.

His own breath came harshly, a blend of exertion and the energy that always surged through him in a defensive response. A few deep breaths and the tension flowed away, leaving a residue of disgust. With a sigh, he moved close enough to nudge the body with a boot tip. The ball must have struck closer to the heart than he'd thought. He leaned over, only then saw the rectangular object protruding from a spot just below a shoulder. Hunkering down on his heels, he closed his hand over a knife tip barely embedded in muscle, tugged and rose, examining the blade before a glimpse of movement caught the corner of his eye.

A figure emerged from the deep-shadowed trees. The fog, denser now, swirled, half-obscuring the figure so that it seemed an illusion. His brows met in a frown. Alex, it had to be. "When in the hell did you get back?" he called, relieved, yet annoyed by the lack of a response. Behind him, heavy footsteps pounded down the slope from the house, a familiar deep voice, Alex's, shouted his name.

Mystified, Stephen moved toward the trees. The mist shifted, stirring as he passed. His eyes stretched wide in stunned disbelief as he made out Chelaine's face, ghostly pale, wreathed by curls coiled tight from the damp. Wearing buckskins, she stood very still, staring past him. He spoke her name again, more loudly, but her eyes remained fixed, trancelike.

Chelaine had acted instinctively. She saw the pistol raise in Edward's hands and of its own volition, her arm came up, flexed, and the blade flew straight and true, striking her target.

She saw a dead body sprawled, but it was another man, another knife, a death in a distant land. Faintly, as if from a far distance, she heard her name. Hands closed on her shoulders, strong fingers whose grasp transmitted anger. At last she blinked, shaking off the haunting memories, recognizing Stephen. In the moonlight, his face registered an odd blend of fury and wonder.

Stephen's fingers closed more tightly, he shook her a little in frustration. "Damn it! Don't you *ever* listen? You were to wait for my return."

His anger made sense, but when she tried to explain,

the words came out soft and disjointed. "You didn't know . . . Alex, he came back and . . ." Her voice faded to a whisper, Stephen's face dissolved, her knees buckled, and a mist darker than the fog clouded her eyes. She felt herself slipping, his arms catching her and then the darkness engulfed her.

Chapter Twenty

CHELAINE STIRRED WITH A SIGH, HER LASHES FLUTTERED, and she winced at the bright illumination of the hall. Stephen carried her toward the staircase with a loping stride that jounced her uncomfortably. A few deep breaths cleared her head before she glanced up, surveying Stephen's features. He looked panic-stricken, his jaw tensed, lips stretched so taut the skin whitened at the corners of his mouth. The expression was so foreign to his nature, she reacted with an instinctive desire to ease his concern.

"Stephen? I'm fine, you can set me down."

He stopped short at the assurance, glanced at her in relief before his hands tightened about her shoulders and knees, a look of pure rage eliciting another wince from Chelaine. "I could throttle you!" he growled, and at that moment, it almost looked as if he might. When she insisted, in a clear, steady tone, that he release her, his dark brows met in an awesome glower before he snapped, "Shut up! You're in no condition to make any demands."

With that, he resumed his march, no longer as hurried but still resolute. Up the stairs they went, straight to his suite, where he paused only to shift her weight and grasp the handle before he shoved the door open with his foot and swept in, heading for the bed. There, with a gentle caution that belied his tensed anger, he eased her down on the mattress, far enough inward to allow him room to settle beside her.

"It was only a faint," she protested, more upset by his menacing scowl than by the brief spell of unconsciousness. "Why are you so—"

"Outraged?" he supplied. "Infuriated? Righteously indignant?"

"Am I to choose the emotion that best fits your manner?" she replied saucily. "They all suit you, but why I can't imagine. A few minutes ago you were overcome with worry and now . . . you're berating me." Her bottom lip pushed out in a slight pout. "If you don't calm down, I *will* faint again."

He met the statement with a smirk, mocking the artifice designed to distract him from a justifiable fury, not only for the shock she'd dealt him in collapsing, but because she'd endangered herself—and him—by her unexpected appearance. "I told you to wait for me aboard the ship," he repeated his earlier words. "Don't you *ever* listen to reason? Christ! If you weren't so weak, I'd turn you over my knee and—"

"I am *not* weak, and I came only out of concern for your safety."

"I knew exactly what I was about, thank you," he countered. "And you are weak, you look . . ." He paused, studying her intently. Chelaine looked very cool and composed, her skin glowing with healthy color. In contrast, he felt drawn, drained by the scare she'd given him. "You said you weren't the fainting type," he said accusingly.

With an exasperated sigh, Chelaine admitted, "There are times it happens to every woman. I haven't before, I likely won't again—especially if you're going to roar and snarl like a wounded bear when I open my eyes." She patted his tensed arm and started to rise, only to have his hands close firmly on her shoulders and push her back. "Let me up. If you don't, I'll—"

"You'll *what*—scream, cry . . . or pout? I'd not be impressed by any theatrics. You'll stay where you are until I've sent for a doctor." Her mouth pursed as she shook her head. "Meanwhile, I will cool my temper enough to hear your answers to my questions." A resigned sigh greeted the intention and she gave in, reluctantly settling in for an interrogation. "What on God's green earth are you doing in that get-up?"

Amused by the fact that his first inquiry concerned her attire, she began to smile, thought better of it in light of his mood, and explained, "I found them in your sea chest and only tried them on to see how they fit." Her brows lifted in a faint hint of accusation. "*You* said you'd tossed them overboard."

"I should have. You've the look of a rebel lad once more." At the inaccuracy of the description, she canted her head slightly in a challenge. Stephen surveyed her figure, noting the clinging buckskin seemed to have shrunk, clearly detailing the swell of her breasts and outlining her curves, and glanced up, amending his judgment. "A rebel girl . . . woman." The corners of her mouth tipped up at the admission. "I thought you'd put all that nonsense behind you. A countess doesn't wear—"

"I'm not yet a countess," she corrected. "And if you don't cease your belligerence, I may not be."

"You will," Stephen said confidently. "Now, you took it upon yourself to leave the ship when I left assured you'd be there to greet my return . . . with eagerness, as I recall. Whatever possessed you to think I needed your help?"

Eagerness. Yes, she *had* longed to keep him from the meeting, still full of yearning despite their lovemaking. They'd promised not to keep secrets from one another. Not only had he deceived her about his true intent, it seemed he had a purpose other than desire in the flare of passion that left her with a feeling of languor. Chelaine sat up, her narrowed eyes a warning, daring him to command her to lie back. "You conniving, blue-eyed devil!" she fumed. He gazed back at her, incredulous and perplexed by her indignation. "You took me to bed just so I would be too tired to question why you had to meet Edward so urgently." Stephen flushed guiltily, but when he reached out to grasp her upper arm, she jerked away. "You're so used to lying, you can deceive me even with your body."

Suddenly *he* was on the defensive. It was not a comfortable feeling, especially when there was a grain of truth to the accusation. "My desire for you was as real as your own," he insisted. "How can you think all I had in mind was—"

"I never said it was *all* you had in mind. We'd been apart for almost three weeks. You managed to satisfy your needs—"

"And yours."

"As well as ease your concern for my 'safety' at the same time," she went on, ignoring his observation.

"How can I ever learn to trust you, when you can't even tell me the truth?"

"And if I had?" He'd recovered from the accusation enough to justify his actions. "Who knows you better than I, Chelaine? You did exactly as I thought you would if I'd revealed the whole truth. I didn't deceive you so much as keep information to myself that would have upset you. How long could you have sat still, worrying about me, waiting and pacing the deck to see if I'd come back unharmed?"

"I have enough respect for your ability to survive anything so that I would have obeyed your wishes," she admitted. His eyes reflected a brief pleasure at the compliment, quickly banished by a resentful glare. "There was quite a bit you withheld."

"Only that I knew Edward had set a trap, to see Alex meet his death before I was to fall victim to a fatal shot from Corbeau. He came to me early in the afternoon, posturing righteously as he confided he'd overheard your talk with Alex. Alex was Corbeau, my adversary —not only that, he would be meeting you this evening, to take you away."

"And you acted shocked, you let him believe his plot would succeed." Chelaine had calmed and imagined the scene, Edward sure of a success that gained him so much, Stephen listening, all the while recognizing his cousin's treachery, determined to see it finished in a face-off alone in the orchard. A just end for someone who could cold-bloodedly plan murder for ambition and greed. "He had no idea Alex was gone, or even that I might turn up."

"Speaking of turning up, you still haven't told me what brought you to my rescue. For all you knew, it was to be a settlement of his efforts to come between us."

A discreet cough, followed by a cleared throat, drew their attention to the open doorway. Alex stood there, one hand propped against the doorjamb. "I can settle that question, if Chelaine doesn't mind the interruption," he said. He glanced past Stephen, pleased to see her looking so well. "You gave us both a fright, Chelaine. I held off sending for a doctor but," his gaze settled on Stephen, he struggled to keep a serious demeanor, "it appears His Lordship might need one. Did Edward manage that?" His nod indicated the bruised jaw and swollen lip.

"No." Stephen hesitated to admit the truth but with a sheepish grin gestured toward Chelaine. "The lady settled an old score, admittedly dealt out a well-deserved punishment for my charade. She knows everything, you can speak your mind in ease. When *did* you return?"

"Midafternoon. But by the time I returned home, it was close to supper. I found Chelaine's ring awaiting me, and while I puzzled over her summons after our disagreement—"

"I owe you for that ruse," Chelaine commented, "even if it was Stephen's idea." She frowned at him. "Really, Alex . . . you overplayed your part. An idyllic retreat on an island, swimming in the Caribbean, lazing on a—" She left off as he asked her forgiveness.

"Accept my humble apologies. Stephen's always led me astray. Even when we were boys, he was forever involving me in some escapade. You'd never know I'm the elder."

"Now that I'm revealed as a bad influence from boyhood on, could we get on with your reaction to the ring?" Stephen gestured Alex into the room, and he came forward to pause several feet from them, stick his hands in his pockets and nod at his cousin.

"I sent David off with the ring and a note. I'm sure Chelaine read my message."

"I did. I thought it might be important. First I found the ring. It was so like mine . . . well, look." She held out both hands. The original was in place on her right hand, its twin, exact but for its less worn, brighter gold, glinted on her left hand. "After I read the note, it became obvious who sent the ring and why."

"And you came riding out for—"

"I rode to intercept Alex, before he might come up from the river and distract you," Chelaine insisted, faintly irritated at Stephen. She'd already told him she knew he could handle himself with Edward. "But Alex wasn't at the landing."

"I might have been if I hadn't puzzled over the fact you hadn't sent your *father's* ring as we'd planned. Not long after I sent David off, I went to the brig myself. And found you'd just left in haste, headed for Hartehill. I went to the house first, then heard a shot and came running."

"What've you done with the body?" Stephen's voice was bland. He felt no remorse, his concern now was how to explain the death and not arouse suspicion. He had enough influence to feel confident that whatever story he offered would be accepted. Staring up at Alex, he missed a twinge of guilt on Chelaine's face. She lay back again, eyes closed.

"I dragged him up through the field and sprawled him on his back by the garden wall. It will seem he came on Corbeau and was shot. We can work out the details later." Alex hadn't missed Chelaine's reaction.

All the talk of death and dealing with Edward's body upset her. "There was only a bit of blood on his coat back, easily missed by a careless examination." His gaze flicked at Chelaine, drawing Stephen's attention to her. "I'm going downstairs for a drink. You don't look like you need company."

Stephen nodded agreement, gazing at Chelaine. He barely noted Alex's departure. Reaching forward, he smoothed a damp wisp of hair back from her forehead. Her eyes opened at his touch, she gazed back with a somewhat dazed look, stirring his concern over her well-being again. "I'm sending for a doctor. You don't look—"

"There's nothing wrong, nothing any doctor can help." She sighed and rose on one elbow. Stephen's hands caught beneath her shoulders, helping her to sit. Suddenly she circled his neck with her arms, resting her cheek against his chest. "I know he had to die," she said softly, "but now I have killed twice." Stephen's hand had stroked her hair. At that confession, he drew back, meeting her eyes.

"*My* shot killed Edward, Chelaine. All you did was jar his aim." Her eyes widened in doubt. "I took the knife from his back. The tip was buried no more than an inch, enough to stick but hardly a fatal blow. And you acted instinctively, for my protection." That reassured her, the color came back into her cheeks. "You're sure you don't want a doctor? Just to—"

Chelaine shook her head firmly. "I don't, not now." She nestled close, secure in his arms. All the misunderstandings and deceit were past, including Edward's death by his own greed. Ahead, she could see nothing but happiness. "Stephen?" His answer was muffled against her hair. "I still have one secret." Suddenly he tensed, but she hurried to assure him it wasn't anything unpleasant.

Once more he pulled away, brushed her hair over a shoulder, and studied Chelaine's face. She looked happy, a little hesitant, and to encourage her he smiled, stretched forward for a kiss, and canted his head, puzzling, "What secret?"

Her lashes lowered. As much as she'd anticipated this moment, Chelaine suddenly felt shy. "I . . . I meant to tell you earlier. I would have if you hadn't left the ship." She glanced up, searching his face before she announced, "I'm carrying our child." His eyes went wide in shock, and she smiled at how incredulous he appeared. "This happens when a man and woman—"

"I know . . . of course, I know, but it never entered my mind." He stared past her, a grin slowly transforming his face, replacing his astonishment. "When did you learn . . . how far along . . ." He hugged her tightly, then suddenly released her, cautious of her delicate condition. "So—that's why you fainted." He recalled her dizzy spell the night of the ball. "How long *have* you known?"

"I wasn't sure until this past week."

"And you were off to Virginia, without telling me?"

Chelaine wagged her head. "If you recall, I had the impression you and Vanessa were lovers."

Stephen laid a curse on Edward's head, though he was already condemned to his reward. He was still dazed. "A child . . . *our* child." His head went back with a laugh of sheer exhilaration at the idea of fatherhood. "And what a child—if she favors you, we'll have our hands full!"

Chelaine stared at him in surprise. "Why are you so sure it will be a girl? I thought of a son." She grinned. "And if he favors you—"

"I know, he'll be born arrogant and demanding."

"You can't *always* guess my thoughts, Stephen. No, he'll be handsome, charming, as wild and reckless as the smuggler who sired him."

Stephen tipped a brow. "I think *that* should remain a secret. He'll be an earl. Lord, I never considered . . . an heir!" He cupped her face with his hands and very tenderly pressed his mouth to hers, in a sweet, loving kiss before he drew back. "Whichever we have, the child won't lack for spirit!" Suddenly a dark scowl shadowed his eyes, his hands slid down to settle at her shoulders.

Chelaine was startled by the abrupt transformation, bewildered. "Stephen—what's wrong?" She thought a moment. "Oh, you're worried, people will gossip."

"I don't give a damn what people think! We'll be wed soon, six- or seven-month babies are common enough."

"Then why are you so upset?"

"Because you risked more than your own life with a hard ride on horseback, and then coming on us when you knew the danger . . . Didn't you consider your condition, the chance of harm to the baby?"

She hadn't, and admitted it with a shake of her head. "All I thought of was the risk of losing the only man I love, ever loved. Stephen, don't look at me so! I'm healthy. And women *do* faint when they're expecting."

She looked so forlorn, his anger vanished and he wrapped his arms about her again, soothing his harsh words. "I'm sorry, love. You frightened me a second time this evening. I spoke without thinking." His hand stroked her hair again and she cuddled against him. "You'll have the best of care, the baby'll be born here, at Hartehill. In this bed. You've no idea how long I've wanted to share it with you." A sudden thought stiffened him, he shifted back to take a glance at her face. "You don't suppose we did any harm, making love . . ."

Chelaine shook her head, smiling. For so worldly a man, Stephen had no knowledge of wives or babies . . . but he would learn of both soon. She had seen her sister midwife and birth enough of them to know exactly what to expect. "We have quite a while to enjoy ourselves . . . and so much lost time to make up for," she assured him. "It will be months before I grow big and undesirable."

"You couldn't look undesirable if you tried." He kissed her again, more passionately this time, feeling her response in the soft parting of her lips. There was untold delight in the knowledge she was his, that within her she carried a spark of life that bonded them forever. Finally, remembering Alex was below, before he was carried away by desire, Stephen drew away. Chelaine pouted, a pretty pout as only she could.

"There's so much to plan. I'll send for Lucy. She and Alex can witness our vows, and then nothing will ever come between us again."

Chelaine nodded. "I can't believe this is true!" she exclaimed. "I'm dreaming again, a happy dream. Dreams never come true."

"They do when two people share the same dream. Have I said how much I love you, m'Lady?"

She smiled. "No, you haven't, but I gathered as much. I'm not yet a countess, Stephen."

"So? You deserve the title, my love. You *are* a lady . . . not just m'Lady, but *my* Lady."

For once, with a docile air, she submitted to his will. "I'll be whatever you wish, *my* Lord Braden." Then, with a tenacious grip, she locked her fingers at his nape and lay back, drawing him with her. His strong, sculpted features dissolved as their contented smiles melded in a kiss that sealed a love born long before, on a dark, wave-swept beach in Acadia.